COLTON THREAT UNLEASHED

Tara Taylor Quinn

Special thanks and acknowledgment are given to
Tara Taylor Quinn for her contribution to
The Coltons of Owl Creek miniseries.

HARLEQUIN®
ROMANTIC
SUSPENSE™

Recycling programs
for this product may
not exist in your area.

ISBN-13: 978-1-335-59390-0

Colton Threat Unleashed

Copyright © 2024 by Harlequin Enterprises ULC

For questions and comments about the quality of this book,
please contact us at CustomerService@Harlequin.com.

Harlequin Enterprises ULC
22 Adelaide St. West, 41st Floor
Toronto, Ontario M5H 4E3, Canada
www.Harlequin.com

Printed in U.S.A.

A *USA TODAY* bestselling author of over one hundred novels in twenty languages, **Tara Taylor Quinn** has sold more than seven million copies. Known for her intense emotional fiction, Ms. Quinn's novels have received critical acclaim in the UK and most recently from Harvard. She is the recipient of the Readers' Choice Award and has appeared often on local and national TV, including *CBS Sunday Morning*.

For TTQ offers, news and contests, visit www.tarataylorquinn.com!

Books by Tara Taylor Quinn

Harlequin Romantic Suspense

The Coltons of Owl Creek

Colton Threat Unleashed

Sierra's Web

Tracking His Secret Child
Cold Case Sheriff
The Bounty Hunter's Baby Search
On the Run with His Bodyguard
Not Without Her Child
A Firefighter's Hidden Truth
Last Chance Investigation
Danger on the River

The Coltons of New York

Protecting Colton's Baby

Visit the Author Profile page at Harlequin.com for more titles.

To the Colton readers, who are the most important and cherished members of the family.

Chapter 1

He'd had sex with her. What in the hell had he been thinking?

Clearly, he hadn't been thinking. Sitting in his office, Sebastian watched her through his window. Weeks had passed and still he watched with too much interest as the beautiful veterinarian left the kennel where she'd been seeing to a pregnant dog after her regular office hours at her clinic in town and headed toward his house. That messy bun—did she always have to wear it looking so bedroom-like?

The long blond hair had been down by the time she'd left his bed. Had she loosened it? Had he? Things had been so intense that night, with Oscar being injured by shrapnel from gunfire. Him calling Ruby in the middle of the night, afraid the heavily bleeding canine was going to die on him.

As if sensing his current unrest, the golden retriever mix—and Sebastian Cross's personal canine companion—grabbed a stuffed octopus and brought it over to shove it in Sebastian's hand. He and Oscar had started Crosswinds together, training search-and-rescue dogs, like Oscar, for people all over the country.

Oscar didn't seem at all fazed by that night two months before. But Sebastian, thinking he'd lost his only family member—pacing in his home while Dr. Ruby Colton worked on Oscar—had been thrown back a few years. He'd thought he'd left the panic behind. And the vet—she'd finished with Oscar that night and had come upon Sebastian in a particularly low moment.

One no other human had witnessed before.

How it had gone from there to…sex…

Wiping a hand down his face, he turned from the window in his office—chosen because of the view of his property—and headed toward the back door off the kitchen. The door Ruby used every time she came to check on Oscar.

He grabbed another quick glance out the kitchen window. When it was light outside, the vastness of his land, the lake at the edge of it, soothed him.

Anytime of the day or night, sight of the kennels did the same.

Neither was enough that evening as he heard the knock on his door.

In the two months since "the night," as he'd come to think of it, neither he nor Ruby had mentioned what had happened. They'd both pretended nothing had. They had to, right? Owl Creek was a small town. And she not only tended to the search-and-rescue animals that he trained, but she also gave free medical treatment to the PTSD dogs he provided to veterans who needed them.

Still…if nothing else, he had to apologize.

To her. To someone.

She was his best friend's little sister, for God's sake.

Wade Colton was the closest thing he'd ever had to a brother. And he'd gone and…

The knock came a second time.

He hadn't been himself that night. A reminder to never, for any reason, allow himself to be around another human being when he was sinking.

Oscar stood at the door, staring at him. With a nod, Sebastian opened it.

And, while the dog gave his doctor an enthusiastic greeting, Sebastian took the few seconds that Oscar gave him to find an easy smile and paste it on.

Shamelessly using Oscar as a distraction, Ruby spoke with real joy to the boy wagging his tail and licking her chin, avoiding the big mountain man with his shaggy dark blond hair and beard. She related to animals so much better than she did to people. Understood them. Fully accepted and embraced their unconditional love as her top need in life.

Steadying the dog with her tone of voice as she told him, "Good boy, stay," she checked his left hindquarter and left shoulder—both areas from which she'd had to remove shrapnel that fateful night two months before. Thankfully, neither had suffered muscle damage.

"He's healed nicely," she said to Sebastian, still running her fingers lightly over the dog's fur. "You're such a good boy," she told Oscar. "No bad guy's going to slow you down, huh?"

She stood then. The next thing on her agenda not quite as easy as telling the man his dog was well. It had to happen eventually. The longer she put it off, the less chance she'd seem at all natural as she met the blue eyes of the man she'd known most of her life as her older brother's friend.

A boy they'd seen only during the summers he'd spent at his family's cabin in Owl Creek—the home in which he now lived.

She remembered quite clearly how he'd left one year in August as a boy and had returned the following June as a man. He'd grown what had seemed like a foot, had a mustache and shoulders that blocked out the sunlight when he'd stood in front of her, teasing her about her crooked pigtails. She'd developed a bit of a crush on him.

Something that had faded as she, too, had changed, grown, become a woman.

So why had she, how could she have…?

Her gaze met his. Neither said a word.

They had to talk about it, didn't they?

At some point?

If for no other reason than to verify that they weren't telling another soul, ever, what had happened. Most particularly not Wade.

Big-brother hassles, she did not need.

Sebastian's smile wobbled a little. She opened her mouth…

And jumped, clutching Sebastian as a painfully loud crack sounded, followed immediately by a crash, and then a squeal and deep growl from Oscar. The canine was on point, staring at the door.

"Was that a gunshot?" The words burst out of Ruby, followed by a frantic "I'm calling 911."

Sebastian was already at the door.

"Wait, Sebastian! Are you kidding? Don't go alone. Wait for the—"

He was out the door before she'd finished her sentence.

With Ruby and Oscar in the house, and all the dogs on the premises at risk, no way Sebastian could wait the ten minutes it would take the police to get from town to his five acres on the lake. He had a woman—and dogs—to protect. Grabbing his gun from the metal cabinet on his way out, he kept his back to the cabin as he rounded the corner.

The unsolved shooting in the middle of the night two months before still weighed heavily on his mind. He was in full United States Marine Corps mode as he moved with supreme precision, darting his head out for only a second, focusing in that second and pulling back as the second came to a close.

With the sun starting to set, his vision was somewhat compromised, but he got the job done.

As soon as he knew all four sides of the house were secure, he darted behind the small medical building to get closer to the kennel. His biggest concerns were the outside stalls and large, fenced-in, play-and-training area. His four employees—a full-time trainer and three part-time assistants who cared for and cleaned up after the dogs—were gone for the day. But a dozen dogs were there. One pregnant and another with a litter of new puppies.

At the back corner of the medical building, he repeated his earlier process, shot his head out, pulled it back.

And, adrenaline pumping with a dose of anger, he

flattened himself against the wall. Someone had completely shot out Ruby's windshield. A red glare blinked on and off in the glistening mess and Sebastian turned to see flashing lights coming up Cross Road—the private drive leading to his cabin. He wasn't fool enough to go after a shooter on his own with the professionals arriving. He just kept watch over the kennels until several officers spread out around the entire training facility, and then, with his same military precision, made it back into the house with his bad news.

"You had no business going out there alone!" Ruby's tone was sharp, instigated by the fear raging through her, as Sebastian came back inside the house.

Sitting on the floor with an arm around Oscar, who was half in her lap, she flushed as she saw the displeased expression on the man's face. "I'm sorry. I have no business speaking to you like that," she amended, embarrassed.

And scared.

And so thankful that he was standing, unharmed, in front of her.

His shrug made her want to hug him. "You're probably right," he said. "Military training doesn't preclude sitting around and waiting for others to save you." He was still frowning, though.

"What?" she asked, standing, fear returning in full force.

"Your windshield's been shot out."

Hers? But…

Brow creased in a hard line, she stared at him. The shots two months before—she hadn't been anywhere near the place. She'd assumed whoever had been responsible then was attacking again…

"*My* windshield?" she asked.

Even if the shooter wasn't one of Owl Creek's citizens, who all pretty much knew her SUV, both front doors had been painted with the emblem and name of her veterinary clinic.

Did someone have a problem with Colton Veterinary Clinic?

Or with her personally?

Mind spinning, she couldn't come up with any viable explanation.

It's not like she had any exes. There was no one whose heart she'd broken who could want revenge. No new girlfriend who could be jealous.

And at the clinic?

She drew a total blank.

Shivered.

Sebastian, hands in his pockets, was squirming a bit on his feet, as though he was having a hard time keeping his distance.

At least, that's the way her mind was currently translating his actions.

Because she was afraid, she knew. Felt uncharacteristically vulnerable.

"I'll need to have it towed," she said then, unnerved by her unusual reaction to the burly man as well. They'd had sex. She didn't want, or need, any complications from the one-night mistake.

Of that, she was certain.

She was a doctor. Had built a hugely successful practice and was only thirty.

No room in her life for the prepubescent girl who'd once had a crush on the kid Sebastian had been back then—in spite of the fact that as a grown woman, she noticed that the inches and muscles and facial hair he'd sprouted were attention getting.

No room, ever, for any full-time romantic relationship. It just wasn't what she wanted.

"As soon as we get the all-clear from the police, I'll help you clean out any personal stuff and drive you back to town." The man had found his voice.

She nodded. Smiled at him. "Thank you."

And felt a niggle in her lower belly when he smiled back.

As it turned out, Sebastian didn't get a chance to assist Ruby with her vehicle clean-out, or to drive her back to town. As soon as word got out that Ruby Colton had called the police after being present at Crosswinds Training when there'd been gunfire—and, of course, it had gotten out, since she was daughter to the man who owned half the town—her brothers had shown up in full protective mode.

Chase and Wade were at Sebastian's door within half an hour of the police showing up. Fletcher, the middle of her three older brothers, a detective with the Salt Lake City police force, seven hours away, was on the phone, demanding answers.

Chase, the oldest at thirty-six and vice president of Colton Properties, went straight to Ruby. Within seconds, while Wade still had Fletcher on the phone, Chase had her on his cell with their mom and dad, assuring Jenny and Robert that she was absolutely fine. She'd heard a shot was all.

She'd been safe inside the house, checking over Oscar, the entire time.

Sebastian heard it all peripherally. Wade, the youngest brother, fellow marine and as a kid, best friend to Sebastian, made a very determined beeline for Sebastian, demanding to know every detail of what had happened. And when the police came in, saying there was no sign of a shooter anywhere on Crosswinds' five acres, all three men had been ready with questions.

It turned out there was a fresh set of what appeared to be male shoe prints, size ten to eleven, out by the main road. It was likely the shooter used a scope, and never actually set foot on Sebastian's land.

Which set off more conversations between those in the room and those still on the phone. Did that mean Ruby had been targeted?

Or was this more seemingly random violence aimed at Crosswinds? And hitting Ruby's car would be more impactful than the previous shot into brick that had sent shrapnel into Oscar, who'd woken up Sebastian in the middle of the night to go out.

Oscar had heard someone outside that night. Sebastian couldn't prove it but was certain of the fact. And he told Wade so when his friend asked again about the previous shooting event.

The February ground had been clear at that time, but with the wind chill, they'd been looking at below-zero temperatures and everything had been too hard for footprints. By morning, the land had been covered with a couple inches of snow. Investigators had never found a shell casing.

And they hadn't yet in this instance, but they intended to keep looking.

While Sebastian was still answering Wade's questions, in between Wade talking to Fletcher, Chase was escorting Ruby out of the cabin. Wanting her off the property as soon as possible.

Sebastian watched her go, saw her look back at him, or at least at Wade and him, with something like regret in her eyes. He felt it, too. Had wanted to be the one to help her. Since the damage had happened on his land.

But when he glanced over and saw the way his friend, who was ending the call with Fletcher, was watching his older brother and younger sister leave, the look of resignation on his face, Sebastian made a sharp return to reason.

Ruby hadn't been looking at him. She'd been watching over her big brother. The sorrow had been for Wade—not due to some ridiculous desire to have Sebastian be the one to take her home.

He welcomed the return to reality.

"How you doing?" Sebastian asked Wade then, a question that, a few years before, would have been completely in line with their friendship.

In the past few years, after Sebastian had left the Marines—they'd joined together, but Wade had stayed in—they'd naturally grown apart.

"Not you, too," Wade said with disgust, turning so that Sebastian's view was of the left side of Wade's face only.

The move, more than the words, spoke to Sebastian. He'd received his share of pity since he'd been back in Owl Creek. Had hated it every bit as much as Wade must. "You think you're less than you were?" he asked quietly. Wade hadn't been back long, but the man hadn't come to see Sebastian yet, or accepted any invitations to meet for a beer.

Anger filled Wade's one good blue eye with such

intensity that Sebastian took a step back. And heaved an inner sigh of relief.

"Hell no. I can still take your ass. You want to give me a try?" Wade half growled, and Sebastian fully understood the note of real frustration in Wade's half-teasing invitation. Growing up, the two of them had taken on each other more than once. Wrestled. Tried to prove who was stronger.

No one had ever been seriously hurt, but they'd each landed bruises a time or two.

"Lead with both fists, man, just like always," Sebastian said then. "You know what you know. That there's nothing less about the man you are or the power you wield with one seeing eye instead of two. It's up to you to show the rest of the world."

Wade grunted. Clearly not looking for any warm feelings at the moment.

Sebastian got that, too. A hundred percent.

"People only know what you show them," he said, anyway. Because he'd learned the lesson himself after his stint in the Marines had ended so abruptly.

And because Wade Colton had picked him up, out of his insecurities, and set him straight every single summer his parents had deserted him at the cabin. Leaving Sebastian with a nanny to watch over him rather than a family to have fun with.

"You told me once that my value was whatever I thought myself worth," Sebastian murmured, remembering.

The words had been with him ever since.

Chapter 2

Ruby was not happy about her vehicle being shot at. She'd been shaken up by being present during the potentially danger-filled episode.

She wasn't buying in to any theories that the violence had anything to do with her in particular. Simply a matter of wrong place, wrong time.

There'd be vandalism at her clinic, or her home, if she was the target. Threatening notes or texts. Some kind of altercation.

She'd lived in Owl Creek her entire life. Had never been in a long-term relationship. Wasn't involved in anything controversial, anywhere. Nor had she ever lost an otherwise healthy patient on her operating table. She'd had to deliver some sad diagnoses. None of them brought any anger toward her to mind.

Even online, her clinic had only good ratings. Not a single one-star anywhere.

She'd spent the evening going over the facts, multiple times, with her brothers and sisters and parents. She answered texts from her uncle Buck, whose ranch Wade had recently started working and living on, and from her cousins, too.

And had eventually given in to the pressure and agreed to spend the night at her folks' well-secured home.

"You're a Colton," her mother, Jenny, told Ruby as she peeked into the room Ruby had picked for the night, one of the four upstairs guest bedrooms in her parents' newest home. The bed faced a wall of windows overlooking the lake. "Being a Colton makes you prey to anyone who could want to hurt any of us. Your father's built an empire. You don't do that without making enemies. Even if it's just someone who is jealous."

Her mother was right, of course.

But that didn't change the fact that, with the shooting of Ruby's windshield, Crosswinds was the logical target. Which meant that Sebastian and his dogs, out there all alone, could be in danger.

She told herself, as she was lying in bed worrying about him, that having been there, hearing the gunshot, was what was keeping her awake.

That and the fact that his programs—both search-and-rescue, and the pets he trained to help veterans with PTSD—were vastly important to her, too.

Plus…he'd been a peripheral part of her summers growing up.

And she'd had sex with him.

No. That wasn't it. And she wasn't going to think about it.

She just needed to make sure that he agreed that they'd never, ever talk about it or tell anyone. Ever.

Then she wouldn't have to worry, every time she saw him, that he'd bring it up. Or she would. That it would somehow show up and stand there between them.

She needed it done.

She reminded herself of this fact when, three days later, Sebastian called to tell her that Jasmine, the German shepherd she'd been checking on the night of the shooting, was having her babies. With three other veterinarians working full-time at the clinic, she was able to take a break and head out to Crosswinds.

Ruby had counted ten puppies on the X-ray she'd done earlier in the pregnancy. Sebastian said she'd only had seven and was straining. Ruby made the ten-minute drive in eight. Pulled up with her brand-new windshield, parked on the opposite side of the little dark green medical building, her own little Crosswinds mini clinic, and ran inside.

Sebastian stepped aside as soon as he saw her, and she went to work. Saw the sack of fluid blocking the birth canal, a situation made worse by the fact that the eighth puppy Jasmine was trying to push out was a breech. Ruby handled both issues without pause, and half an hour later, she stood over the litter, telling the big mountain man, with his shaggy hair and beard, and who was clearly worried about both Jasmine and her newborns, "You've got ten healthy pups there."

She cleaned up. Grabbed her shoulder bag, intending to leave Sebastian with the newborns he was perfectly capable of looking after. "I'll send the bill over," she told him. The search-and-rescue portion of Crosswinds was funded by the individuals and organizations that needed the dogs and paid for her services. Usually, she took the time to make out the charges on the computer that was set on the counter for that purpose.

For all he knew, she was pressed to get back to the clinic. Truth was, she wasn't feeling like herself around him.

"I'll walk you out."

She nodded, though being alone around him was what she was trying to avoid. At least until the jitters from the gunshot the other night dissipated a bit. But he was probably right. The conversation had to happen.

Since he clearly had a plan in accompanying her to her vehicle, she waited for him to start.

"I want to pay for your windshield."

What? Not at all what she'd been expecting.

"Insurance covered it. And no. It wasn't your fault."

"The police are looking into Crosswinds being targeted," he told her what she'd assumed all along. And yet, her insides tightened uncomfortably at the news. For Sebastian. And the dogs. "I guess there've been a couple of anonymous complaints about the noise. When one dog barks, they all think they have to get their two cents in." He shrugged.

"Anonymous noise complaints?" she asked, slowing her steps as she frowned up at him. "You're on five acres, ten minutes outside of town. Who's close enough to hear anything?"

His nod didn't feel like a good thing. "That's what I said. And what everyone else seems to get. Which apparently points more to the fact that I'm being deliberately targeted for some reason. They're looking into that now. They didn't find a shell casing the other night, either, so right now, all they have to go on is a size-ten shoe print. It's not like there are traffic cams out here.

And we have no way of knowing if the guy came from town or the opposite direction altogether."

The tension in her grew. Sebastian, the dogs, his programs—they helped so many people. And after burning herself out at the clinic, on call 24/7 for years, she'd hired more people and had been finding her own personal energy and joy return as she volunteered for Crosswinds's PTSD dog-placement program.

"Have you had any disgruntled customers?" she asked. "Someone whose dog didn't perform as they thought it would?"

He shook his head. As she'd known he would. Sebastian personally guaranteed the satisfaction of his clients. His dogs served as they were trained, or he took them back and found them good homes as pets. In all the years he'd been in business, it had only happened once that she knew of.

"I've opened my life up to the police," he said then. "We've had multiple interviews and they're following up on everyone I can ever remember knowing…"

"What about back in Boise?" she asked then. Sebastian had grown up in the city, two hours away from Owl Creek, summering at the cabin on the five acres that was now his permanent home. Property that had been in his family for decades. "Your father was a doctor, right? Maybe something to do with one of his patients?" She was grasping, she knew. Just needed him to have the answers that would bring his nightmare to an end.

"Again, the police are investigating every possibility…"

"What about cousins?" She knew he'd been an only child, but… "Is there someone who felt cheated by you getting the family property?"

He shook his head. "I'm it, in terms of family."

The words were like a punch to her solar plexus.

She couldn't imagine…with five siblings and four cousins right there in town, all growing up together—sometimes all ten in the same house—the idea of having no one…

"What do the police say?" she asked, caring much more than she wanted to. He was a friend of her brother. Not her own intimate concern. Peripheral. Not personal. No matter how many times she'd repeated the words in the past two months, her heart was not getting the distinction.

But Ruby knew she had to.

She'd had enough friction in her home growing up. Her parents, while respectful of each other, weren't close. So she'd basically had two different authoritative sources to deal with on her own, going back and forth between the two, to get any sense of what was expected from her. Then, being one of six growing kids, with bright minds and a ton of energy, and add in her aunt and uncle's broken marriage and her mother trying to compensate for her own twin leaving her husband's brother by taking care of his four kids…

She had enough family to last her a lifetime. And an aversion to sharing her home on a permanent basis. Except with the various animals she fostered.

Which meant that any personal feelings she might think she was experiencing for a man with whom she'd had sex were just going to have to go away.

She didn't want them.

Sebastian watched the expressions flit across Ruby's face as he told her the current police theory was that the culprit was exhibiting behavior that was escalating. Going from bogus complaints to random gunshots.

He couldn't read her. She'd always been such a curious mixture of compassion and aloofness…and not just with him. Growing up, Ruby had been the one who didn't join in. Who preferred to make her own entertainment—reading a lot of the time—rather than jumping in a boat with the rest of them and shooting out across the water.

Didn't much matter what she was thinking. His missive was going to be the same.

"You have to stop coming out here until we get this resolved." He put it right out there. The other night…if she'd been in her SUV when the bullet had hit…

No.

"I've got puppies to watch over," she told him, chin high, as she stood up to him. She didn't even give him so much as a shake of her head, to let him know she was disregarding his wishes. "Fletcher told my parents that if this guy was out to hurt someone, he'd have done so," she continued. "Oscar's injury aside," she added. Then just kept talking. "This person had no way of knowing that Oscar was even out there. That was an anomaly."

The police had said the same. And Ruby Colton was acting as though if she just kept on talking, not giving him a chance to get a word in, she'd change his mind.

"This is my property," he butted in when she took a breath. "All that matters here is what I say. And I'm not going to take a risk with your life…" He'd been up all night that first night after her car had been shot. Dealing with cold sweats and a mind filled with images of what could have happened.

"So you're going to let all the people relying on

search-and-rescue dogs miss out? And all the veterans needing dogs to help them live normal lives…they just go without?"

She had spunk. It got his ire up.

And his appreciation, too. In spite of himself.

"Believe it or not, Dr. Colton, we raise a lot of healthy dogs here who will get along just fine without your services for the time it takes the police to find this guy." He was smiling. Crosswinds needed her. She knew how grateful he was for her help—most particularly with the volunteer veteran program. But his gaze bored into hers, as well. Her safety was nonnegotiable.

"Like today?" She upped her chin another notch. "You confident you'd have ten healthy puppies right now?"

"I only called you because I knew you were coming out to check on Jasmine, anyway," he told her. "And the police say that the perp's pattern, based on the shootings and the complaints, is to hit weeks apart. But this is it. Now. Today. No more until whoever is out to get me is in jail."

"My parents still think the shooter could be after me. With all of the public fundraising I've been helping with, everyone knows how much the work out here, the services Crosswinds provides, means to me."

He hadn't thought of that. If the police had, they hadn't said so.

He wanted to fire her on the spot.

And knew it wouldn't do any good if someone was already after her.

"I don't buy it," she told him. "If someone wanted to hurt me, they'd be going after my clinic. Putting up bad reviews. Accusing me of letting an animal die. Flattening my tire while I was at work…"

She stopped as he cocked his head, frowning, but half smiling, too.

"What?" she asked.

"You sure you aren't the perp?" he teased, even knowing it was in no way a joking matter. Just…someone had to ease the tension.

"I've…given this a lot of thought over the past few days. Having my windshield wiped out, and then dealing with each member of my family—every one of them a know-it-all, mind you—I've had to shore up my defenses. My car was shot at while I wasn't in it. And it wasn't even on my property. That does not mean I need to go into hiding."

He opened his mouth to argue with her, but she got the next word in first. "What about you?" she blurted. "You're right here, going on with your life, running your business, and every single one of the occurrences has to do with this place. Yet, you aren't shutting down."

"I can't shut down. Too many people rely on—"

"Exactly," she interrupted. "So what makes my life more valuable than yours?"

He had an answer for that. But the challenge shooting at him from those unrelenting green eyes kept his mouth shut.

For the time being.

She climbed into her SUV. Shut the door on him. Started the engine.

But he and Ruby Colton weren't done talking about the matter.

And when they were, he intended the last words to be his.

Chapter 3

Ruby had no cause to visit Crosswinds that next week. Sebastian emailed photos of the puppies feeding, telling her that Jasmine and the gang were doing great.

She'd already released Oscar from her care.

He had no new dogs arrive.

And she knew he was deliberately trying not to need her.

There also hadn't been any other signs of unrest in her life, or, according to Wade, Sebastian's, either. Things at Crosswinds had been running smoothly, with no upsets all week.

And yet, she was still feeling…jittery.

Because she needed to talk to him. To get things back on an even keel. Before Wade noticed the tension between them. The last person she'd ever want to know about her fantastical mistake with Sebastian Cross was her overprotective brother. Wade was a strong adversary on a good day. But with having his entire life upended after being blinded in one eye, with his career in the Marines no longer an option, he wasn't in a good place mentally.

Sitting in her office on the second Thursday in April, waiting for her two younger sisters, who'd called to say they were bringing lunch to share with her, she wondered if she should drive out to Crosswinds after work. Just get everything with Sebastian out in the open. It was not her way to let things linger, or fester, unless doing so let them slowly evaporate into the ether.

Having sex with a client, who was also her brother's close friend, didn't seem to be something that would fade away quietly.

She wasn't acting like herself.

Hence, her sisters bringing lunch to share with her in the middle of their busy weekday schedules. Checking up on her. Or just wanting her to know they cared.

Either way, after the shooting ordeal at Crosswinds, she wasn't going to convince her family that she was fine—her usual, untroubled, independent self—until she started to feel that way again.

She had to talk to Sebastian.

Hannah and Frannie, twenty-eight and twenty-six, respectively, came in together. Hannah was carrying a reusable insulated bag bearing the logo of her catering business, and Frannie had a cardboard holder with three cups of coffee from her bookshop café.

Unusually happy to see them both, she stood to help divvy up the goodies they'd brought, taking a foil-wrapped package out of Hannah's bag, hoping for her sister's signature grape-laden chicken-salad wrap, and caught the scent of coffee when Frannie removed the lid and set a cup in front of her.

One whiff, and the jitters she'd been feeling turned into cold sweats. Her head swam.

And she opened her eyes to see both sisters staring at her with panicked gazes.

One on each side of her chair. A hand each on the arms of her chair.

Her chair.

She'd been standing.

"What's going on?" she asked, hearing the weakness in her tone.

"You passed out, that's what!" Hannah, the no-nonsense Colton, stated emphatically. "We need to get you to the ER."

"I'm fine," Ruby said, sitting up. Waiting for the light-headedness to return. "Seriously," she added, when it didn't.

"Come on, Ruby," Frannie, the quiet bookworm, and baby of the family, said, her hazel eyes imploring. "You don't just pass out for no reason."

"You're a doctor," Hannah added, her green-eyed gaze no less impactful. Because looking into Hannah's eyes was like looking in a mirror. Colton eyes. Similar to their dad's eyes, and exact replicas of Uncle Buck's. "You know this isn't normal or fine."

She was a doctor of veterinary medicine. Not a doctor for humans.

But because Hannah's point was valid, she agreed to let them drive her to the clinic in town. Just to get her vitals and fluids checked. It made good sense.

And would reassure her little sisters so that they

didn't go running to their mother with the news of Ruby's little mishap.

"It's the stress," she told them as they waited for results of the urine and basic blood tests, which would, she was sure, show no infection. "I haven't had much of an appetite."

"I knew you weren't fine," Hannah said, sitting on her right, leaving the chair on the left to Frannie. "You could have been in that car for all the shooter knew. If he shot from as far away as the cops said he did. Of course, you're overwrought."

"The stress from everyone watching over me," Ruby said dryly. "I love you all so much, you know that, but eleven of you, twelve including Uncle Buck, texting me at least once a day…"

Hannah glanced at Frannie, across Ruby's perfectly healthy frame. "Yeah," she said. "We should have been better organized about that." Her middle sister's tone held definite I-told-you-so isms.

"Hannah wanted us on a schedule, so there'd be a timeline," Frannie allowed. "Fletcher said it was better, since you live alone, if we each just check in throughout the day."

Her words dropped off. And Ruby didn't know whether to laugh or groan.

As it turned out, she didn't have a chance to do either as the physician's assistant who'd seen her entered the small exam room.

The first thing the woman did was glance at Hannah and Frannie, then her gaze landed on Ruby. "Is it okay to talk in front of your sisters?"

Frannie gasped, clutching Ruby's left hand so tight that she felt her baby sister's nails digging into her skin.

"Of course it is," Hannah said, covering Ruby's other hand with her own.

Just laying her palm there. Warm. Supportive.

She met the medical professional's gaze. "Yes," she said calmly. There was nothing a simple urine or basic blood test was going to show in such a short period of time. Her vitals had been fine. But then she'd been certain of that before she'd come in.

The PA looked only at her and said, "You're pregnant."

She couldn't be.

It had to be a mistake.

As soon as she got to her own transportation, she was going to get a home pregnancy test—out of town, so no one would see her buying it—and prove the PA wrong.

Sitting in the front passenger seat of Hannah's car, Ruby continued to feel the weight of her sister's open-mouthed, disbelieving stares—just as when they'd been in that tiny room at the clinic.

A room that was now forever ingrained in her brain and would probably give her nightmares in the years to come.

Huh. Her, pregnant?

The woman who knew one thing about herself for certain.

She couldn't ever see herself wanting a husband.

Let alone raising a family.

She could not be pregnant.

"Who is he?" Hannah's question came the second she closed her driver's door.

"There is no *he*."

"You had yourself inseminated?" Frannie asked from the seat directly behind Hannah.

"Of course not. Either of you see me as the mothering type?"

"Yes," they answered in unison. Shocking her so much, she turned to stare at each of them in turn.

"You know the last thing I want is to get married and have a family."

"I know that's what you say, but you'll make a great mother, sis." Hannah's tone was unusually soft. Compassionate. The woman was so in love with little Lucy, she figured everyone would feel the same after giving birth. "Now, who's the father?"

No way. Uh-uh.

"No one."

Sebastian Cross wasn't even her lover. He most definitely was not the father of the child. Even the one that only existed in one PA's words and on a chart.

Charts could be corrected.

Words, maybe not forgotten, but the mistake could be forgiven.

Yes, that was it.

There'd been a mistake. Picking up her phone, she dialed the clinic. Asked to speak to the doctor. Insisted on holding, was still holding when Hannah pulled up at Colton Veterinary Clinic, parked and turned off her ignition.

"I didn't even know you were dating anyone," Frannie said, as they all just sat there.

"I'm *not* dating anyone." She didn't even try to keep the exasperation out of her tone. And then, as reality hit her, she filled with total panic.

Her sisters thought she was…

Turning in her seat, phone still to her ear, she stared them both down. Hard. A big-sister, I'm-seriously-going-to-tell-every-secret-you've-ever-had stare. "Do not breathe a word of this to anyone," she said then. "I mean it. Not Mom. Not anyone."

There was no compromise on that one.

She saw the glance Frannie and Hannah shared. It didn't bode well and did nothing to calm Ruby.

"I'm serious," she said. "My medical information is private."

Frannie shook her head. "But, Ruby…a baby…"

Ruby cut her off with a glare. "It's a mistake," she said. "Which is why I'm waiting to speak to the doctor in charge today. And even if it wasn't, this is my business to share or not, to handle how I see fit, not yours."

She was dead serious.

Hannah, the only mother among them, sighed. And Ruby drew her first easy breath since the PA had made her ridiculous announcement. "Just tell me that you weren't…forced, or…"

In light of the recent happenings at Crosswinds—her car being shot at, all the worry her family had shared on her behalf—she felt Hannah's concern to the bone. "I swear to you, sweetie, no one has ever touched me, like that, without my full cooperation."

"So you did sleep with someone," Frannie said softly. "Who is he?"

"No one," she said again, calmer now. "It's a mistake."

Hannah still sat, door closed. She was the one Ruby knew she had to contend with if she wanted her secret kept. Frannie was naturally quiet. Reserved.

"I won't say anything about the baby," Hannah said

then. "You're absolutely right, it's your secret, your business. But if you are pregnant, your secret's going to start showing itself before too long."

Hannah had been there and done that.

Ruby nodded, looked at Frannie. "You'll keep this to yourself?"

"Of course, I won't say anything." Frannie looked as though she wanted to say a lot, though.

"Say it wasn't a mistake…would you have it?" Hannah asked.

Ruby knew what Hannah was really asking. And was fairly certain her sister wouldn't judge. Whether Hannah agreed with Ruby's decisions or not, she would want to be supportive. "I wouldn't *not* have it," she said softly.

And had to escape the car before she threw up all over her sister's upholstery.

A week had gone by since the shooting of Ruby Colton's windshield and her subsequent visit to deliver Jasmine's last three puppies.

A week without seeing her.

Sebastian was still on edge. Someone had shot up his property. Twice. Causing damage both times. First the shrapnel hit Oscar—though, arguably, that had likely been collateral damage, not intentional—and then Ruby's windshield had been shattered.

And the complaints…

Who was out to get him? When would they hit next?

The not knowing was getting to him—maybe that was the perpetrator's goal?

Give him an enemy to fight, and he'd get the job done. Sitting around waiting for an attack from an unknown source that could come without warning?

All the Marine training in the world wasn't going to prepare him for that.

Not well enough to suit him, at any rate.

So he focused on the training he excelled in—search-and-rescue. Each dog generally took two years of weekly training before being ready for a search-and-rescue mission. At Crosswinds, he had canines at every level of training, all the time. Those just starting out. Those almost ready to go to work. Some had handlers who came to Owl Creek, stayed at one of the motels in town that gave Crosswinds a special rate and came out to the facility to work with the dog before taking them home.

Search-and-rescue wasn't an easy business. Or a cheap one. He ran a highly accredited, elite organization. Yet, a lot of handlers were volunteers. Sebastian did what he could to keep his costs down for them. His property, while outfitted as well as the best training facilities, was all basic brick and wood buildings—all painted one color. The military green he preferred.

And he did as much of the training himself as he possibly could.

The second Thursday in April, he'd spent the morning and midafternoon at Buck Colton's ranch. One of the golden retrievers, Elise, a relative of Oscar, was at the tail end of avalanche training. He'd needed to take her to an unfamiliar site, with another dog and avalanche tools—spikes and shovels—lying around.

Malcolm Colton—Wade's cousin—and Malcolm's SAR dog, Pacer, had helped with this particular session many times.

They had ridges dug out for that purpose. Sebastian would bury Malcolm in one, under a couple of inches of dirt with full breathing capability, and give his trainee—that day, Elise—Malcolm's scent, while Pacer was given a different smell to follow and went off for his prey. The idea was for Elise to ignore Pacer and all other distractions to follow Malcom's scent, and then be willing to dig to get to him. For which she'd get a treat.

The girl performed in record time. Every single time they repeated the exercise. Getting to Malcolm, and then racing straight to Sebastian to lead him to her find.

At one point, when the burial point was on a steep incline, she stayed with the uncovered body and barked until Sebastian came to her.

Sebastian was just heading back to his truck, with Elise trotting, head high, at his side, when Wade came out of the barn. He called out to Sebastian.

In jeans, a long-sleeved denim shirt and cowboy boots, Wade walked with the same sense of command he'd displayed in his US Marine Special Forces uniform, black eye patch and all.

"Quick question for you," Wade said, petting Elise's head as he reached them. "My sister Hannah just called. She says that Ruby's been dating someone, has some boyfriend, but won't say who. Hannah thinks this might be the guy who shot out Ruby's windshield. Said she was really odd, to the point of angry, when Hannah asked her about him. None of us had any idea she was dating anyone. Did you?"

Sebastian shook his head immediately.

Ruby had a boyfriend?

A development he'd never even considered.

Relief didn't flood him, as he'd expected it to.

She might have mentioned that detail.

Sleeping with another guy's woman was not his way.

And could cause unforeseen complications—like a guy targeting her at Sebastian's place.

"Anyone who's been at the kennels that she might have had contact with?" Wade continued to grill him. "She's been spending so much more time out there, and with the handlers you have coming in…"

He thought over the people who'd been in and out of Crosswinds, when Ruby might have been there, who might have taken exception to Sebastian's friendship with her, from before Oscar was shot.

That's when the violence had started. With Oscar's injury.

But the complaints had started before then.

And had continued.

She'd slept with Sebastian while she'd been seeing someone else?

Gut clenched tight, he had to admit it made sense. They could have taken offense at how much time Ruby spent with Sebastian's dogs. Maybe not believing she was just seeing the dogs. The jealous boyfriend…shooting up his place in the middle of the night. Complaining about noise. Then still seeing his girlfriend's vehicle there until dawn?

Maybe she'd explained she'd just been there for Oscar. Had sworn that nothing else had happened. She'd sure been eager to pretend that it hadn't.

Maybe the guy had seen her with Sebastian again.

Made sense that the violence would have escalated.

And most definitely fit shooting out Ruby's windshield while she was parked there.

"I can't think of anyone," he told his friend honestly. Sebastian was reeling from the sudden turn of events. Did the guy know Ruby had slept with him?

How could she not have at least told him she had a boyfriend?

If the perp was this violent without knowing the full story, how much further would he go if he found out they had slept together?

"How sure is Hannah that she has one?" Sebastian asked, careful to keep his question completely casual. Curious. But, because of the violence, concerned, too.

"She's positive. She wouldn't say how she knew but she told me that her proof was one hundred percent positive. She's worried sick."

Sebastian didn't blame her. After that news, he was, too.

Worried about the potential for more violence, worried about Ruby's safety. And a bit concerned about the incredible disappointment coursing through him.

He'd never have taken Ruby Colton for one to screw around on her boyfriend.

Or to have sex with Sebastian and not tell him she was in a relationship.

Not that the sex meant anything.

But with the violence, her windshield… They'd talked about possible threats. About any potential enemies.

Why hadn't she at least told him about her secret possibility?

For that matter, why did she have to keep it secret at all?

That question led to an unpalatable, and yet possible answer.

The guy was married.

And Sebastian's day had just gone down the toilet.

Chapter 4

Ruby talked to the doctor at the clinic.

And after work, she went back to the medical facility on her own for a second urinalysis.

She'd had a period since she'd slept with Sebastian. Granted, it had been light, but that happened occasionally, based on her workload and stress level.

And since making the hellacious mistake of having sex with her older brother's friend, she'd been fairly stressed.

Besides, they'd used a condom.

She hadn't been kidding, or doubting herself, when she'd been so adamant with her sisters regarding her test results.

She'd known they couldn't be right.

And being a doctor, she also knew that sometimes test

results were skewed. A faulty test strip. Or technician. Both happened, even in the best hospitals and clinics.

Then she'd thrown up.

Something she hadn't done since she was a kid.

And she'd gone into full doctor mode. Symptoms. Tests. Results.

When symptoms contradicted each other, test a second time, just to be sure.

And there she was, walking out of the clinic, just after seven, having watched the test being run, and the results appear, right along with the doctor.

She, Dr. Ruby Colton, DVM, was pregnant.

And in two years' time, there was only one man she'd had sex with.

Once.

She had to talk to Sebastian.

Thought about calling him.

A charged conversation like the one they were bound to have…might be better over the phone.

Easier, at least.

In her car, she glanced at the second set of test results. And knew she had to drive out to see Sebastian. He deserved to see the results, both sets of them.

She stopped by her office and made copies of both test forms she'd received that day, put her own in a folder and folded his and put them in her satchel. She lifted the leather bag up to her shoulder, and, with a "have a good evening" to the evening staff, she left.

On a mission.

A distasteful one.

The best way to handle those were to get them done immediately. No overthinking.

Just complete the task.

Keeping her mind on her meeting with Sebastian, trying to find words for the conversation that would result in the least drama, she felt like the ten-minute trip out of town to his place lasted for hours. She found no words.

Every sentence her mind started sent her into panic mode and she had to abort the effort.

Abort.

She wasn't going to do that.

She'd told Hannah she wouldn't even before she'd been pregnant.

Before she'd known she was.

I've got this paperwork I feel I should show you, Sebastian, out of courtesy, but it doesn't require any involvement from you at all. Not even a name.

The sentence appeared as she pulled up Cross Drive.

No one knew she'd slept with him.

No one ever had to know.

Yes. That thought worked better than any other one she'd had since throwing up in her own clinic's parking lot.

Drawing up by Sebastian's back door—because coming from the medical building or the kennels, the back entrance was the one she always used, not because she was afraid to leave her car in view of the road—she pulled open the screen door to administer her customary two short knocks.

The mission was underway. Would soon be complete.

"Eeoowooah!" The male holler rent the air, filled with anger. With gut-wrenching pain. Sending shivers up and down her spine. Instinctively pulling the screen to her body, crouching up against the wooden door keeping her from the house, she glanced at the yard around her.

And toward the kennels.

The sound came again. Animalistic.

Clearly coming from the house. Heart pounding, thinking only of the pain inherent in the sound, she turned the doorknob. Felt it give. Hurried inside, already reaching for her phone.

And saw Sebastian sprawled back in a recliner, eyes closed, with an open laptop on its side on the floor.

"Yaawwwah!"

She jumped back as the horrible sound came from his throat, just before he threw a heavy fist at…nothing.

And it hit her.

Sebastian. In the Marines, just like Wade.

Early discharge.

His head was still, his cheeks and lips skewed right, then left, the muscles scrunching one way, then the other, like he was cringing from one side of his face at a time. All of it hiding beneath the light beard.

She'd taken a training class on PTSD before Wade came home. Mostly for herself. She'd needed to know what her adored older brother might be going through.

Sitting at attention, Oscar watched Sebastian. Glanced at her. And back at his owner. The retriever was a search-and-rescue dog, not one trained for the veterans Crosswinds also served.

She couldn't get close or risk being hit. But Oscar could. She'd seen the dogs in training. Had helped train some over the past few months.

Moving behind Sebastian's chair, she motioned for the dog, pointing for him to sit beside the chair. The big mountain man was striking up, out, with the movements he was making. Oscar's head was below the arm of the chair. Oscar knew to nudge Sebastian's hand for a treat. She waited.

And felt tears fill her eyes as, less than a minute later, the dog, hearing Sebastian cry out, nudged his owner's hand.

Sebastian woke up, his eyes glazed at first, and then crystal clear as he focused on Ruby, moving out in front of him.

She'd never felt less welcome anywhere in her life.

"What in the hell are you doing in here?" Sebastian heard the accusation in his tone, wasn't sure he had the wherewithal to withhold it.

Wasn't sure he wanted to try.

"You have no business being here," he said, angry. With her, yes. Because she was there. Because she'd slept with him without telling him she had a boyfriend.

Because, with everyone working so hard to find out who was behind the attacks at and on Crosswinds, she hadn't said a word.

But most of his anger was aimed at himself.

He'd been gone again—had slipped into the hell that was the part of his life no one ever saw. Or knew about.

"I wanted to talk to you," she said, sounding like some doctor, not the compassionate woman, the friend, who'd been offering so much of her time to Crosswinds. "I heard you holler out…"

Seeing his computer lying sideways on the floor, he snatched it up. Closed it. Stood. "How long have you been here?"

"Long enough."

And didn't that just put the plunger on anything good about the day.

"Yeah, well, I'm fine—you can go now." Oscar nudged his hand and Sebastian went to get the dog the treat he'd already asked for once.

Wait. Oscar nudging his hand…had woken him. He looked at Ruby.

"I made him sit by you," she said. "I didn't know what else to do…"

She cared.

That mattered.

Not for any reason he could come up with.

But it did.

And it hit him why he couldn't seem to get by what had happened between them two months before. It wasn't the sex calling to him, although it had been—yeah—but…she knew.

She'd sat with him, held conversation like any other time, making no mention of the panic attack he'd been suffering. She'd just…brought him down. By being herself.

She knew.

And he wasn't sure he was sorry.

He had no idea what to do with that.

"Oscar's a search-and-rescue dog," she said then, as if his dog was the issue at hand.

He nodded.

"Because you don't want anyone to know you need one trained for…"

"I don't need one," he said gruffly. Then leaned on the corner of the wall, one ankle crossed over the other, as if entertaining in the near dark, while standing, was a normal thing.

Ruby turned on the light by his chair.

Sat down in the one just like it a few feet away.

"How often do you have them?"

He sat, too.

Why not. The day couldn't get any worse.

"I hadn't had one in more than a year." He'd told her the truth, was glaring at her again. "Until the night Oscar was shot. Or rather, the night after that."

He'd had the panic attack first, the night of the shooting.

And sex. He'd had sex that night, too.

With a woman who had a boyfriend. Possibly a dangerously jealous one.

How could she not have told him?

Not only because his place was being attacked, but also…to protect herself? Why wasn't she telling anyone? Didn't make sense to him.

But then, he wasn't at his best.

Not even half best.

"But you had them when you first came home?" Her softly uttered question hit him in a weak spot.

He needed to get rid of those.

All done. No more.

"I was called home to deal with the deaths of both of my parents, who'd been killed in a car accident, what do you think?" he asked, not kindly.

He had to get rid of her before he did another thing he'd regret. Like telling her how someone else knowing, having *her* know, seemed to lighten his load some. Even while it made him feel weak.

His anger didn't seem to reach her. She didn't tense. Didn't stand to go.

The woman didn't even frown at him.

He deserved some kind of facial disapproval, at least.

"What memory does the sound of gunfire trigger for you?"

He nodded. Reminded himself that he was not happy with her. The boyfriend, and all. And said, "Wade and I joined the Marines together, but, as you know, we ultimately served separately." What the hell. If he had to get it out, might as well get it done with.

Better that then get into some wimpy-feeling personal conversation about her having sex with him while she was involved with another man.

Or having sex with him at all.

"I ended up in Afghanistan, along with a buddy, Thane, I'd met at boot camp. Like me, he was an only child. Had no other family. One night we were drinking. A lot. Too much. We were shipping out the next day and he asks me what's the single most painful thing I could ever remember dealing with to date. You know, like he was thinking about the pain we might be walking into."

Her eyes aglow with warmth Ruby sat up straight. Like her shoulders weren't going to bow, no matter what he said.

Like she could take it.

Maybe even wanted to take it.

And it struck him… She could be using him to better understand her brother who'd just returned, seemingly broken. He'd like that.

To help Ruby help Wade.

"I told Thane about Jerry."

"That spaniel you had when we were kids?"

"I had him until I was seventeen," he told her. "He was a rescue dog, and sometimes I felt like he'd rescued me, not the other way around. I was home alone a lot growing up. A lot. But when Jerry came, it was

different. I had someone to greet me at the door. Someone who was as happy to see me as I was to see him."

He stopped. Helping Wade was one thing. Becoming a sap...not.

"Jerry had been abused. All he wanted was someone
to be kind to him. He was the most gentle living being
I've ever known." *Move on.* "So I told Thane about the
night Jerry died," he said, finishing.

The End.

"What did Thane say to that?"

Right. The point he'd been getting at. "He told me
about the night his dog, Bear, died. It gave us something in common. An understanding of what we could
be walking into," he explained, completely serious as
he met her gaze. "We never mentioned our dogs, or that
night again, but it was like we knew. And the knowing, the accepting that life could hurt like hell, gave us
strength to get the job done. To do what we had to do to
try to prevent, or stop, others suffering so much worse."

Her gaze was glued to him. He wasn't sorry.

Until he remembered that she had a boyfriend.
That Hannah Colton had irrefutable proof of a man in
Ruby's life.

What was it about the woman that sucked him in?
Made him someone he was not? He didn't want to con-
nect.

Not with her, definitely. But not with any other
human being, either. Not like that.

"You're about to tell me that Thane died over there,
aren't you?" Her words fell like cotton balls around
him. Over him. Soft. Tender. Until there were so many
of them he knew he could suffocate.

"I was about to not tell you that he died lying right

next to me in a dirt-filled cove we'd dug out of the side of a mountain," he said, standing.

Time for her to go.

She didn't take his hint. Didn't get to her feet and head to the door. Instead, looking up at him, she said, "You can cross-train Oscar. I'll help if you'd like. No one has to know…"

Cross-train… Oscar nudging his hand…

"He can help stop the nightmare at its onset," she said, telling him something he knew better than she did. He just hadn't figured himself for needing the help.

He lived alone. There was no one to protect from his very private, very personal struggles. It wasn't like he dozed off on the job.

Or out to eat.

She was getting too close, pushing herself way too far in.

Hands firmly on his hips, Sebastian did what he had to do. Shoved her right back out again with an accusatory tone that left no room for doubt. "Why didn't you tell me you have a boyfriend?"

Chapter 5

"Excuse me?" Ruby stood straight, completely affronted at first, and then just worried about him. Was he still in the clutches of his nightmare? Thinking she was someone else?

It was the only thing that made sense.

"That night we had sex, you were seeing someone else." His words would have been her worst nightmare if she'd ever gone off the rails far enough to have dreamed it.

Completely shocked, she stood there with her mouth open. Couldn't think of a single thing to say.

"Wade told me," he continued.

Wade? It was like she'd walked into the twilight zone.

"My brother Wade?" She'd gotten the words out. That was a start.

"Of course, your brother Wade," Sebastian said, still

standing there, all burly mountain man. His hands, which had been on his hips, had dropped to his side.

She didn't know what that meant, either.

"It's not like what we did meant something," he said then. "It was a reaction, I get that. Something that happened in the moment without thought. And I get that you didn't owe me anything. The anonymous complaints, even the gunshot that caught Oscar... It could have been him, if he's the jealous type and didn't like the time you were spending out here. But still, we hadn't done it yet, so I can even get your silence until that point. But when the shot went directly through your windshield. That night everyone thought it was personal. The way Chase whisked you out of here, insisting you stay at your parents'. And Fletcher was all over the case. Even the police were asking about everyone we knew, or had known. You didn't think to mention this guy? Just in case?"

She had to go. Get out.

He was out of his mind. Slamming her.

She headed for the door.

And... *Wade*?

Sebastian had to be hallucinating.

She got herself outside. Door shut behind her. Was peripherally aware that Sebastian wasn't following her. And slowed her pace long enough to take a full deep breath.

All of the reading she'd done on PTSD, and she hadn't seen a thing about waking hallucinations that were set in real time.

But there was paranoia...

He had to still be in the throes of the demons that ate at him. Lying next to his best friend as he was shot, watching him die. And immediately following, to be called home to the sudden deaths of his parents—his only living relatives.

She couldn't leave. Not until she was sure he'd climbed his way out of the personal hell she'd found him in the night of the first gunshot. She'd thought his panic then had been induced by Oscar's being shot.

She should have known it was more than that.

And Wade.

Did her brother know that Sebastian was struggling with PTSD-like symptoms?

Was that why Wade's name had entered into Sebastian's rant?

Her having a boyfriend was just ludicrous. No way anyone in her family would spread around that claim.

And…the baby.

For a few minutes there, she'd forgotten.

She was pregnant.

From one night that, in Sebastian's own words, meant nothing.

She couldn't even get a one-night stand right, and he thought she had a boyfriend?

She stumbled on the way to her car.

She had to tell Sebastian about the baby. But not right now. Not until his mind was clear.

But she couldn't just leave him like he was, either.

Heading to the only place she felt welcome at the moment, she entered the medical building with the key Sebastian had given her long ago. Was greeted by Jasmine, who, instead of wagging her tail, whined from inside her large, round two-foot-high fencing, and stared up at Ruby.

Her first thought was that the dog knew, too. That

Sebastian had told her canine patients that she had some secret jealous man who was shooting up the place. Jasmine had walked over to the blanket-covered matting where her puppies slept.

Was nudging at a makeshift bed.

All personal thoughts fleeing, Ruby stepped over the fencing and kneeled next to Jasmine. "What's the matter, girl? What are you telling me?" she asked. She'd come in to check on the puppies—or just to play with them for a second, to get her equilibrium back.

And maybe to have a heart-to-heart with the new mama, feeling a bond with Jasmine.

But as she started to check over the puppies, her heart began to pound. Three of them weren't well. At first, she thought it was the last three she'd birthed, but looking at the markings, she knew it wasn't. Which made no sense.

Phone out of her pocket, she dialed Sebastian immediately.

"I'm sorry, Ruby. So sorry. I had no right to come at you like that—"

"Come down to the clinic," she said, breaking in on him. "Three of the puppies have weak heart rates, raised temperatures and they're panting hard. We need to get them into town, where I have everything I need…"

Where she could do blood work. Run urinalysis. Start IVs.

After dropping the phone, she was already gathering up the babies. Grabbing a box filled with supplies, dumping them onto the floor, to use the box as a carrying bed for them. Had them settled, had picked up her phone, her satchel and was at the door, when Sebastian appeared.

Taking the box from her, he didn't speak. Didn't even look at her.

She didn't look at him, either.

At the moment, their drama didn't matter.

There were lives at stake.

Sebastian drove.

Ruby wanted to be able to watch over the puppies, and he was glad to have her do so. Was thankful that she'd been there.

That, even after his supreme rudeness, she'd gone down to check on the puppies.

"You think they're going to make it?" he asked.

"It's too soon to tell. They aren't convulsing. That's a good sign." She hadn't taken her eyes off the puppies since she'd climbed into the back seat of his truck, right after he'd loaded their box there.

None of them were spoken for yet. He didn't even know if they'd have the characteristics necessary to be search-and-rescue trained.

But if they weren't suited to SAR, they could still make great service dogs for the too many veterans who needed them. Or companions to kids who might need an extra friend.

Like himself?

He'd like to blame his harsh words to Ruby on the nightmare she'd helped pull him out of. She'd calmed him, and he couldn't explain that to himself in any way that didn't set him on edge.

He'd been fighting the effect she had on him as much as he'd been reeling from the news that she had some secret guy in the wings.

Whether the guy was the one vandalizing his place or not.

And that's where his defenses flew sky-high. Why on earth—other than as the possible source of the violence—should Ruby not telling him about her boyfriend matter to him at all?

The only thing that needed to matter right now was the health of the puppies she was tending to. He'd called one of his employees, Andy Martin, to head to his place and sit with Jasmine and the other puppies, to watch over them just in case any of the others started exhibiting signs of unconsciousness, rather than mere sleep. If they couldn't be woken up.

He pulled up to the back entrance of the clinic as Ruby instructed, was out of his seat the second he'd turned off the truck, flinging open the back door and reaching for the box, while Ruby climbed out her side.

She hadn't said what she thought was wrong. He didn't ask. Didn't want to distract her.

He just assisted, following all her instructions to the letter, as she checked vitals, drew blood, looked in noses and mouths.

He knew enough about dogs to write a book. About breeding them. Raising them. Training them.

Medically, he only had enough knowledge to be deeply concerned. Three lives... In all his years at Crosswinds, he hadn't lost one.

She'd told him to stay with the puppies while she went to the lab. Was back sooner than he'd expected.

"They've been poisoned," she said, as she worked over all three dogs with an efficiency that left him in the dust. "It's some kind of petroleum-based something," she explained, no longer asking for his help. "Maria, one of my most experienced techs, is on her way in. We need to get IVs started, but first, I'm administering an absorbent demulcent. We don't want them to vomit. Petroleum-based poisons can do permanent damage to the lungs…"

He held up his hand. "Hold that thought," he said, and then, phone in hand, dialed Crosswinds to check on Jasmine and the other puppies, only hanging up after being assured that all were breathing fine, had normal temperatures and heart rates.

As he hung up, he heard the back door open and shut.

"It might be best if you wait in my office," Ruby said then.

She had other help. Didn't want him around.

He got it.

Knew he deserved her rejection.

Headed to the door.

"Sebastian?"

He turned back in time to see her glance up at him. "If we caught it in time, their chances are good. Only one in one hundred healthy dogs die of poisoning that's caught in time. We should know within a couple of hours, at the most…"

Their chances were good, not great. They were dealing with less-than-two-week-old puppies. Not healthy grown dogs.

And petroleum-based poison? Like paint thinner?

The puppies were in a secure crate. No way they could get into anything.

If Ruby hadn't driven out to check on them, if she hadn't continued on to her task after he'd been such a jerk to her, those puppies would have died.

After turning on the light as he entered Ruby's office, he sat on the edge of the desk and called the detective who'd been assigned to his case. He'd been given a number to use, day or night. Glen Steele, the detective who picked up, said he'd send a team out to Crosswinds immediately.

After hanging up, Sebastian called Andy to let him know the police were coming.

And then, with too much pent-up energy coursing through him, he stood again, knocking a folder he hadn't even seen to the floor. He was going to do as she instructed, wait for her in her office. But cooped up in one room when someone had been on his property? Poisoned puppies?

Who did that?

It took a special kind of sickness to attack babies of any kind.

He picked up the folder, telling himself not to let his thoughts venture back to Ruby dating such an individual.

Whether the perp was someone she knew or not, Sebastian's property had been invaded again. Someone had actually been inside a locked building. Purposely attacked innocent puppies.

His employees had all checked out already, as he'd known they would.

Who else had been at Crosswinds since he'd stopped to see the puppies after dropping Elise back at the kennels upon returning from Colton Ranch?

A piece of paper had half slipped out of the folder. Sebastian opened the folder to right it.

The police would once again interview each of the four Crosswinds employees. Get an accounting of anyone they'd seen on the property.

And…

What was that?

Express Medical Clinic.

Ruby's name typed clearly on the first line.

He noticed that part last.

After he'd seen the result marked positive.

She was positive for something.

He closed the folder quickly. Put it back on the desk.

Didn't want to process what his one accidental glance had seen first.

Pregnancy test.

Chapter 6

It was almost eleven that night before Ruby walked into her office. She'd called Sebastian earlier. Told him he could go. Maria had offered to drive her out to pick up her SUV when they were through, but she'd declined. She could call any one of her brothers or sisters to take her, yet that night, or, she finally decided, in the morning.

She wasn't eager to have another conversation with Sebastian Cross that night. Whatever he'd been going through, whether it had been real or the result of an episode triggered from his past, she'd felt as though she'd been stabbed by his words.

Hurt beyond one friend speaking harshly to another.

She'd been hurt like a woman got hurt by a man she'd slept with. As though there'd been something romantic between them.

Because she was pregnant?

The knowledge had surfaced to taunt her any time her head hadn't been filled with medical thoughts over the past couple of hours of monitoring puppies. And waiting.

She was pregnant.

Couldn't wrap her mind around the test results, the fact that they said what they did. Let alone get any further along than that.

The doctor at the clinic had told her to make an appointment with her ob-gyn sooner rather than later. At two months, there were many things they could determine already.

And she needed to be on vitamins.

Some of it she'd remembered from going through Hannah's pregnancy with her.

Nothing that felt at all real to her.

Or as if the information was part of her own life.

The three puppies were showing marked signs of improvement. She expected them to be just fine.

And wanted to just go home to bed with that victory the last thing on her mind for the day.

Instead, she was going to her office to sleep on the couch. The pillow and blanket she kept in the closet for that purpose would do just fine. She'd already set the alarm on her phone to wake her every two hours.

She opened her office door, ready to give up her concerns and rest, and stopped. The one person in the world she absolutely did not want to talk to that night was still there. Sitting on what was supposed to be her bed in about five minutes.

"I thought you went home." Over an hour before. She'd told him to go.

He'd never actually said he would. He'd just asked after his puppies.

"You said the little ones would need two-hour checks throughout the night." He didn't stand, or grab keys from wherever he'd stashed them, or make a single move to vacate what was soon to be her bedroom.

"That's right." She stood in the doorway. No way she was going to be in a bedroom with the man. Not ever again. "I've already set my alarm."

"You can't be getting up every two hours. You need your rest."

What was he? The veterinarian police? As well as the dating general?

"You need to go."

"I need to apologize," he said instead, his hands on his jean-clad thighs as he met her gaze straight on. His beard was like a picture frame to the straight line of his mouth.

Drawing attention to his lack of smile.

"I want to tell you why I overreacted as I did tonight, except that I have no idea how to do that. But I know I was one hundred percent wrong and I'm truly sorry."

She wasn't in the mood to be forgiving.

She was tired. Hurt. And apparently pregnant, too.

"I just want you to know, if you need anything... I know your family gets a little overwhelming for you sometimes, and, you can, you know... If you need someone to spout off to..."

What the hell? He couldn't still be hallucinating?

Was she?

She moved into the room far enough to drop down to her chair. With the desk in between them. An office, not a bedroom. "What on earth are you talking about?"

"You were there for me that night Oscar was hurt. And then again tonight. You've seen me at my worst—at least more of it than anyone else has ever seen. And… I'm hoping that… We're friends…"

"Sure. I guess we're friends," she said, truly confused. And too tired to figure things out. "What's going on, Sebastian? Are you sick or something?" Were his struggles more than residue from his past? Was it something physical? Something that was going to get worse?

Her heart pounded and her stomach felt sick.

"I know," he said.

She frowned. Tears of frustration pushed at her. She held them back and asked, "Know what?"

"I was on the phone, leaned on your desk. I accidently knocked the file off, Ruby. I saw the test results."

The file. Results.

Her gaze landed on the only such item on her desk. The one she'd left when she'd folded up Sebastian's copies of the paperwork and put them in her satchel.

Cold, hot, nervous as hell, panicking, she stared at him. He was so calm.

And offering to be there for her?

"You know?" she asked. Was this something he wanted, then? Something he'd welcome?

She hadn't, for one second, considered that possibility.

They'd never even been on a date.

He was Wade's friend.

His nod was slow. Seemed to be filled with compassion. "Does the father know yet?"

She blinked. Shook her head. Wanted to stamp her feet. Or kick something.

"What do you mean 'does the father know?'" she asked, her tone low. Filled with warning.

He shrugged the big strong shoulders she'd run her tongue all over. "About the test results. They're dated today. And you were at my place shortly after you'd have finished here." With a sideways nod of his head, he kept right on talking. "This boyfriend... I figure, since you're keeping him a secret from your family... there might be some challenges, and in spite of my earlier words tonight, I just want you to know that I'm here to support you in..."

"Stop it." She bit out the words. Stood. Everything he'd thrown at her earlier cascaded down on her. Along with the boatloads of hurt his words had generated. "How could you think that of me?" She raised her voice. Didn't care. "Aside from the fact that we owe each other nothing in the dating department, how could you possibly think that I'd have some secret guy and, in the light of ongoing events, not tell anyone?" *Or, in light of the fact that we had sex, not tell you?* The words were there, wanting to be said. She stifled them for all she was worth.

"Hey, I'm just an innocent bystander here. My earlier outburst aside. I still take full responsibility for that."

"Move on, then. Tell me how you've drawn such a demeaning conclusion about my private life."

"I was at Colton Ranch today," he said, looking as weary as she felt. "With Elise."

He'd been avalanche training, she translated, with a definite lack of patience.

"Wade came up to me and asked me if I knew who the guy was. He thought maybe it was someone you'd met through Crosswinds. Like a handler who'd come in for training, or something."

"What?" The scream filled the hallway of the vacant clinic as she sank back down to her chair. "Has the whole world gone mad?" Or was it just her small part in it?

Pregnant? Her brother claiming she had a secret boyfriend? Sebastian accusing her of putting everyone at risk by not exposing the guy to the police investigation?

"Wade said Hannah came to him today. She was apparently really upset. Which, for Hannah..."

Ruby slumped back, every bit of energy draining out of her.

Hannah had promised not to mention the baby.

"According to Wade, Hannah had irrefutable proof that you've got a secret boyfriend, and they both think that he might be the one after you. They're afraid your secret is putting you in danger."

Which was why Sebastian had been so upset earlier.

At least one thing in the world made sense.

Until she thought about telling the man sitting on her couch, who was being so kind to her, that the baby he thought belonged to someone else was his own.

Her stomach jumbling with nerves, she waved toward the lone folder on her desk. "That was her proof," she told him, slowly. Hoping maybe he'd figure things out on his own and need some space as badly as she did.

That he'd just go and leave her alone.

Because alone was how she was going to have to handle the next phase of her life. Even without thinking ahead, she'd known from the instant she'd heard the second results that she was going to be doing it by herself.

Maybe she was hoping they were going to point at folders, then talk around the issue and leave it at that.

When he sat there, looking at her expectantly, she said, "I fainted this afternoon. Hannah was…"

Sebastian sat forward, frowning, his gaze creased with concern. "You fainted? Are you okay? And you've been standing out there all night tending to my dogs? You should have said something."

He was a compassionate man. She'd known that about him…always. The way he was with dogs—he got them, just like she did. Accepted, and gave the unconditional love without reservation.

"I'm fine," she said, looking at the folder then, not at the man across the room. Thankfully, Sebastian was taking his seat again. Him towering over her was not a good thing for her equilibrium, either.

"Apparently the smell of coffee is going to be off my list for a while," she said inanely. Something she'd only just realized. "Hannah and Frannie were here having lunch," she continued, buying herself time because she was too tired to just take charge and get what was coming, over with. "They insisted we head over to Express Medical, and I did so just to quiet their fears."

"You didn't know?" More of that compassion was showing from his eyes. She hadn't realized how much she'd noticed that about him.

Because it was always focused on his dogs. Or people his dogs rescued. Or the veterans who needed his dogs.

She shook her head. "I was sure it a mistake, and told them both so. And forbade them from telling anyone about the false result. I went back for a second test after work. To prove myself right."

Would he piece it together now? She'd had the test and then driven out to his place.

Sitting forward, Sebastian rubbed his hands together, lightly, as though uncomfortable. "So...who is he, Ruby? Why the need for secrecy?"

He still didn't get it.

"It's you, Sebastian."

It's you, Sebastian. He couldn't have heard her right.

No way did his name have anything to do with this one. Coming at her with accusation in his tone—yes. But...being a secret boyfriend?

Because he sure as hell couldn't be what she was trying to tell him he was.

No matter what.

He was going to live without human beings in his home for the rest of his life. That decision had been made years ago.

His dogs were his family.

Being a secret boyfriend, one who still lived alone... He could, perhaps, in the future, wrap his mind around that one, but...

He shook his head.

There was just no way.

"I used a condom," he said quietly. Careful to be respectful of any emotional state her news would have flung her into. "A fresh one. All three times."

Three times in one night.

What a night that had been.

"I know." Ruby nodded, seeming far calmer than the situation warranted. "That's one reason I was so certain the test had produced false results."

One reason. There were others? He waited to hear

them. Needed to hear them. To build his case against what she was trying to make him out to be. It wasn't happening.

When she didn't elaborate, he pushed. "What were the other reasons?"

"My cycle. I've had it."

Oh. Maybe a bit too much information there. For a friend trying to be supportive. That was maybe better left to the secret boyfriend.

If there was one. The thought hit like a brick to the face. He was generally an intelligent man. Quick to grasp what was in front of him. "Hannah was there to hear the test results," he said slowly, piecing it all together. "She couldn't tell anyone about the diagnosis, and so she did the next best thing. She went to find out who the father was."

"That's my guess. It sounds like Hannah. Definitely my no-nonsense little sister."

Ruby looked tired. More than tired. She looked… lost.

He had to go.

It's you, Sebastian. Even if he'd heard her right— which he wasn't sure he had, but he wasn't asking—she had to have confused him with someone else.

Maybe if he wasn't there, she'd call the father.

Maybe she couldn't call him. If he was married. Was at home with his wife. Maybe he even had other children. Clearly, if she could tell the father, expose their relationship, she wouldn't be sitting here talking to Sebastian.

She trusted him. The knowledge felt…good.

But no way could he take on this problem. He couldn't be what she was trying to make him out to be.

And trusted that she'd see that. She'd just received the news. Was still in shock.

Remembering both times she'd come upon him when emotional unrest had him at his worst, he leaned forward, elbows on his knees, and said, "Are there any more reasons?" For him, rational talking helped. Focusing on the reality right in front of him, little pieces at a time.

"I've only had sex once in two years. The odds are just too incredulous to believe."

Once. In two years.

She'd meant two months, right? Only once since him?

He stared at her. She was staring right back at him. Gaze clear. Not happy. But clear.

It's you, Sebastian.

He stood up and strode out.

Chapter 7

Ruby hadn't given Sebastian's potential reaction a whole lot of thought. She hadn't even been able to land on one of her own, let alone imagine his.

However, him calmly walking out on her, without a word, was a complete surprise.

Sitting there at her desk, at nearly midnight, with most of the city outside asleep, she'd never felt more alone in her life.

Hannah, damn her, had been worried, trying to watch out for Ruby, to help her deal with a situation she'd clearly not been tending to well herself. And Ruby loved her for it. But her sister had just put the weight of twelve Coltons on her shoulders, when she wasn't even handling the tiny weight of one growing inside her.

Denial was the first stage of grief.

Was it a stage of life, too?

Was she grieving the loss of the life she wanted?

Or just giving herself time to process?

She heard steps in the hallway. Grabbed the gun her father had made her learn how to use and keep in her desk drawer, because she was a Colton and you never knew...

And saw Sebastian standing in her doorway, the box of puppies in his arms.

She didn't say a word. The little ones were his. And out of imminent danger. Being with their mother would be a good thing. And Sebastian would remain with them all night. She didn't have a doubt about that.

Instead of saying whatever goodbye she'd figured he'd come to say, he walked into the office. He glanced at the gun she held, but didn't hesitate as he stood directly in front of her desk.

"These are the babies in my life," he told her. "The only babies I can ever have."

After sliding the gun back into its place, she locked the drawer with the switch on the underside of her desk. "I'm not asking anything from you, Sebastian," she said, feeling steady with the words.

She hadn't consciously thought about it, but there it was. Sitting right with her.

"Like you, I didn't expect or want this, but I knew this afternoon that if the positive result was accurate, I was going to have the baby. My choice. Made completely without you. We—you and I together—don't have to do anything differently, change anything about our relationship. We work well together, and... I hope, as you said tonight, we're friends, too..."

He shook his head. Opened his mouth and, not ready for his rejection, she blurted out more words. "I can do this alone. As we've already established, I have a huge, nosy, caring family who will butt in all the time and help me. Even when I don't need it." She smiled. It hurt her cheeks.

Everything she was saying hurt, too.

She'd drawn a metaphorical picture of the way she'd wanted her life to look. She was in the middle, a spinster. The cacophony of growing up in such a large family, the tension between her parents, her mother's hurt feelings, the distance…and then Aunt Jessie and Uncle Buck… The idea of bringing any chance of any of that into her own home…

In the picture, Hannah's sweet Lucy had been the little love of her life. Being an aunt fulfilled her motherly instincts just fine. And her practice, the animals who consumed her days and a lot of her nights, too, took up most of the rest of the space. With just enough room left over to fit every member of her family and Owl Creek's citizens. The town was her picture frame. The pieces of wood that supported her, kept her together.

Sebastian seemed to shrink as he stood there, silently holding his box. The puppies were sleeping. She'd noticed that immediately. And were breathing normally.

"You deserve a stable, loving husband. Your children, as much or more so." When he finally spoke, the words carried calmness. Truth. "As you witnessed for yourself earlier tonight, I can't provide that. Not because I don't want to, or because I'm not willing to. Not because I wouldn't give my all to try, but because it's out of my control."

If Oscar was PTSD-trained…or Sebastian got a second dog that was…

She stopped the thought short. No wishing for stars in the sky on a sunny day.

"It's okay," she told him. "I don't want a husband, Sebastian. I've never had a long-term relationship because I didn't want one. I'm thirty and single by choice." The words came easily. There was a new catch in her heart as she said them, though.

And a hose filled with panic blowing a gasket inside her. How did a strong-minded, independent woman like herself accept the fact that she'd had no choice in the biggest matter in her life? Keeping the baby was a choice.

But getting pregnant? She'd taken precautions and...

"That night..." Sebastian said, as though reading her thoughts. Her gaze darted to him as he continued, "If it hadn't been for my panic attack, we'd never have..."

No, they wouldn't have. But... "I wanted to." He had to know that she hadn't been completely selfless that night. Sex asked too much from her to just be a distraction.

For a second there, his eyes lit up and he grinned. Her lower belly responded.

Then he sobered. "That panic attack is precisely why I can't offer you..."

"I wouldn't accept it if you did," she told him quietly. She didn't want any marriage. Let alone one born out of pity or obligation—which was what her parents' marriage had been. Or had become, by the time Ruby was old enough to be aware of such things.

Maybe all marriages became that, inside a home's walls. How did anyone really know?

"I'll be that friend I spoke about a little bit ago. When I was thinking there was a boyfriend..."

She nodded. A little smile flowered inside her. "I'd like that."

And now, he should go. Since he was taking the puppies back to Jasmine, she could go home and get some rest.

Except that her car was at his place.

She most definitely was not going back there. Not this late at night. Without an emergency to tend to.

Besides, her little two-bedroom house on the lake was calling to her. It was all hers. And only hers.

Sebastian wasn't leaving. "I should be there when you tell your family I'm the father."

Her family and Sebastian—her father and Wade and Sebastian—in the same room when she announced that she'd gotten knocked up by mistake and was going to be a single mother?

She could feel the tension all the way up to her ears. The pressure...

"Can we leave that thought for another day?" she asked him. "Let's wait at least until after I've had my first appointment before we tell anyone anything..." There could be something that would prevent the pregnancy from continuing. She was still in her first trimester. Could miscarry.

And did not want to.

A strange sense of grief had hit as soon as she'd thought of the possibility of losing the baby. So much so that she issued a quick, silent and very fervent prayer to the fates that her fetus was healthy.

The sensation took over her entire being. That need for the little raspberry-sized being growing inside her to be well.

Not understanding herself, or life in general, she settled for a "thank you" to Sebastian when he agreed to her request.

Him being the father of her baby would be their secret.

For the moment.

"Would you mind giving me a ride home?" she asked him then, thinking his ready acceptance would be a given. After all, she was carrying their mutual result of the choice they'd made together to have sex. He could provide some transportation.

Didn't mean she needed him. Or wanted his help.

It was just the way the math added up.

Sebastian was so far out of his element that he couldn't find himself. He saw the immediate steps in front of him and took them.

He got the box of sleeping puppies settled in his truck, waited for Ruby to climb in and started the engine.

Looking out the windshield, the future hung before him. Drive off the lot and down the mile or so to Ruby's little house on the lake. He'd been by it countless times. Had never been inside.

His child would be living there.

The thought came and he sat with it.

He wasn't going to be a husband, or a live-in father, but he was going to have a biological child in the world.

It didn't compute.

He'd made his decisions. Set his course.

But sometimes, as had happened with the tragic deaths of his parents, life went off course. He was going to have to adjust.

He couldn't change what he couldn't change. His occasional panic attacks. The unpredictable nightmares. His need to live alone.

But he had a lot of rerouting to do.

The child would come first. What was best for the life he and Ruby had created.

And Ruby was his responsibility, too. In part. Since she was housing the child—over the next seven months, but after that, too.

He'd call his banker in the morning. Start the work on a new financial plan.

And someone was out to get him…and possibly her. A vision of the completely shattered windshield—one bullet in the exact right spot—on her vehicle, not his, shot through his mind as he pulled into Ruby's driveway. Saw the dark house with the huge lake right behind it.

Someone could swim ashore…hide in the reeds, then behind the trees in her yard.

He got out when she did. Reached for the box of puppies.

"What are you doing?" she asked, stopping at the front of his truck on her way to the sidewalk leading up to her front door.

"Based on the poison information you provided, and on some evidence found at the scene tonight, Glen Steele determined that the puppies were being poisoned when you pulled up to my house. That it's likely all the puppies, and Jasmine, too, would have died if you hadn't arrived when you did. This guy's for real, Ruby, and he's escalating."

"And you're afraid to go home?"

How could a woman's scrunched-up face look so cute to him in that moment?

"Hell no. I'm uncomfortable leaving you home alone, especially arriving this late, until we know more."

The set of her chin didn't budge. "What on earth does the time matter? If I'd come home earlier, I'd still be here now, this late."

Right. If she'd arrived home alone, and someone had been watching...

He had to get himself together. Focus.

"I'd still like to stay," he said quietly. How could he protect her if he wasn't there?

"I don't want to be rude, Sebastian, but you are not staying here. I'm going inside. Alone. And I'll have someone bring me out in the morning to get my SUV. I appreciate your concern. I know we're both a bit off-kilter. I'm glad we're going to be friends through all of this. And there's no way I'm risking more intimate moments with you right now. Good night."

He stood there and watched as she turned, walked slowly, steadily, up to her door, went inside and shut the door behind her. He watched until he saw lights come on.

And then he drove around a bit and checked back.

Once. Twice.

Thinking about her. About the baby she was carrying.

Needing a battle plan.

Finding no ready answers.

Sometime after one, he caught a glimpse of himself from the outside looking in. A guy in a truck, driving the same roads, watching a house, when he needed to be getting three puppies back to their mother, checking everything over, setting his alarm for two-hour intervals and stretching out on a mat in the medical building that had been invaded by a would-be killer that night.

The police were on the case. Ruby was a Colton, a member of the family that owned half the town—they'd definitely be watching over her. Robert would have already seen to that.

She wasn't telling anyone he was the father of the baby yet. She hadn't even been to the doctor to confirm that things were in place to progress normally.

He had some time to figure it all out.

Ruby called for an obstetrician appointment in Connors as soon as she was up and showered Friday morning. And was lucky enough to grab a canceled appointment. She'd intended to catch a ride out to Crosswinds to get her vehicle, but there'd been a text from Sebastian saying he'd had it delivered. When she checked him on it, she found the SUV locked in her driveway.

She had the keys.

He must have had it towed.

Which couldn't have been cheap.

When she started to wonder how he'd explained the choice to the truck driver, she shook her head and pushed the thought away. Didn't matter to her what someone else had said to another. She had her vehicle.

The forty-five-minute drive to the medical complex where she'd been going since she was a kid calmed her.

She was taking action. Gathering information. From there, she could determine her next step. And the one after that.

She was taking control of her life, rather than letting life control her.

She was getting away from Owl Creek, shrapnel in Oscar, poisoned puppies, a shot-out windshield, the secret-boyfriend drama created by her sisters... and Sebastian Cross. For the morning, she could just breathe.

And she did so fairly well, remaining calm and in charge of her life, right up until she was lying on the table for the ultrasound her doctor had just ordered. The procedure had been part of the canceled appointment Ruby had snagged, and the timing was right.

Wasn't it great how that all worked out? Saved Ruby a trip back.

Except that she wasn't mentally prepared. Not for the procedure—she'd have worn pants that were easier to slide down to her pelvic bone to make room for the Doppler to travel in the gel. And she wasn't ready to be face-to-face with the screen that would make the inconceivable a medical reality to her.

Internally, Dr. Evelyn had said, everything looked perfect. Things that were supposed to be changing inside of her were doing so right on target and as well as she liked to see them.

According to the doctor, she was most definitely pregnant.

Ruby still couldn't grasp the concept in terms of herself. The past twenty-four hours were like an out-of-body experience.

She felt the gel. Heard the technician explain things she already knew. Ultrasound was ultrasound, whether you were using it to diagnose human bodies or animal ones.

Frozen, lying stiffly, her arms tense at her side, her fingers clenched into fists, she stared at the ceiling as the procedure began.

Concentrated on the sensation of cold jelly spreading over her stomach. The there and then. Not the what-would-be.

Tried not to hear the deafening lack of sound as the technician's silence permeated the room.

Find the fetus. Measure. Determine that everything was normal. She listed the woman's duties as far as she could think through them.

A muffled thump sounded in the room. Again and again. Rhythmically. Booming through every wave in Ruby's eardrum. Faster than she normally heard.

But it was undeniable just the same. Her head turned of its own accord. Her gaze landed on the grayscale image on screen and she couldn't look away.

There it was.

She saw it immediately. Analyzed every inch of material on the screen. Knew exactly what she was looking at. And diagnosing.

Her. Alone. By herself.

The uterus looked great. The fetus. Perfectly positioned.

And that sound, muffled and seemingly so loud…

"We have a heartbeat," the technician said, pleasure in her tone.

Stating the obvious.

And Ruby burst into tears.

Chapter 8

Sebastian checked on the puppies several times that day, finding irony in the fact that he was tending to babies he owned when he'd never be a father to his own child.

The child couldn't know about their biological connection. Sebastian could be a friend to Ruby and nothing more.

But he could assist Ruby in any way possible. He'd already spoken with his financial advisor, who was setting up a trust fund for the child that Ruby was carrying.

In her name.

And by noon, he was convincing himself that it would all be okay. When problems arose—as they always did—he and Ruby would work them out, with her having the final say.

If he didn't take ownership over the situation, he'd be okay.

What he did intend to get to the bottom of was the escalating vandalism on his property.

Three puppies had almost died.

He wasn't going to sit back and wait for more to happen. He needed answers, even if he had to find them himself.

Calling Glen Steele, he asked for a full rundown of what the police had found the night before, what they made of the evidence and what more he could do to assist.

They'd found a partial smudge of a footprint not far outside a window in the medical building. The window facing the kennels had shrubbery beneath it, which made the footprint unusual. They'd also found some freshly fallen greenery. The window had been found unlocked and had been opened recently, with no obvious signs of a break-in.

Which made no sense to him. The windows, most particularly in the medical building, were always kept locked.

The poison had been administered, they believed, through puppy treats. A tainted one was found several feet from the building, on the way down to the lake.

To that end, Sebastian arranged to have surveillance cameras installed along the shore of his land by nightfall. He wasn't sure what good they'd do, since the culprit had managed to avoid all cameras around the kennels and medical building, but it was worth trying. He threw away all the dog food on the premises and ordered new options to be delivered by feeding time that night.

But he didn't figure that that would make any difference, either, as the puppy treat found in the grass was not anything he'd had on site.

Clearly, his place was being targeted. For what reason, no one knew. The police weren't completely ruling out Ruby as a target, either. Though they were less worried that the attacks had anything to do with her, they noted that she'd been present during the last two of them.

They had acknowledged that perhaps her presence, her arrival at his house the evening before, had prevented the rest of the puppies, and possibly Jasmine, from being poisoned as well.

Her arrival. She hadn't been at his house to see to the puppies. She'd seen the puppies only because she'd walked out on him when he'd been such a jerk to her.

She'd been there to tell him about the baby.

It was no mistake that he'd been in the throes of a nightmare. Fate intervening, showing him why he couldn't be a father, before he found out he'd biologically created a human being.

Still didn't explain his emotional overreaction to Wade's news the day before. His friend had questioned him before the nightmare. After his session with Malcolm and Elise, Sebastian had been feeling good.

But because he'd thought Ruby had had a boyfriend when she'd had sex with him, he'd suddenly felt sucker-punched.

Come at her like a pubescent boy.

At a time when she'd needed him to be a support.

It was just more proof to him that he was best with dogs as his family, not people. His parents, a high-profile thoracic surgeon and a well-known philanthropist, had been gone more than they'd been home when he was growing up. That, coupled with the summers he spent away from his school friends in Boise and being made to stay at the remote cabin at Owl Creek with a nanny, meant that he'd pretty much been a loner his whole life. Not unhappy. At all. He'd always been treated with care and respect. He'd loved Owl Creek. And had had every advantage in Boise, too. He'd had Jerry. The spaniel had been his constant. Winter. Summer. Boise. Owl Creek. Always home. In his room every night.

Until the year he'd graduated from high school. And then he'd joined the Marines, where he'd been a member of another family.

Several times that day he thought about calling Ruby. Felt compelled to do so. But knew the desire was driven by his own selfishness, not with her best interests in mind.

Just as his insistence that he was going to stay with her the previous night had been. It would have made him feel better to be there protecting her from whatever boogeyman might appear out of the ether. In making the choice, he hadn't considered how having him there in her space would have made her feel.

Maybe growing up the only child of wealthy parents had made him a spoiled brat.

He didn't give in to any of his instincts to drive into town and check on Ruby, either. He'd texted her Friday night, just asking how she was.

Saw her text back: Fine. And let it go.

And on Saturday, he got back to dedicating himself to work that helped others survive traumatic situations. Jaxon Walker, a new handler, had arrived in Boise the night before, was driving to Owl Creek Saturday morning to check into a hotel in town. He would be heading out to Crosswinds to meet Echo, the two-year-old male search-and-rescue shepherd that Sebastian had been training for him. Jaxon, a detective with the Buffalo, New York, police had been referred to Sebastian, and if all went well, Crosswinds could be training another dozen dogs through Jaxon and his contacts.

As Sebastian headed to the kennel to prepare for the first session between Jaxon and Echo, he got a thrill considering the potential successful searches, with the future lives saved by his dogs. Similar to the way he'd felt the first time he'd put on his Marine uniform, knowing that he was willing to give his life to fight for his country's safety and freedom.

Protecting and saving lives—those were his callings. And they were good ones. He just had to make sure that he didn't let his enthusiasm to care for others overstep onto Ruby's rights to live her own way.

Even while he spent the rest of his life doing what he could to protect her and the child she was carrying.

Not an easy task he'd set for himself, but one he was up to, he was sure. Easy had never been his way.

As it turned out, Jaxon Walker, clearly as eager as Sebastian to get their association started, showed up more than half an hour early. Sebastian hadn't even gone in to spend his usual few minutes with Echo yet.

Energized by the other man's enthusiasm, he invited Jaxon into the kennel with him, and gave the man a general spiel about the work they did, pointing out various training areas. He was still several yards from Echo's kennel when he heard whining and crashing up against a kennel door.

Instantly alarmed, his mind immediately going to Jasmine and her puppies, Sebastian called for help and had everyone on site checking every kennel for signs of a distressed dog.

He headed straight toward Echo, was relieved to see the dog standing and wagging his tail at his door. Still a few feet away, noting the dog's empty water bowl, he made a mental note to talk to Bryony—his youngest employee, at twenty—who'd been in charge of watering that day.

And then, as Echo started to whine and jump up at her door, he frowned.

"Down," he said firmly. "Echo, sit." Basic commands the dog had followed without fail since his eleventh week of life.

When Echo continued to ecstatically greet his approaching visitors, a sense of foreboding came over Sebastian. Something was wrong.

Very, very wrong.

His hunch played out in the worst possible scenario over the next twenty minutes—which was as long as Jaxon Walker hung around Crosswinds.

Echo, once out of his kennel, ran around uncontrollably. Sniffing. Digging. But not on cue, and not at anything that mattered.

The dog wouldn't come. Jumped up on Sebastian for treats. And ran off playing with another dog in training.

Jaxon, obviously disgusted, told Sebastian that he was not only taking Crosswinds off his list, but was also going to spread the word to other law enforcement as well, and strode out.

It was the single most awful moment of Sebastian's career with Crosswinds.

And he did what he had to do.

He called Ruby.

* * *

When she saw Sebastian's number come up on her phone, Ruby almost didn't answer. His text the night before had been…nice.

Welcome, even.

And enough.

Other than her clients and patients and employees, she didn't want to see anyone—most particularly not him.

So much so that she'd done nothing to stop the spread of her sister's secret-boyfriend saga. Or the amateur detective work her family was engaged in to find her out.

Let them spin their wheels, waste their time and fail, she thought.

At least it would keep them off her back for a couple of days. Time for her to come to terms with the fact that her world had been irrevocably changed…forever.

To accept that she wasn't going to be living the life she'd planned.

And to figure out why her heart was so protective of, so incredibly caring about, a tiny floating mass she absolutely hadn't ever wanted.

She was trying to wrap her mind around the fact that she was going to be a mother. That in roughly seven months' time, she'd be dealing with breast feeding every two hours, diaper changes and…

The phone had quit ringing.

But it started up again.

"Hello?" Sitting at her desk, trying to get her breath back from the gulp she'd just taken, Ruby figured it was better to answer a call then have the man on her doorstep.

If indeed, he had any intention of coming anywhere near her once he'd had the time to process her news.

"Ruby?" His voice had an unsettled tone. If he was just making an assuage-the-guilt call, she'd put an end to that immediately.

"What do you need, Sebastian?" she asked in her calmest, most professional voice.

"You."

Her heart leaped. To the ceiling. Stuck there.

"Out here," he said, loosening her emotions from their elated state, crashing them to the ground.

It had to be hormones, she thought briefly, before she sat upright. "What's wrong?"

She should have known, should have sensed…

"It's Echo. He's out of his head. Won't follow commands, won't…"

He'd had Echo's handler, some bigwig cop from Buffalo, coming in that day. "I'm on my way," she told him, her bag already over her shoulder before she dropped her phone into it.

Letting her receptionist know that she was out on a call, made it to Crosswinds in seven minutes. Pulled up next to the kennels and headed straight for Echo's caged room, before noticing the confusion out on one of the training courses.

Echo, running and playing with another dog, Lucky, who'd been in training for months.

Lucky, bless his heart, was sitting at attention, on command, while Sebastian and his other trainer, Della Winslow, were trying to corral the shepherd.

"Hey, Dr. Colton, I was just in Echo's kennel, filling her water again—it was empty and I'd just filled it a couple of hours ago. She'd thrown up in the back of it, behind her bed, and I found this in it..." Bryony, in jeans and cowboy boots, held up a couple of pieces of dark paper, and Ruby's heart sank.

After thanking the kennel assistant, she grabbed a handful of dog treats and ran out to Sebastian and Della, slowing as she neared the door to the training area, where they had Echo at least semi contained.

Barely glancing at either of the humans, she held out the treats, calling to the wild dog. Whether it was the new voice in her immediate vicinity or the word *treat*, Echo, looking toward Ruby's outstretched hand, stopped long enough for Sebastian to get hold of the dog's collar and Della snapped on a leash.

Within minutes, Ruby had the dog in the medical building, with Sebastian beside her, holding Echo steady while she listened to the dog's heart rate. She administered activated charcoal and waited in the building while Sebastian turned the dog over to Della and the others to watch over her for the next several hours.

As soon as he returned, Ruby held out her hand. "Bryony found this in Echo's kennel," she said, handing him the crumpled and stained pieces of paper she'd brought back with her.

"Dark chocolate?" He looked from the paper to her. "A fifteen-ounce package?"

"We have to assume he ate it all," she told him, finally, for the first time, meeting his eyes. "It could kill him, Sebastian. I don't think it will. He's young. His heartbeat is rapid, but not alarmingly so. He vomited afterward, so that's a good sign. Hopefully the activated charcoal was introduced soon enough to counteract the theobromine and caffeine in his system."

He nodded. Held her gaze. And it was like he was

talking to her. Out loud. She heard his frustration. His worry. His pain.

And his anger, too.

Still watching her, he pulled out his phone and dialed Glen Steele.

"We've got the type of chocolate, the amount purchased—we have to be able to get something off from this, even if we have to go to every store in town ourselves," he said after hanging up with the detective's assertion that he was on his way out.

At first, thinking his *we* meant him and her, Ruby's heart swelled. With him. For him.

And then she realized that he'd been using a generic *we* to encompass everyone working on the case.

"I'm going to stay a while," she told him then. Because she didn't want to leave. Not him. Not Echo.

She didn't want to sit home by herself on a Saturday night, knowing that she was taking on the biggest challenge of her life and would be doing it all alone.

"If he does go into cardiac arrest, the ten minutes it would take me to get here could be a matter of his life or death."

From chocolate.

Sebastian didn't argue. Because he wanted her there? Felt a sense that she should be there, with him, as she did? Or because he was too distracted to argue? She didn't know.

"It could just be one of your employees brought it to work and…"

"No food in the kennels, ever," he said.

She hadn't been sold on the theory, anyway. Who'd drop a fifteen-ounce bar of chocolate and not notice? Or carry one in their pocket while they were working? It wasn't like a bar that size would fit in a normal pocket.

"I'm guessing he got a hold of it, that it was given to him sometime before daylight," Ruby said then, needing to help him. To fill the silence that was growing too deep. "It can take hours for a dog to react…"

"Before anyone got here," Sebastian said. "Every single attack has been in the dark. I just don't get it. What is this guy trying to prove?"

"You said the police think he's trying to sabotage Crosswinds for some reason. To run you out of business."

"It's one theory." He was watching her again. Really watching. Her eyes, her face, down her body and back to her eyes. "And it makes a certain kind of sense. This thing with Echo definitely cost me today—and who knows for how long into the future." He told her about the detective's parting remark regarding spreading the word among other police departments to take Crosswinds off their list. "Who am I hurting out here?"

Her heart lurched at the tone in his voice. And she took a step forward.

"Don't let him get to you, Sebastian. Don't let him win. He made a mistake, giving Echo the whole bar, paper and all. Maybe you're right and the police will be able to find him through its purchase. And even if they can't, he left behind tangible evidence this time."

He nodded. "Thank God for you," he told her then. "He hits and you swoop in and save us, three times now."

Because he'd called her, yes. At least two of the three times. The puppies two nights before—well, that had been…not him calling her.

She'd been there for an entirely different reason.

And she and Sebastian were going to have to talk more about that.

But not yet. Not with Detective Steele on his way.

"I didn't save you today," she said. "You still lost Jaxon, but, if you'll allow me to, I can call him while he's still here in town. I can explain from a medical perspective why the dog was acting as he was."

Shaking his head, Sebastian pulled out his phone. "That's something I can do myself," he told her, and walked out of the building.

Because that's how he worked. Doing everything he could possibly do by himself.

Just like her.

Independent loners. Both of them.

Which didn't bode well for the baby they'd created.

Chapter 9

Jaxon Walker agreed to another trip out to Crosswinds. He'd already driven back to Boise, hoping to catch an earlier flight out, but said he'd check into a hotel instead and let Sebastian know when he'd be in Owl Creek the next day. While Sebastian had been adamant about keeping the attacks against his business out of the news and away from his clients, he'd told the detective what had been going on, and instead of losing a client, he seemed to have gained another law-enforcement person with a mind to discuss the case and the motive.

All anyone could think of was that someone needed revenge against him. Or, as Jaxon had pointed out in their phone conversation, perhaps against his mom or dad. The property upon which he'd built Crosswinds had been in his family for generations. It was all that was left of his parents' estate. Sebastian had used a chunk of his inheritance to renovate the cabin and build Crosswinds, as well as to support himself until he'd grown the company into the elite training facility it was. The business was lucrative. And he'd invested well himself. Had more money than he'd ever spend. No one but his financial advisor knew that. He didn't care about spending the money. He needed the security.

Maybe, until he'd made a success out of Crosswinds, no one had known there was anything left of Sebastian's parents to go after.

It was the most workable theory Sebastian had heard. And when he'd shared it with Ruby after the police left, she'd agreed with him.

"Your father was a doctor, so maybe there's someone who lost a loved one he couldn't save—a kid who's now grown, who maybe had a hard life after their parent died." It made sense. Better sense than anything else he'd heard to date.

At Jaxon's suggestion, the police were already broadening their search into his parents' lives. For all Sebastian knew, one or the other of them had had an affair and there was some illegitimate child who was jealous that Sebastian had everything. Maybe it was someone who had just, in recent months, discovered their heritage through one of the popular DNA-testing organizations.

The thought was out there. He recognized that.

And yet…the uncertainty lingered.

He stood in the kennel with Ruby, watching Echo, who'd calmed dramatically and whose heart rate Ruby had just pronounced a little high, still, but within normal range. Sebastian felt a twinge of resentment when his phone rang.

Because…what? He wanted a minute alone with the

woman he'd already determined he didn't want to be personally alone with?

The call took all of thirty seconds. Phone still in hand after he hang up, Sebastian told Ruby, "James Greenaway just quit." One of his three part-timers, James had been cleaning out the kennels. "He said that three interviews with the police was enough. He didn't do anything wrong, but they're treating him like a suspect. He wants to be done."

Sebastian could have argued, tried to reason with James, talk him back to work, but he hadn't. He didn't blame the kid. And hoped that James had nothing to do with the attacks. He'd hired him right out of high school. Had had hopes of moving him up to assistant trainer in another year or so.

Still standing there in the dimly lit structure that housed the dogs' separate living quarters, Sebastian called Steele one more time to report James's resignation.

"It's probably going to make the police look at him harder," Ruby said as he disconnected that call. She still didn't seem to be in any great hurry to leave.

He nodded, not liking the feeling of helplessness that had been pervading his life over the past weeks. First Oscar's gunshot injury, then Ruby's windshield, the puppies, and Echo…

A baby.

"How exactly does putting you out of business, if this is what the guy's trying to do, help him any? You still own the land. And five lakefront acres with the newly remodeled, enlarged and updated home…"

"Unless he's just bitter and trying to make me suffer as he has." Before killing him? And filing for a possible inheritance? The only way that worked was if there was another biological child...

He stared at Ruby.

"What?"

"I set up a trust for...the child. It's in your name, so you can use the money however you see fit without having to go through any hoops."

"I don't need your money, Sebastian." In her jeans, tennis shoes and long-sleeved short black shirt, she stood up to him. Didn't back away.

And he said, "It's done, Ruby. You can choose to use it or not, and whatever is there when the child turns eighteen will belong to them." But something else had just occurred to him.

"On Monday, I'm going to be drawing up a will." He'd write it yet that night. Sign it. In case something happened to him over the weekend. "Everything I have will go to the child in the event of my death."

Her frown, the rush of emotion in her gaze, held him captive. "Don't talk like that," she said. "This guy... they're going to stop him."

He nodded. Wasn't fearing for his life.

He was just figuring out how to be a father to a child he couldn't live with or raise.

She had to get out. Get away from Sebastian's magnetism. His conscientious heart.

He wasn't offering to be an active father to her child. She wouldn't accept if he had been.

So why did his distance, and yet his immediate help with money and wills—legal, lawyerly things—hurt?

He was the only person in the world other than herself who knew that he was her baby's father. The only one who could share that with her.

And he was thinking about money and wills.

She understood.

Admired him.

And had to hold back tears because…his actions left her feeling utterly alone. In a building filled with him. And dogs.

How could she possibly feel bereft surrounded by any of her beloved four-legged beings?

"I need to get back," she said, maintaining her calm as she started for the door. She was not going to make a scene. Or give Sebastian any reason to doubt that she could be pregnant with his child while remaining friends and maintaining a healthy working relationship.

At the door, she smiled at Della, who was coming into the kennel, and when the trainer spoke to Sebastian, Ruby just kept on walking.

With all the outside lights still on in the training areas, she could make her way on her own as though the sunshine still lit her way.

One foot in front of other.

To her waiting SUV. Paid for. In her name. Her property. Hers. And, soon to have a car seat in it, would be the baby's main mode of transporation, too.

The little flip-flop in her heart at the thought was… nice.

Realizing that her vehicle looked a little lopsided was not nice, however. Hurrying, wanting to get out of there before Sebastian came to find her—or, maybe worse, didn't—Ruby looked at the back driver-side tire with a sinking sensation that went far beyond having a flat.

The tires were less than a year old. Still under warranty.

Didn't mean she hadn't punctured one. Driven over a nail. It happened.

But that it would go flat right now? Another injury to her vehicle at Sebastian's? After dark?

She knew what he was going to think, even before she called him.

Truth was, she was having a hard time not going there herself.

Their vandal had struck again.

But to what purpose? And how? The lights had been on.

Around the kennels. Not behind her car. And not down by the lake.

"It's just a flat," she told Sebastian when he came jogging over from the kennels.

"Steele has officers coming back out just to check the area," he told her. "And for now, you need to stay away from Crosswinds."

"Don't be ridiculous, Sebastian. This one is probably not even an attack. Why just do one tire?" And only her car?

"I don't know why." His tone held the frustration she could read on his expression as he bent to the tire, shining his phone light all around it, following with his hand. "I don't know why any of this is happening. But I do agree that one flat tire seems to be a bit of a de-escalation. Why risk getting caught for one tire?"

Unless the perpetrator had been interrupted again. Like with the puppies.

From his squatting position, he came back with, "How could anyone have known that Echo was the one dog that would cost me the most, today of all days?" He looked up at her and then added, "I can't find anything. Not a nail, or an obvious cut." Moving around to the back, he opened the hatch and the flooring to access the spare tire.

"You don't have to change that," Ruby said quickly. "I'll call…"

"Are you serious?" The look he gave her was long and hard. "I know how to change a tire. And would do so for anyone who got a flat on my land."

With a nod, she silently acknowledged her overreaction, with a note to keep a better watch on herself.

"You don't think Echo was just a random choice," she said then. Sebastian had a real issue going on. One that involved both of them. One they could actually talk about.

"Do you?"

She didn't. The handler in town, the potential for so many more clients… "But how would anyone know that?"

He hauled out the tire, set it standing up right next to him, holding it with his jean-clad knee. And met her gaze. "I know, right?"

Only someone who knew…

"You think James is doing this? But why?"

"Maybe not doing it, but he could have been passing on information. Even unknowingly. Just talking about work…"

She loved that he was trying to think the best of his young, ex-employee. And wasn't so sure that James couldn't be behind the vandalism. "His dad died in Afghanistan, did you know that?"

He nodded. "We talked it about it once."

"Maybe he's jealous that you came back. That you're building something great here, and helping other veterans better their lives, when he's struggling to make ends meet."

He shook his head, then said, "Maybe, but it doesn't make sense. I've been paying his community college tuition."

She hadn't known that. Flooded with warmth to know that he'd do such a thing. And remembered the baby she was carrying.

One who wouldn't have a father, but would have Sebastian paying college tuition.

"I went to the doctor yesterday." She didn't plan the words. They just fell out. And when she heard them out in the open, she started to panic. She didn't have answers yet. Didn't want to talk to him again until she had herself firmly settled wherever she was going to land with her new life. "There was a cancellation," she said, starting to babble. "A woman who'd also had an ultrasound scheduled, so I was able to get it all over with in one quick visit."

There. It was done. Time to move on. "What do you need me to do there?" she asked, pointing toward the spare tire he was still holding. When he didn't answer, she looked up at him. The struggle in his gaze grabbed her.

"I can just send someone to get the vehicle in the morning," she said inanely. "Catch a ride home with Della."

"Do I ask what you found out? How it went?" He seemed stupefied. Frozen.

"I don't know." She barely got the words out.

"I feel like I need to know."

Her heart soared for the second it took her to get a hold of it. "Then I guess you should ask."

She didn't offer the answer. He had to need it badly enough to seek it.

Instead of asking, he set about changing her tire. Like a madman in a race to save his life. Bolts flew out, tire off, tire on, bolts back in. All without a noticeable breath.

Tool loaded back in her spare-tire compartment. Floorboard replaced.

He finally spoke. "Steele asked that you leave the tire, for now. As possible evidence. Just in case."

She nodded. "Thank you." She didn't look his way as, hugging her satchel to her side, she reached for the driver's-side handle.

"Is everything okay?"

Freezing with one foot on the floor of the car, the other still on the ground, she faced the windshield, not Sebastian, and said, "Yes."

She moved to sit down, but stopped again as he asked, "What did the doctor say?"

She'd told him to ask. Implied that she'd answer. "About what?"

"Everything."

Ruby took her foot back out of the car, but left the door open, leaned herself against the frame and part of the seat. Ready to fall in. To get away.

"I'm eight weeks along, everything looks perfect— her word, not mine. She said I needed to start prenatal vitamins, and that she'd see me in a month." She left out the part where she'd said Ruby might experience some fatigue, and to get enough rest. Those were both on her.

"And the ultrasound?"

Ruby stared at him. "We're really going to do this?"

His expression didn't harden, really, but it grew less tentative. He crossed his arms. "You said to ask."

"Why are you?"

With a shrug, Sebastian met her gaze, his face half-shadowed by the bright lights on one side of him and darkness on the other. "I have no idea," he said, sounding like the words had been wrung out of him.

And once again, her heart relented. "If you're feeling guilty, Sebastian, don't. This isn't on you. My choice. I don't need a man to complete me. I'm as independent as you are. I don't know why this happened. The odds are so completely against it. We only did it one night. It was my first time in years, and we used condoms. The chances are minuscule and yet…"

She heard herself. Grew instantly self-conscious that she was babbling again, and finally said, "I'm okay doing this alone."

"I don't think it's guilt that's pushing me to know."

Oh. She stared at him, her mouth suddenly dry as her heart pounded. Not in any way that felt good. "What then?" she asked.

When he shrugged, shook his head again, she wanted to sit down, shut the door in his face and gun it out of there.

Which made about as much sense as him just shaking his head at the important answers.

"How was the ultrasound?"

A *fine* came to mind first. Succinct. Followed by a dramatic exit. She waited herself out. "It was amazing," she said, finally telling him the truth. "I look at those films all the time, and so seeing, not only a human one, but my own body, with that tiny orb of life in my own uterus…"

Her throat clogged up with tears and she had to stop. Swallowed. Blinked. Took a deep breath. Needed to show him how strong she was. How capable.

And then she looked at his face, the set chin, unsmiling mouth, eyes wide…and glistening.

"I heard the heartbeat," she told him. Felt her own chin trembling and sat down. "That was it," she concluded, all business, a doctor in her own right. Her own field. "Thanks again for changing my tire," she said, then shut the door, started her vehicle, pulled away and…

Left him standing there.

Unmoving.

The first glance in the rearview mirror was a mistake.

The second one, curiosity.

The third, just plain not smart.

If she lived twenty lifetimes, she was never going to forget the sight of that big mountain man, the father of her baby, standing all alone.

Chapter 10

A razor-thin spike was found in Ruby's tire. A matching piece had been retrieved from the ground nearby. While there was a small chance that she'd brought the spike in with her, the bigger probability was that the shard had been put in her normal parking spot on the chance that she'd drive over it.

Not a life-threatening event. Not even a potentially dangerous one. At most, she'd have had a slow leak, rather than the more rapid one that had transpired.

Sebastian wanted to believe the flat tire on Saturday night was just a fluke. But his gut was telling him otherwise. No one but Ruby parked next to the medical building.

She parked there every single time she was at Crosswinds.

Her windshield being shot out, and a tire flattened,

definitely seemed to him to have both been done on purpose. Aimed at Ruby.

Other things—the puppies, Echo, the complaints, Oscar—were clearly meant to hurt him. Or, at least, Crosswinds.

And on three of those occurrences, Ruby had saved the day.

Her windshield had been shot out after she'd saved Oscar.

Then the tire flattened after the puppies were poisoned. And her unexpected arrival that evening had most likely prevented the rest of the puppies and Jasmine from also being poisoned.

He didn't want to find out what would happen to her if she returned to Crosswinds after saving Echo. Most particularly after Jaxon Walker paid for the dog and made arrangements for a couple of more weekend training sessions before taking Echo back to New York.

Maybe the perpetrator didn't know that yet, but Sebastian had to figure he would.

By the following Thursday, Sebastian had received three calls through Jaxon Walker's referrals, resulting in at least one sale. And every time something good happened for Crosswinds, he got more tense. Wondering if his stalker, as he was beginning to think of the vandal, would somehow find out and make him pay.

Or, God forbid, go after Ruby again.

The police had followed leads and were watching young James and checking out his associates. But so far, nothing had clicked. The chocolate bar that had poisoned Echo, their most concrete lead, was sold in every tourist shop in town, in hotel gift shops and in the local grocery store, too.

The biggest issue on Sebastian's mind was getting the mystery solved, the threats stopped, before word of Ruby's pregnancy got around. They hadn't spoken since she'd driven away Saturday evening, but he'd texted her every day. Asked how she was feeling. If she'd had any more light-headedness. How her work was going. And she'd responded promptly.

Almost as if they'd made an agreement that it would work that way.

He could go about his life knowing that she was working normal hours, eating well and feeling fine.

But he needed to speak with her. He didn't want any mention of the baby or pregnancy in writing that could be seen, hacked, or looked up by law-enforcement officials. Was he paranoid? Hell, yes.

It was all going to come out. She'd start to show. Her family wouldn't rest until they knew who the father was.

And Sebastian wasn't going to hide from his responsibility, either.

But she wasn't showing yet.

And had sworn her sisters to secrecy.

Dialing her on Thursday afternoon, her early day at the clinic, he half expected his call to go to voice mail. Was pleasantly surprised when he heard her pick up.

"I won't keep you long," he began. "I'd just like to suggest that as long as you aren't showing, as long as we can keep the situation under wraps, I'd rest a lot easier if we could do so."

Her pause made his gut clench.

"Ruby?" he asked when no response was forthcoming after several seconds of dead air.

"I don't intend to tell anyone you're the father, Sebastian, so you can rest easy." Her tone was not friendly.

"It's not that," he quickly clarified, while feeling kind of offended at the same time. Though, to be fair to her, he'd made it quite clear that he wasn't going to be a father to the child. "I've been working with Steele, walking every inch of my property, watching cameras, going over names and faces of people I don't even remember having ever met, getting a daily rundown of James's activities, and everyone he speaks to publicly at least, to see if we can put together any pieces. Until we find something, I'd feel a whole lot better if no one knew you were pregnant."

Silence met him again. It occurred to him that maybe they should have had the conversation in person. "So far, there's no definitive sign of my father having an affair, but I allowed Detective Steele to search all my parents' past financial records and there are suspicious local hotel bills. None of them close to any hospital where my dad might have been dealing with an emergency. There'd always been corresponding restaurant bills. And, in many, if not most of the instances, my mother's credit card showed up in use across town. There are hotel bills for her, too. So maybe they just both had meetings, dinners where they might be drinking, and made mutual decisions to get rooms. Could also be that they were both having affairs, but I know for certain she wasn't pregnant because she had to have a hysterectomy after I was born..."

He paused to breathe. And to check his phone to see that there was still an active connection to Ruby's.

"Who was home with you when both of your parents were gone?" The question hit him from left field. Who cared? It was so long ago.

"By the time I was twelve, no one. Not in Boise."

He'd been plenty big enough to take care of himself. "At the cabin they always hired someone, to keep house and cook as much as anything else. And in Boise, when I was younger, I think at least one or the other of them always came home at some point. There was always someone there when I woke up in the morning." It had all seemed normal to him. He'd had Jerry.

Even when his parents had been out, one of them had always phoned at bedtime.

He'd been fine. Blessed, in a lot of ways. He'd learned independence. Self-sufficiency. Responsibility.

He'd also become a loner.

And if he'd had his way, he'd have had parents who wanted to be at home with him, not out living their lives even though it meant leaving him alone.

Now his own kid was going to grow up with an absentee parent.

He was getting way off track.

"We've been lucky that the attacks have either been misses or uneventful up to this point," he told her, rushing to wipe away any images he might have just planted in her brain. Needing to get them out of his mind.

"But this guy has been at this more than two months. And if you take the anonymous complaints into account, it's been closer to four. There's no reason to believe that he's done. Other than your flat tire, Steele and his team believe that the attacks are escalating. If this guy is going to all this trouble to hurt Crosswinds, to get back at me, can you imagine what he'd do if he knew that you were carrying my child?"

He hadn't meant to put it quite that way.

"I just think, due to your association with me, it would be safer if no one knew you were pregnant," he said, finishing with the only thing he'd really needed to say.

"You're afraid that, if this person gets desperate, the baby could be a target."

It sounded fanciful when she spoke his fear aloud. But… "Yes."

"I agree."

At first, he thought he hadn't heard her right. But then she continued, "Hannah and Frannie have been driving me crazy, but I've warned them that they're going to lose me if they say anything before I'm ready. For their silence, I'm having to put up with one or the other of them bringing me at least one meal a day and sharing it with me. They want to see me eat. And, you know, one owns a café and the other a catering business, so there you go."

She sounded as though the love of her siblings was a huge hassle. But he heard other undertones in her voice, too.

"It's nice being spoiled a little bit, huh?" he asked softly.

To which she said, "Good night, Sebastian," and hung up.

Leaving him with a smile on his face.

Ruby was still asleep at 5:30 Friday morning when her phone rang. Recognizing the number as the Crosswinds kennel line, she picked up immediately.

"Ruby? Della, here. Sebastian took Elise out night training last night and isn't back yet. I just arrived to find the kennel flooded. The sprinkler system won't shut off. All the dogs are partially submerged. I have no idea for how long. They're all responding to me, but…"

Already out of bed and throwing off her nightshirt, Ruby said, "Get them to the medical building, cover the floor with cloth, mats, anything. I'm on my way…" Then she dropped the phone and got herself out the door. They'd been having unusually warm weather, in the fifties and sixties, but it still got down below freezing at night.

As soon as she was in the SUV, she voice-dialed Crosswinds, instructing Della to get the blow dryers used for grooming and, on the low, not hot, setting, dry the dogs as quickly as she could, starting with the puppies. Bryony was there, helping, and Sebastian, Della told her, was still out of cell range.

She drove as fast as she felt she could safely drive. That early in the morning, with dawn not even a promise on the horizon yet, she had the road mostly to herself. And when she noticed a car coming up behind her, just leaving town with her, and keeping pace, she allowed herself to put a little more pressure on the gas. While dogs weren't in as much danger of immediate physical distress as people were in such situations, they were still at risk. And the dogs she was on her way to save would go on to save human lives.

The car behind her was gaining on her, so she sped up more. The sooner she got to the dogs, the better. But when the other vehicle still stayed on her tail at twenty miles over the speed limit, she slowed down instead, hating the time lost, but wanting to let whoever it was pass. For all she knew they were on their way to a human medical emergency.

She watched impatiently as the headlights moved to the passing lane, checked out of habit to make sure nothing was coming from the opposite direction that could crash with it and almost didn't see when the vehicle, another SUV, based on its size, started to cross back over the line. Putting on her brakes, she swerved, keeping the wheel turned hard to the right, and managed to do a complete circle in the shoulder, and get herself safely back on the road in time to see the other vehicle's taillights rush off in the distance.

Thankful that everyone was okay, hoping the other party made it safely to their destination, she slowed down to signal her own turn.

Racing up Cross Drive, she had a moment's unease, seeing herself hurrying to the rescue again, after another bad thing happened at Sebastian's training center. Assuring herself—hoping—she was just overreacting to the near miss on the road, she still cautiously parked directly in front of the medical building. In view of all cameras, and anyone out and about at Crosswinds. Once inside, she forgot about her vehicle completely as she quickly looked in enough mouths, saw enough pale gums, to know she had an emergency situation. Instructing Della in how to assist, she prepared, and began to administer, warm intravenous liquids to the dogs from smallest to largest, puppies first. Took temperatures of the ones showing sluggishness, and warmed water bottles to pack around the ones waiting for treatment, with layers between the bottles and the dog's skin.

By the time Sebastian called in, she'd taken the temperatures of every dog on the premises, and Della reported to him that every one of them showed some sign of hypothermia. Echo and a few of the larger dogs were warming just with the water bottles. Ruby was just finishing up the last of the IVs. She'd been monitoring heart rates and felt that every one of the dogs, including the new puppies, was going to be fine.

But only because Della had come in early. And thought to call Ruby immediately.

She couldn't be certain that the faulty sprinkler system was due to what Sebastian now called his stalker. But as she assessed the damage, looking at all the dogs that could easily have been lost, that possibility loomed larger inside her. It gave the early morning emergency an additional sense of dread.

Detective Steele arrived before Sebastian did and quickly drew the same conclusion that Ruby had. He stopped by the kennel briefly to say that the attacker had likely struck again. The locked box controlling the thermostat in the kennel had been cracked. It was possible the unknown subject had turned up the heat high enough to trigger the sprinkler system, but more likely that he held some kind of lighter up to a sprinkler head, and then only used the thermostat to turn off the heat. They'd know more once they got inside the computerized thermostat.

Sebastian, the lines under his eyes making him look worn out, burst into the medical building minutes after Steele headed back to the kennels. "They're okay," she said at his first frantic look around the room. Della had gone with the detective, to give him access to the office attached to the kennel by a bricked hallway.

The big mountain man nodded, but walked from dog to dog, starting with the puppies, squatting down in front of each one, feeling feet and tails, calling all the newborns "little one" and each of the adult dogs by name. Asking how they were doing.

Ruby watched with a lump in her throat.

Hating what was happening to Sebastian.

His animals were his family. His only family. He placed every one of them carefully. Like a parent sending his children off to college. He followed up with them all after they'd found their permanent partners as well.

For a brief second, watching him give his all to his dogs, she was swamped by a wave of jealousy. Because her own child wouldn't get the benefit of Sebastian's undying attention or unconditional love.

The thought passed and by the time she left the medical building late that morning, helping to transition the dogs back to their kennels, she and Sebastian were working seamlessly together again, exactly as they had for the past several years.

Walking out of the kennel with him to get some lunch, she was feeling better than she had since before Oscar was hurt. Seeing a way for her and Sebastian to be friends, to take on challenges, and work through them together.

They were passing her car, on the way up to his house, when he stopped. "What's that?" he asked, pointing to a clod stuck in one of her wheels. And then, walking closer, they could see the dirt stuck in her bumper, too.

"That's from the three-sixty I made in the mud this morning," she told him, hoping again that the party who'd been more in a hurry than she'd been, had made it to wherever they were going safely. As they started walking again, she told him about the incident.

"He was probably drunk," Sebastian said. "You should have called the police."

If she'd had any inkling that the vehicle was out of control, she definitely would have. The person had almost run into her, had effectively run her off the road. Why hadn't she considered alcoholism for the excessive speed?

Filled with panic for a second, she worried that her failure to alert police might have gotten someone killed. But she slowed down her thoughts to go back over the morning's incident more carefully.

"There was no sign of any lack of control," she said aloud. Checking herself. "The vehicle stayed steady in the lane the entire time it was behind me," she recalled slowly. "I kept watching it because I was going so fast and it was clearly coming up on me. Not like someone who was racing, just like…someone—" catching up to her "—in a hurry."

She'd been in a rush. Had she transferred her own tension-inducing motive to the other car?

Before she could answer her own question, Sebastian was on the phone, talking to Glen Steele again, relating what Ruby had just told him.

"He's on his way over here," Sebastian told her, hanging up. "He wants to speak with you, and he wants to see your vehicle before you drive it again."

She nodded. Kind of glad at the moment that the morning's odd event was getting looked at again.

And hating the shadowed look that once again marred Sebastian's face.

Chapter 11

Leaving Della and Bryony with the dogs, Sebastian insisted on following Ruby back to Owl Creek after Steele was done with her. The detective had not only taken photos of her car, but he'd also taken the dirt clumps, too, in case that could help prove how she was forced off the road.

Ruby thought his following her home was overkill. He'd received the message loud and clear. From the looks she'd sent him, and from her repeated words, too.

He'd just nodded. And climbed back into his truck. He'd been out half the night. Had to get back to the dogs. He felt like a sitting duck, just waiting for the next bullet to hit.

He had to talk to Ruby.

And he'd wanted her off his property the second Steele had said she was free to go.

They'd had grilled-cheese sandwiches at his place while they'd been waiting for the detective. She was going home to shower and change before heading into work for her afternoon and early evening appointments.

He didn't like that, either, but knew that he had no say on that one.

Just like he wasn't packing up and taking his dogs and going into hiding, he couldn't expect Ruby to curl up under her couch and quit living.

Steele had stressed that if the perpetrator wanted Ruby gone, he'd had plenty of opportunities to try to make that happen. Same went for Sebastian. It continued to appear as though someone was out to sabotage his business.

To what end, he had no idea.

He was considering finding other boarding for his dogs until the stalker had been caught. He'd already, at Steele's suggestion, hired three full-time, armed and bonded security officers from Boise to patrol the kennels at night. Two patrolling outside. One inside with the dogs.

The sprinkler system would be reset and ready to go by dinnertime.

The kennel was going to be kept locked, day and night, with only Crosswinds employees and security allowed inside.

And Ruby was to be nowhere on the premises.

She waved at him as she pulled into her driveway, as though she thought he'd just drift off into the wind.

He pulled into her driveway behind her, instead. She'd opened the garage door, and he was standing inside the garage when she got out of her car.

"Sebastian, what are you doing?"

Glancing around, he said, "Can we go inside for a

second? We probably don't want anyone to see us having a fight." He just put it right out there.

And with one look at him over her shoulder, she led him inside.

"What's going on?" she asked, the second her door was shut. The garage led into a laundry room, and she didn't lead him out of it. Instead, with her satchel still on her shoulder, she faced him down right there by the washer.

"You are not to step foot on Crosswinds again," he said, every bit of frustration inside him seeming to roll out with the words. "If you do, I'm going to press charges for trespassing."

Okay, that was more than he'd intended. But the woman and her independence and her refusal to let him help her and the baby inside her…were upending him a little.

"I know I can't dictate your actions and I have no say in where you go or what you do, but I do have a say on my own property."

To his utter astonishment, he saw tears brim her eyes. What the hell?

With a nod, she turned to head into the kitchen, telling him to let himself out.

"Wait," he called behind her, following her to the kitchen door, but going no farther. He wasn't invading her home unless she invited him in. "Ruby…"

She turned then, no sign of the tears, but her gaze was filled with something worse than disappointment. Sadness, maybe. Accompanied by resolution.

"It's okay, Sebastian. You have to do what you have to do. I knew the baby was going to be a problem for you. And you were quite clear that you couldn't be a part of their life. It stands to reason that, since right now the two of us, the baby and I, are one, you can't have me in your life as well."

What the...? He took a step. Stopped. "Ruby," he called softly. "I'm doing this so you and the baby will be safe..."

With another nod, she met his gaze, looking sadder than he'd ever seen a woman look. Or that's how it felt to him. "I know. You're afraid you'll have an episode and one of us will get hurt..."

Well, that. But... "That's why I'm never going to marry or have a family, but...you, and the child, will always be welcome to call on me anytime, day or night." He told her something he hadn't yet come to terms with on his own. And yet the words rang with such truth, he accepted them fully. "I hope we'll stay in contact," he continued, working things out as he went along. Feeling...freer for having said them.

And then, before things got rocky, said, "This no-trespassing thing...it's only until whoever is after Crosswinds is caught. This *person*," he growled, "obviously knows who you are, and knows that every time he tries to create a situation that hurts me, you're there, fixing things. You heard Steele say it almost seemed as though the perp lay in wait this morning, watching to see if you'd head out to Crosswinds, and was out on the road, ready to stop you from saving the dogs."

Sebastian had barely been able to remain standing there in calm conversation when the detective had let that piece of information drop.

"We don't know that for sure," Ruby responded, finally speaking, taking a step closer to him. But when he looked her in the eye, she glanced away. As though the theory made sense to her, too.

"You'd already figured that out on your own," he challenged her.

When she glanced up again, she met his gaze and nodded.

He took a step. Stopped. "May I come in?"

"Of course." The tone of voice, like there'd never be a question of his welcome, sent warmth through parts of him that felt like they might just freeze to death.

Walking up to her, he took her hands in his. "I'd die if anything happened to you because of me," he told her, letting honesty guide him. He had nothing else left but raw truth. "And now, with the child, and these attacks...how do I fight the unknown? It's like I'm this tense bundle of potential screwup with no power to do anything about any of it. Except this. I can forbid you from coming to Crosswinds, until we know it's safe."

She smiled then. A wide, slow, warm smile.

And Sebastian figured he'd won the round in a battle that was never going to end.

Ruby had a call from Detective Steele while she was in an appointment that afternoon. And listened to his message as soon as she was free.

Police had found evidence of a large vehicle parked in some brush behind leafy trees, about a mile outside of Owl Creek, on the road to Crosswinds. The vehicle had been facing to pull out toward the dog-training facility. They could tell by tire tread and track depth that the vehicle had to be at least a full-size SUV. Which was exactly what she'd thought it to be.

There was nothing on traffic cams in town to show anyone in an SUV driving from town toward Sebastian's after the bars closed. And no traffic cams a mile out of town.

She hadn't even finished the message when a new call coming in interrupted the voice mail. Seeing Fletcher's name pop up, she answered immediately.

"I'll be in Boise by eight," he announced as soon as he told her hello. "By the time I rent a car, that should put me at your place by around eleven."

"What?" she asked, dropping down to her desk chair, with a glance at her watch. She had two more exam rooms with patients waiting.

"Didn't Steele tell you? I've taken a leave here and I'm heading to town to help Steele figure out what in the hell's going on there. You could have been killed today."

Her heart fluttered with love and gratitude at the same time it tightened with tension. She didn't need her family overreacting. Or thinking she couldn't take care of herself.

In her current circumstances, she needed as much time apart from all of them as she could get.

"I didn't hear his full message," she uttered inanely. "I was listening to it when you called. And you most definitely don't need to fly home for this."

"I'm already at the airport," he said. "Finding criminals is what I do, sis. One of my own is being attacked— no way I'm not going to be there."

The tone of voice, and the words, stopped any other protest she might have made. Because she knew it would be pointless.

"Do Mom and Dad know you're coming?"

"Not yet. I was planning to bunk with you tonight. I'd like to hear everything you can remember, about all of it, in your own words. Tonight. Without anyone else interrupting. That way, I hit the ground running tomorrow. I'll move in with Mom and Dad tomorrow night."

She nodded. Realized he couldn't see her. And said, "I'll have the coffee on," before she remembered that the smell of the stuff made her nauseous.

She'd stop and pick up some beer for him instead. Or fix him some tea.

And then get him the heck out of her house before he figured out that she wasn't drinking alcohol, or caffeine, and threw up if she smelled coffee.

Detective that he was, Fletcher would figure out her secret and then all hell truly would break loose.

Call him over-the-top, but Sebastian was bunking out at the kennels Friday night. He sent the third security officer outside with the other two. One was watching the road frontage. Another patrolling along the lake.

And the third had the buildings.

He was on a cot with a sleeping bag, with Oscar's bed beside him, right in the middle of the kennel building. Or he would be. He'd also brought in lawn furniture, including a small table, and sat, sipping a beer and reading a book about prenatal care on his tablet.

If he was going to protect, support, he had to know the dangers. He'd expected to struggle, had bought the six-pack to relax him through it. But, still on his first beer, he was more fascinated than agitated. There were possible malfunctions, to be sure, but Ruby's age and physical condition allayed most of the concerns.

The birthing process he was familiar with, having birthed many puppies over the years. He wouldn't be there, of course, but...

His phone interrupted the thought.

Ruby.

"Something wrong?" he asked, picking up in the middle of the first ring. She didn't randomly call him. Ever.

"Why would something be wrong?"

He could come up with dozens of reasons, both stalker- and pregnancy-related. "No reason."

"I'm just finishing up here at the clinic and wanted to check in on the dogs." Which he should have figured from the get-go.

"I just did rounds half an hour ago," he told her. "All gums look healthy and pink. Everyone's eating, responding to stimuli, and the puppies' temperatures are all normal." She'd left a thorough list with Della.

"Thank goodness. I'm so glad to hear that." She sounded glad. Genuinely happy, in fact. Which gave him pleasure, too.

"So, what did you have for dinner tonight?" he asked—a personal question that would never have occurred to him to ask until she got pregnant. She'd told him earlier that it was Hannah's turn to provide the daily meal and she was bringing Lucy along to the clinic to share it with her.

"Grilled chicken salad with, I think, every vegetable known to man in it. And pudding for dessert. I need my dairy, after all." He heard the note of sarcasm in her tone—and pictured her smiling.

"I picked up takeout when I went in for some beer."

"I had a juice box. Lucy said she got to share one of hers with me."

Her five-year-old niece. He'd met the little girl several times. She was a cutie. He'd never, ever considered what a child of his own would look like.

Until that second.

"Have you heard from Detective Steele?" she asked then, sounding a whole lot more tentative. In light of their earlier conversation in her kitchen, he suspected.

"About the fresh tire tracks hidden in brush and trees a mile outside of town?" He'd been right to ban her from his property. He was not going to back down on that one.

"Yeah. Did he tell you about Fletcher, too?"

Sebastian's brow raised. "No."

"He took a leave of absence and is flying in to help Steele. He lands later tonight and will be staying at my place until morning, when he's moving to my parents' place."

"He heard about your road incident today."

"Yeah. Steele called him. After the windshield thing, I haven't told my family about any of the stuff at Cross-winds. But apparently Fletcher, one detective to another, had asked to be notified if there were any further actions against me. Steele didn't think the flat tire qualified, but this morning's run off the road did."

"You don't sound happy about his arrival."

"I don't need my big brother disrupting his entire life over something the local police can handle. Something that I dealt with quite fine this morning, I might add."

He'd stopped to look at the tire tracks in the dirt not far from his place. Could retrace her three-sixty. Standing there alone in the dirt, he'd been angry as hell that it had happened, frustrated that he couldn't stop the jerk from getting near her again, and impressed, too, at her driving skills. He'd been thankful she'd kept herself alive.

Not something he wanted her to have to be doing. Ever again.

"Fletcher's a decorated detective, Ruby. Him and Steele working together—they're going to catch this jerk. The sooner that happens, the better."

Her pause gave him pause, until she offered, "As you said, he's a great detective. And… I have secrets I don't want my family to know about yet."

Ahh. Sebastian finally caught up to her. With a screech. Knocking his palm against his head.

"If you feel like you need to tell them—"

"I don't," she interrupted before he'd figured out how to finish the statement.

She had every right to tell her family anything she wanted them to know. He needed a plan to weather the backlash.

Once a Marine, Always a Marine. War in Afghanistan, raising search-and-rescue dogs, a stalker, an unexpected pregnancy. He needed the best training he could get, the ammunition and the battle plan.

"I need some time to myself. To figure out what I want and need, regarding the future, before I have a dozen people telling me what's best."

He couldn't imagine the tension in that particular situation.

"I guess that's where I'm lucky," he told her, glancing around at his own family. Reaching down to pet Oscar, who rose immediately and nudged his hand. "I have listening and support, but no advice givers."

Hearing the words aloud, he didn't feel that lucky, and said, "Advice can be good, you know. Different perspectives sometimes show you something you didn't think of yourself."

"I'm all for advice," she said with a chuckle. "But with five siblings, four cousins and two parents and an uncle all coming at you at once, it's hard to hear any one piece of advice."

For a second, he envied her. *Hard.* "You also have five siblings, four cousins, two parents and an uncle who have your back," he said softly.

Hence, her big-brother detective taking a leave of absence to find whoever was putting his sister's life at risk.

"It's kind of funny," she said, her words coming back softly. "You and me, two totally independent people, who live alone because we want to, who dedicate ourselves to our careers, which both happen to revolve around animals, and yet we come from completely opposite backgrounds."

"I guess it just goes to show you that no matter the upbringing, we are who we are."

"Yeah, as long as we can find ourselves…"

Or until life threw you a curveball you weren't sure you could catch.

"I'm sorry, Ruby. So sorry."

"Sorry?" Her tone stronger. "For what?"

"I'll get backlash, a hell of a lot of it from your family, I imagine, once they know I'm the father of this unplanned pregnancy. I expect there's a good chance I'm going to lose my closest friend over it. But my life is still going to be just me. Independent. Heading up a family of dogs. While your whole future has just changed course. It's not right."

"It's my choice."

"What?" She'd chosen to… Wait, had he…?

"To have the baby is my choice," she told him. "To keep it is my choice. If nature were different and you were the one carrying the embryo we created, the choice would be yours. And you'd make the one that suited you best."

True. "It still doesn't seem right."

"Then maybe you need to do more thinking," she told him. "I've learned that if something doesn't feel right, I'm probably not where I need to be, or doing what I need to do, or with who I need to be with."

"You live a second life as a shrink?" he asked, with a friendly chuckle he hadn't heard in a long while. Hadn't realized he'd lost the ability to just relax and converse.

"No one is preventing you from being a father to this child, Sebastian," she said then, as though he hadn't just lightened the moment. "A lot of fathers don't live with their children, many don't ever have them for overnight stays, but they're still important entities in their children's lives. They're present for the choices, the big events, for some smaller moments. For giving advice…"

Sneaky, the way she'd brought that advice bit back to him.

In new light.

He took a sip of beer. Made note that he wasn't jumping up out of his chair and moving on to whatever he could find that needed to be done.

"I'm not asking, Sebastian. I fully understand if this isn't your choice. I don't blame you. I won't hold it against you. I just…"

"I'm not hating the idea," he said. And then quickly added, "I'm also not seeing it yet. Can we…revisit what this might look like?"

"Anytime you're ready."

He wasn't there yet. But he wanted to be.

Which scared him way more than any stalker ever would.

Chapter 12

Ruby's late-night interview with her big brother was nice. Really nice. Fletcher's questions, the way he led into them, opened her mind to a little more detail. Nothing that identified a suspect, or a motive, but Fletcher seemed pleased with the result.

More than that, he'd treated her like an equal, someone fully capable of taking care of herself. The relief was palpable.

The validation was more needed than she'd known.

And it all came crashing down the next morning, when Hannah burst into her office even before she'd seen her first patient.

"This is it, Ruby." Her shoulder-length dark blond hair flew around her and her green eyes shot daggers. "I just heard that Fletcher's in town to help the police figure out who ran you off the road yesterday?" When

Hannah's voice rose a notch, Ruby got up and closed her office door.

Her office was secluded, down a hallway from the rest of the clinic, but there was no way she wanted anyone hearing the conversation.

"You shouldn't be here," she told her next younger sister, standing by the door, arms crossed against her white doctor's coat. "I wouldn't burst in on one of your catering events."

"Not even if my life was in danger and you knew I was hiding information that could lead to my intended killer?"

"No one is trying to kill me."

"Fletcher wouldn't be here if he didn't think otherwise."

"I think he's just trying to make certain that it doesn't get to that point," Ruby said, leaning her backside against her desk. "The police are pretty certain that I've only been targeted because I'm at Crosswinds. I'm not going back there until this is cleared up."

Hannah's mouth stayed closed. The fire brimming in her sister's eyes spoke for her. She met her gaze to gaze. Had fought the battle many times over the years. Intended to win.

And then, Hannah said, "The police, and Fletcher, don't know that you're hiding a man for some reason. And that you're carrying his baby." Her sister kept her voice low.

That was the only credit Ruby could give her.

"Let it go, Hannah." The warning was implicit in her tone.

When Hannah looked down, Ruby filled with remorse, but didn't back off from her position. "It's going to be okay," she said.

Hannah's eyes glistened when she looked back up. "I know. Because if you aren't going to tell, I have to, Ruby. I can't shake the idea that some guy might want you gone because he doesn't want it known that you're pregnant with his child. I don't care if he's married, or famous, or whatever reason you have for keeping him secret. It's not worth your life…"

Ruby started to speak, but Hannah cut her off. "I'd never be able to live with myself if I stayed silent and this guy got to you."

Sitting down, Ruby took a deep breath. Hannah's valid claim was changing her tactics. But not her decision. "He's not going to get to me, Hannah." She met her sister's gaze, held on steadily.

"So…" Hannah closed in, perching on the edge of Ruby's desk, closer to her. "You admit that there is a *he*."

"No." Ruby crossed her hands at her waist, needing her calm to be the only thing that showed. "I'm not in any kind of a relationship. I told you that from the beginning."

"You're not still going to try to convince me that you aren't pregnant, are you? Because when I tell the family, you're going to have to lie to them, too, and then when you start showing, everyone's going to know you lied to their faces."

She got the message.

Hannah was hurt that she was lying to *her*.

And she'd made her point.

"I am pregnant," she said aloud, shocked at the fissure that passed through as she heard her own words. Not an entirely unpleasant experience. "But I still need you to keep it a secret for now, Hannah." Her tone was no longer commanding. "Please. Just until we figure out what's going on here. I don't want whoever is behind these attacks to know about the baby. I don't want to give this jerk more bait."

Hannah's head shake put knots in Ruby's stomach, as did her sister's words when she said, "I can't keep that promise anymore. There's something not right about this guy. So you aren't in a relationship anymore. It's clear that two months ago, you were having sex with him. And this is the kind of motive you read in the news all the time."

Always-practical Hannah.

But her sister had known her own share of heartache. Which she'd taken on the chin. And grown up out of the ashes to make a great life for herself and her daughter.

Ruby met Hannah's gaze again. "I know the father is not behind this, Hannah. I am as positive of that as I am that Lucy is your daughter."

She was that serious. Hannah seemed to be considering Ruby's words, giving them weight, but then she shook her head. "Maybe he wants you back. He's doing this to scare you back into his arms."

"I know him, Hannah. And he knows about the baby." The words came because they had to. "But we aren't in love. Neither of us want to get married. Him even more than me and you know how much I've always cherished my space alone at home." She couldn't tell Hannah that the father was being stalked and both Ruby and the father feared that if anyone knew he had a child on the way, that child could be in danger. But she had to get her sister's promise of silence. "Please," she said then. "Just give Fletcher a few days to work on these attacks. As soon as the person is caught, I'll tell Mom and Dad myself."

"And the father...he's okay with that?"

"He's not thrilled by the idea. After all, we're the Coltons, you know?"

Hannah's answering nod, the look on her face, held total commiseration at that point. And Ruby said, "But he knows it's the right thing to do. And I get the feeling he's going to insist on it once this violent behavior is solved.".

"So he knows about the attacks?"

"Yes."

Hannah nodded again. She didn't look like she was ready to be done yet, though. "So why won't you at least tell me who he is?"

"Because we need some time to figure out how our parenting situation is going to work. Time without anyone else even knowing that we're going to be sharing a child." She met her sister's gaze head-on. Hannah knew all about the trials and tribulations of parenthood. "I'm going to retain full custody," she added. Something else Hannah would understand, being a single mother herself.

Hannah's face softened then, and she headed toward the door. But turned when she reached it. "By the way, Mom wanted me to remind you about Uncle Buck's birthday party next week. It's going to be at the ranch instead of in town because so many people accepted invitations. Mom asked me to cater it."

Ruby wasn't in a partying mood. Most particularly when one family member or another was bound to bring her a glass of her favorite wine and wonder why she wasn't sipping from it. But she nodded. Congratulated Hannah on the job offer.

And wondered, but didn't ask, if Sebastian Cross had been on the guest list.

And if so, had his name been on the acceptance list as well?

Sebastian had a visit from Fletcher Colton on Saturday. Watching the broad-shouldered man walking toward the training pen, seeing his dark hair, worn a little long, he was struck by the fact that Fletcher's niece or nephew was going to be Sebastian's biological child. Would the baby have blond hair like Sebastian and Ruby? Or darker hair like Fletcher and Wade? He and Ruby both had green eyes. Wade's were blue.

He had no idea what eye color the rest of the Coltons had. Including Fletcher.

Until the man got closer.

Green.

Sebastian was probably going to have a green-eyed kid.

Giving a "sit" command to the Labrador he'd been training, Sebastian held out a hand to his long-time friend's older brother.

Finding himself fighting a load of guilt, unable to shake the fact that he was the father of the man's younger sister's unplanned baby. If Fletcher knew...

When Wade found out...

Glen Steele, as the lead on the Crosswinds case, had called to let Sebastian know that Fletcher would be coming out. The Utah detective had been deputized by the Owl Creek Police Department in order to officially help find Ruby's attacker.

Being the father of the unborn child who could be in jeopardy with any further attacks, as well as the owner of the property involved and the friend of the woman who'd been put at risk, Sebastian kenneled the Lab and walked Fletcher around the property, pointing out every place an attack had happened. Fletcher pulled out crime-scene photos and Sebastian walked the other man through every one of them.

Gave him a full tour of the kennels. Introduced Ruby's brother to every one of his ten adult dogs. Including Fancy, the two-month-old shepherd mix Sebastian had determined had the scent skills to be trained for search-and-rescue. "I've got a few people who foster potential trainees for me," he told the man. "Ruby's friend Kiki Shelton and her grandfather, Jim, have agreed to take Fancy."

There, he'd put Ruby on the table.

Gotten the fact out there that Sebastian was indirectly responsible for Fletcher's presence in town.

As the two headed down to walk the shoreline, where, Steele was certain, the unknown assailant had been accessing Sebastian's land, Fletcher said, "This nastiness aside, you've saved my sister's life, man."

Sebastian pulled on his beard at that thought. If the man only knew...

When he knew...

"That woman had always had more of an affinity with animals than with people," Fletcher continued. "Probably had something to do with the way we grew up—has she told you about that?"

Indirectly. There'd been too many opinions, he knew that.

"You know that our mom's a twin, right?" the detective asked, his mind seemingly only half on the words he was saying as he perused every inch of land upon which they walked, while keeping an eye on the horizon, and occasionally turning to look back toward the house and other buildings, too.

"I didn't know that," Sebastian said. He'd been a summer pal of Fletcher's younger brother. They'd fished. Challenged each other to dive off docks into the lake. They'd shared freedom from parents—they hadn't sat around and talked about them.

Partially because Sebastian didn't do that with anyone. Or hadn't, until recently. With Ruby.

When a guy didn't want to share, he didn't put himself in a position to have sharing expected of him.

"Her name is Jessie. She was Uncle Buck's wife."

That was news. "The woman who ran off and left him with four kids to raise?" You didn't live in Owl Creek without knowing some of the history.

Buck and Robert Colton were brothers. Buck went off to the army, leaving Robert to take over the family's hardware store in town. Buck came back, sold his share of the store to Robert and used the profits to buy Colton Ranch. Then Robert saw Owl Creek's potential to grow into a tourist area and spent his profits buying land cheap and purchasing buildings in town under market value. When the market turned around, he'd amassed a small fortune of land and rentals.

And that hardware store now served as the lobby for Colton Properties, though Robert had left a lot of the shelving and the register in place for posterity's sake. He'd added two additional floors, still with the red-brick facade, but all decked out with modern offices and the best of technology. A newcomer couldn't miss the place. Other than the town hall, it was the tallest building in Owl Creek.

And Fletcher had been about to tell him something about Ruby's upbringing that had made her better with dogs than with people. He could argue that point, no matter what reasoning Fletcher gave. Ruby most definitely worked her magic on people as well as dogs. He had personal testimony to confirm that.

But he had no intention whatsoever of sharing. So he didn't ask any of the questions he suddenly had.

Fletcher had stopped to take a couple of photos with his cell phone. Of the house, and then, of the lake. From midyard.

"I think Mom always felt guilty, her sister leaving Uncle Buck that way, and with Dad traveling so much, she'd cart us six kids over to the ranch, to help Buck out with his kids and things around the house. We'd spend nights there, with Mom tending to all ten of us at once."

Sounded chaotic. Somewhat fascinating.

Why hadn't Wade ever said anything about that?

Or had he, and Sebastian hadn't thought it a big enough deal to remember?

He hadn't known Ruby well back then.

Hadn't been making a baby with her.

"Rubes, being the middle child in our family, and the same age as Uncle Buck's youngest, Lizzie, kind of got lost in the shuffle, I think. Or just figured the dogs were less trouble than putting up with the rest of us."

Sebastian figured he should feel guilty about listening to Ruby's older brother profiling her, but he was too interested to stop the man.

"We all saw veterinary science as the perfect choice for her," the detective jumped ahead before Sebastian was ready to leave the past behind. "Problem was, that's all she wanted. Worked seven days a week, on call twenty-four hours. She was starting to show signs of burnout until she began working at Crosswinds so much. Volunteering with your PTSD program gave her something she'd obviously been missing. She's more relaxed. Has hired a couple more doctors for her clinic, and, from what Mom and the girls tell me, she's taking complete days off, and sometimes whole weekends."

Like the weekend, two months before, when they'd dealt with Oscar, and then made a baby together?

Fletcher wasn't going to be thanking Sebastian, or thinking he'd saved anything, once he knew the truth. And to that end...

"I've got an idea to try and draw this stalker out," he said. He'd come up with the plan the night before. Lying on his cot, awake in the middle of the night, thinking about Ruby's near miss on the road the morning before.

He intended not only to draw out the fiend who was trying to ruin him, but also to keep the unknown assailant busy at Crosswinds, where Ruby absolutely would not be.

"I'm going to run a huge ad campaign for Crosswinds. I've already contacted a marketing firm my mother worked with in Boise. They'd offered to help before, but I'm already at capacity and don't need the publicity. Anyway, a film crew will be out from a local station in Boise to film what we do, interview me, that kind of thing. The crew will be made aware of the situation and will all be privy to the danger before accepting the job. They'll be provided bodyguards. We'll be doing other videos as well, paying social-media influencers to air them. I've got an ample supply of photos and some videos of our dogs out in the field. We'll be asking for permission to use those and include them in the campaign." They'd almost reached the shore. He just kept talking. "To begin, though, the firm is going to hit Owl Creek hard, with news that the marketing firm is honoring me and my parents for a lifetime of service to our communities. They wanted to do that when my parents died, but I needed my privacy."

He cringed at the idea, but to draw out the stalker, trap whoever it was and end the threat of violence... he'd do whatever it took.

"They'll get posters designed and printed, with the idea to put them up on trees on public property coming in and out of town, not involving any individuals or businesses. The plan is there. Ready to roll. I just want police buy-in before I give the final go-ahead."

They'd reached the shore. Stopping, Fletcher turned to Sebastian. "You're taking the offensive, egging him on, rather than waiting for him to strike again."

"And again," Sebastian said, nodding. "I've got three armed security officers here at night. I can bring in a day shift as well. And will work around the clock, if I have to, to keep running things here without staff, if it comes to that. I started out alone. I can do it again."

"You can afford all of this?"

Sebastian shrugged. "I'd spend my last dime if that's what it took to put an end to the reign of terror. This individual went after Ruby," he said, unable to keep the boiling anger out of his tone.

Fletcher studied him. Sebastian, holding the other man's gaze straight on, was up for it and then some.

"Let me talk to Steele," Fletcher said then. "While a bit more elaborate than I'd like, I think we can work with what you're planning. We'll need to assign extra officers to the case and I don't know what kind of staff he has on hand. And maybe we hold off for a few days. Steele's been looking at those hotel bills your father charged. He's got some leads on a woman who was also known to be there. And she later had a kid. A boy. Let us get a look at him."

Sebastian fell back against the tree behind him. Leaned there.

He'd been right? He had a half brother?

Who'd pushed Ruby off the road and could have killed her? And the child?

"Sorry, man," Fletcher said then. "Steele led me to believe you kind of figured your father had been having an affair."

Right. Fletcher would have no idea that he'd been thinking about Ruby at the hands of a deranged guy who resented Sebastian so much he had to take him down.

"I threw it out as a possibility," he said, straightening. "I never suspected it before now. I'm an only kid. The idea of a half sibling…"

"I've got five siblings, and the idea of a half sibling out there somewhere would throw me for one, too. Wrapping your mind around that one…hell, you gotta see your parents, your whole life different…" Fletcher was walking again.

Clearly trying to put a witness, and a friend of his brother's, at ease.

Sebastian would be at ease when the stalker was locked behind bars.

When he knew Ruby and the child were safe.

Until then, he was at war.

Chapter 13

Ruby awoke Sunday morning to a text-message notification.

Thinking it was Sebastian, who'd been the last one to text her the night before, just to ask how she was doing, she rolled over and picked up her phone.

A smile on her face.

Not a horrible way to wake up.

The man got her. He not only accepted her right to make her own life choices, but he also understood her independence. Her need to be a single decision maker.

Not part of a twosome.

Lying on her back against the pillows, giving her stomach a chance to wake up before she started whirling it around, she held up the phone and tapped the text icon.

STAY AWAY.

Two words. All caps.

And her heart was pounding.

Sitting up, she pushed Fletcher's speed dial. Nodded when her brother told her to stay put. And away from windows.

With him on the phone, she walked to the bathroom attached to her bedroom. And when he hung up, she tapped Sebastian's icon.

He wasn't the police. Or part of the investigation.

But he was her partner, of sorts, on the new route her life was taking. If something happened to her, to the child she was carrying, he'd lose his own biological offspring.

"I just thought you should know, because Crosswinds is involved, that I got an eerie text a few minutes ago. Fletcher's on his way over."

Dawn was barely breaking on Sunday morning. He was probably still in bed.

"I'm on my way to Connors. Elise is bleeding. I've got a tourniquet on her, but I think she might have slit a vein—"

"Connors?" she interrupted, her text message an issue for later. "You bring her here, Sebastian. If it's a vein, she might not make it to Connors."

"I'm not involving you or the clinic…"

"Bring her to my house," she said. "I have my kit here. And anything else I need, someone can get for me." She was pulling on jeans and a sweatshirt as she spoke. And, as she heard a car outside and peeked out, added, "Fletcher's here. Bring her to me, Sebastian," she said, hanging up.

She wasn't going to argue with him. Elise might not have that much time.

Ruby already had a sheet in hand as she gave her

phone to her brother and went straight to the kitchen table, covering it.

"Sebastian's on his way with an emergency," she told him. "One of his dogs, whose handler is arriving this week to pick her up."

Frowning, Fletcher, whose hair was standing up at the back, in a bedtime cowlick, didn't say a word as he asked for her phone's password and then typed it in.

She ran for her bag, then laid out supplies.

Fletcher came closer. "I don't like this."

"I don't, either," she told him. "But it's the best I can do. He said a vein's been cut. Depending on which one, she could bleed to death before I can help her. She might need a transfusion…"

"The text, Ruby. I don't like the text."

Right. Fine. Neither did she. "You figure that out, I'll work on this," she told him, thinking of the girl she'd birthed two years before. Of all the hours of training Sebastian and Della—and her cousin Malcolm, too— had put Elise through. The golden retriever had shown more promise, from the beginning, than any of Sebastian's other dogs. She was going to a group of mountain rangers who lost lives every year when they couldn't find missing people in time.

"A dog is hurt and right afterward you get a text telling you to stay away?"

The thought had crossed her mind.

"We don't know that the two are connected," she told him. "If Elise got cut digging, I'm saying the chances are slim. But in any event, I *am* staying away. And ultimately, this guy is after Crosswinds for some reason, not me. Or Sebastian, either. If he was a murderer, why not just take out Sebastian and be done with it?" She was busy arranging, running a silent checklist through her mind. Preparing an IV. Antibiotic. Getting sutures ready. "This isn't just a dog I'm hoping to save here, although I'd do the same if it were. This animal is going to save human lives. It's her calling. And I'm not going to have people die because I got a text message."

Her text notification sounded again. She glanced at Fletcher, who was watching her screen.

"Sebastian's here," he said, and headed toward the door to the garage.

She heard the double garage door open. Listened while her brother told Sebastian to pull in. Counted seconds while she heard the truck's engine shut off and the garage door close.

And counted more as the men carried the injured dog into her.

"She's conscious," she breathed with relief. She showered the girl with praise, with reassurance, even while her heart thudded at the sight of the blood-soaked bandage around Elise's left ankle. "There's blood on her right foot, too," she said, taking a brief glance, seeing cuts, as she unwrapped the gauze around the dog's left front leg.

"Sebastian, stay at her head, comfort her. Fletcher, keep tight pressure right here." She moved her brother's fingers about an inch above the gauze.

And five minutes later, they were all breathing huge sighs of relief. Sebastian's quick thinking and the tourniquet had made the injury less catastrophic. "It's the cephalic vein," she told the two men, relieved to find that only the superficial vein had been nicked.

It took a while longer to dig small pieces of glass out of several cuts and incisions on Elise's lower front legs. She was still assessing damage, tending to immediate medical concerns, when Fletcher told Sebastian about the text Ruby had received that morning, finishing with, "I need to know what happened."

With a swift hard look to Ruby, and a new frown marring his brow, Sebastian said, "She's due to leave us this week. I was running her through all the courses one last time, in the dark, just to be sure I felt she was completely ready. Instead of hitting the spot where I'd buried her scent, she stopped on a hill and began digging frantically. Next thing I know she's spurting blood…"

Fletcher, who'd been dismissed from pressure application a few minutes before, pulled out his phone. Tapped. And then said, "Get a team out to Crosswinds." Talking to Sebastian, her brother received and relayed exact location coordinates to, she assumed, Glen Steele, and then hung up.

"Aren't you going to join them?" she asked Fletcher, adding a second, and final, stitch to another left-foot wound.

"You received a direct warning to stay away, Ruby. I don't think the guy cares about geography at the moment. He wanted you to stay away from the dog."

"Because every time he strikes, you save the day," Sebastian added through clenched teeth.

They didn't even know yet if the two were connected, which she pointed out, only to have two strong male voices come back on her at once.

Ruby felt ganged up on.

And…loved, too.

The text warning to Ruby had come from a burner phone. Off a local tower. No surprises there. But frustrating as hell.

Once again, Sebastian had to call an elite client and explain that his dog had been attacked, and would not be ready for delivery as soon as expected. Thankfully, he was dealing with law enforcement, and once they knew the details, they were not only willing to wait for Elise's cuts to heal, but were also offering suggestions to catch the fiend who'd deliberately harm dogs.

And a third piece of great news—Ruby found no muscular damage to the dog at all. If a small piece of glass hadn't pierced Elise's vein, her wounds would have been mostly superficial. Not that he gave his stalker any credit for that one.

The police had quickly located the spot where Elise had been digging and Fletcher had left to check it out, asking Sebastian to stay with Ruby until they knew more.

The hole Elise had dug was on an incline, coming up from the shore of the river. The land was fenced as part of a training course, and didn't appear to be obviously breached, but someone could have climbed the fence. The enclosure was made to keep young, eager dogs inside, not to keep humans out.

Steele had found pieces of steak with shards of glass embedded in them, buried just inches underground in three different locations along the incline. All out of range of cameras.

Clearly planted there.

And not for a good purpose.

Whoever was after him was smart. Watchful. And vigilant.

And, as Fletcher had pointed out on one of his calls to Sebastian, the subject seemed to have a lot of time on their hands. Or, as the visiting detective had suggested, the stalker worked second shift and Sebastian was the man's current after-work activity.

Ruby's brother had another interesting theory. That the person they were after had a place along the lake. Possibly even in view of Sebastian's property. The police were checking rentals. Not a small task, considering the tourist mecca Owl Creek had become.

Fletcher, in going over the case files the night before, had found another possible suspect as well. He'd been looking for anyone who'd had a history with both Sebastian *and* Ruby. There'd been a man a few years back who'd claimed to be a veteran in need of a PTSD dog—part of the volunteer portion of Sebastian's outfit. Veterans received trained dogs for free. The guy had lied about his military service. He'd never served his country and had no medical records to show he'd received any treatment, or even had a consultation for the stress disorder.

Ruby had been the one to raise doubts in the beginning. She hadn't liked the way the man related to the dog they'd been about to give him. There'd been no bond at all. More like someone who was going to turn around and sell the dog for a nice profit.

His name was David Pierce. Sebastian remembered him. According to police, the guy's last known address was the county jail, dated a few years before. He'd been in for a misdemeanor swindling charge of some sort. Meaning it had to have involved less than a thousand dollars. He'd disappeared upon his release.

Moved out of state.

Fletcher was attempting to find out where.

Sebastian was sitting at Ruby's kitchen table, his truck still in her garage, relating the gist of the most recent telephone conversation he'd had with her brother. Ruby was going over the dog's paws with a bright light, a magnifying glass and tweezers, looking for small shards of glass she might have missed.

It was her third time doing so—giving Elise breaks in between—and she was still finding little glints that turned out to be more shards.

"I remember him, too," Ruby said slowly, as though her mind was only half on her words. "The guy gave me the creeps. The way he didn't even seem to see dogs as living beings. He never looked any of them in the eye. As I recall, he didn't even talk to them."

Listening to her, Sebastian smiled. In some ways, the woman was his twin. Who else judged people by whether or not they spoke to dogs? Or looked them in the eye, as opposed to just looking at them?

"I like Fletcher," Sebastian said then, the other man's integrity pushing at him. Hard.

"Yeah." Ruby rubbed an alcohol-soaked pad on the paw she'd just been picking, and, praising Elise, helped the dog down. "I kind of like him, too," she said then, returning to her conversation with Sebastian.

Sebastian dropped to the floor with Elise, petting the girl, and said, "I'm thinking we should let him know about the baby."

He'd spent a good bit of time soul-searching after his meeting with Fletcher the day before. "When something doesn't feel right, it means you're in the wrong place, or with the wrong people, or doing the wrong thing," he said, paraphrasing her words to him during their Friday-night phone conversation. "It doesn't feel right to me that he doesn't know that when this guy goes after you, it's not just your life that's in jeopardy."

"Would it make any difference to his policing?"

It would not. The answer was a no-brainer. Fletcher would protect his sister's life with everything he had. Period.

"It could change how he thinks about me," Sebastian said, feeling a bit less proud of himself in that moment. "When he finds out…knowing that I knew…"

When had he ever made choices based on others' opinions of him?

But then, he'd never had his own biological kid's potential aunts and uncles swarming in the background, either.

"It doesn't make you any less trustworthy." Ruby's tone held the confidence that made a lot of people just nod their heads and do as she said.

It wasn't the tone that got him. It was the fact that she'd known what he'd been thinking. Or how he'd been feeling.

Which, strangely enough, brightened his mood some. "Just as a heads-up, which one of your three brothers is most likely to come looking for me with a baseball bat when they find out?" he asked, sending her a raised-brow look. With the beginnings of a grin.

There they were, with a stalker, threats, Elise hurt… and talking things over with her made the burden seem lighter.

"I'm guessing Wade," she told him, her tone holding no humor at all. "He won't hit you with it, though."

He'd already known that part. He and Wade had taken care of proving their physical superiority over each other as kids. Both had won some and lost some.

"He's not at his best right now," Ruby said, and Sebastian nodded.

"I tried to talk to him, but he's not ready," he told her.

"Plus, you guys have been close since you were kids. I'm guessing he's going to take our situation a little more personally than the rest."

"Because we aren't getting married."

"Yeah. I can see him taking offense that you don't think I'm good enough for you."

His hand on Elise's back paused. "You don't think that do you?"

"Do *you* think I think you aren't good enough for me?"

She didn't look at him. Didn't even slow her cleaning and disposing of the supplies she'd just used.

And he knocked off another reason to feel bad from his list. Ruby didn't want marriage any more than he did. He'd have thought the relief at that one would be palpable.

Finishing up with her supplies at the table, Ruby dropped down to the floor on the other side of the retriever. Elise wagged her tail, looking none the worse for wear.

Because, once again Ruby had saved Sebastian's day.

When he needed to be the one who saved hers.

Chapter 14

With Fletcher home, Jenny Colton had insisted on having Sunday afternoon dinner with all her kids at the table. There was no way Ruby had been able to get out of going. Everyone was worried about her, and they needed to see that she was fine.

Her dad and oldest brother, Chase, who was vice president at Colton Properties, talked business. Fletcher and Wade took the boat out for a while. Her mom and two younger sisters talked cooking and food and coffee drinks. And Ruby played with Lucy.

She'd been worried that Hannah or Frannie would blow her secret somehow, even by trying to talk to her alone and being overheard, but neither one of them sought her out. Jenny had been too busy helping to plan the food for Buck's birthday celebration and both of her sisters were deeply involved with that. Apparently, Frannie was providing a full bar of coffee drinks to go along with dessert.

Sebastian had taken Elise and gone home shortly after noon. Della had been planning to train, but with the police there, she had fed the dogs and worked inside the kennel instead. And from what Fletcher told her at dinner, Sebastian had decided not to do any more training until he had someone out to check every inch of the other courses.

Fletcher insisted on having Colton Veterinary Clinic inspected as well. He brought in a K-9 officer, which Ruby saw as total overkill, but she had to admit she felt safer going into work Monday morning knowing that the place had been checked for any booby traps.

She wasn't so much afraid of being physically hurt. But living with the constant threat of criminal activity disrupting daily life and hurting dogs was taking its toll on her. She could only imagine what it was doing to Sebastian.

And she figured that the stalker had intended the emotional distress as much as anything physical he'd done.

Which meant, she thought, that the unknown assailant was after Sebastian, not her.

Sebastian had asked her to text when she got home Sunday night. She did, hoping that he'd call. He just texted back instead.

And she figured that was just as well.

He thanked her for letting him know and telling her that Elise had been out in the exercise yard several times and was doing just fine. He kept things on a less personal level.

More their usual style.

Other than the vein bleed, the retriever's wounds had all been fairly superficial. Because Sebastian had been out there to stop the dog from digging any further for the blood-covered meat she'd found.

Fletcher had let her know quietly after dinner that the blood on the meat had tested as human.

But as gruesome a warning as that sounded, he, Steele and Sebastian all figured it was the sign of a thorough stalker, someone who knew that human blood would be most likely to attract a search-and-rescue animal, not a warning of more human bloodshed to come.

They were testing the blood for a DNA match, though. Hoping that they'd have a lead on the assailant within a few days.

That blood could be the mistake they'd been waiting for.

And before she could fully begin to plan the next phase of her life, she needed the stalker caught. Overkill, maybe, but she was growing more and more adamant that she didn't want the person to know that she was carrying a baby. And most particularly did not want him even suspecting that it could be Sebastian's.

Still, having been with her whole family, in her parents' home, playing with Lucy… She couldn't help thinking how the family dinner would look next time Fletcher came home. If he waited for his next yearly vacation. There'd be a playpen, a car seat. She'd be breast-feeding. Changing diapers. And holding a baby. Her mom would be taking charge of the infant, holding baby cheeks up to her own and talking that sweet talk again…

Elation welled in her, mixing with panic. And other

things, too. Excitement. And an odd combination of sadness and regret that she didn't understand.

Which had led her to wanting to hear Sebastian's voice. To talk to him. Telling herself she yearned for him in particular because he was the only one who knew her full secret. Who had an idea of what her future looked like.

But Monday morning, as she left for work, seeing the empty place in her garage where his truck had been parked the morning before, she realized that it was a good thing she and Sebastian hadn't talked the night before. With emotions running abnormally high, they could lead themselves into a place neither one of them would want to be when the dust settled.

And the last thing she wanted to do was trap a man into being there for her.

But it wasn't just her who'd need him. Ruby might be the only visible occupant of her vehicle, but she wasn't the only living human there. She wasn't alone anymore.

Ever. Not even for a second.

And while her child would grow up, and apart from her, that new life forming inside her would always be a part of her.

The concept was mind-boggling.

Every aspect of her life was going to change.

Driving along the lake through her hometown, Ruby started to see the businesses differently, too, just as she had her parents' house the night before. The Tides, the high-end restaurant located on the lakefront, was rented out frequently for weddings and special occasions. Jenny had thrown a party for Ruby on the large open patio there when she'd graduated from veterinary school.

Would Ruby be arranging a high-school graduation party in that same space in eighteen years?

And Tap Out Brewery, with its local brews. She'd had some good times there, eating pub food with friends back before they'd all gone their own ways and her work had become her life. The place turned into more of a party venue after 8:00 p.m. Would she be driving by to make certain her teenager wasn't getting sucked into drinking underage?

As the muscles in her stomach tightened with tension, she passed Hutch's diner. And relaxed some. Hutch had always only made breakfast, but it was the best. She'd been going there since she was a kid. Hutch had been gone for four years, but his wife, Sharon, still ran the place, with the help of their son, Billy.

And maybe Ruby's child would one day join her at the clinic. Just like Chase had joined Robert at Colton Properties. And Wade and Malcolm both worked with Uncle Buck at Colton Ranch.

She'd love that. To have her own little one grow up to love animals, to want to care for them with her. And even after her.

There was a sense of permanence in the thought. Of continuity. For years she'd been pushed by the sense that if she didn't work hard all the time, her clinic wouldn't survive. The idea that it could possibly thrive even after she was no longer there was…nice.

Coming up to the newest addition on Main Street, she pulled over in front of the long, narrow three-story brick building and turned off the SUV. Frannie's bookstore and café, Book Mark It, wasn't open yet, but her sister had offered the night before to have tea ready for Ruby on her way to work if she wanted to stop.

Frannie hadn't said, but it would be decaffeinated. Because... Frannie knew.

And while Ruby could make her own morning beverage at work, and normally would have just to save the time, she went inside to see her little sister, instead.

Sebastian wasn't waiting on Ruby's brother, or anyone else, to start his lure-the-stalker-out campaign. He'd wait to involve anything in Owl Creek, but the filming, and interviewing was going to begin on Monday. And the first segment would air in Boise later that week. He'd called Andy, Bryony and Della to let them know they needn't come into work.

Not Monday, for sure. And, if they chose, they could take off until the Crosswinds attacker was caught. He couldn't require people to risk their lives.

Della refused to take any time off. And she brought her own two-year-old search-and-rescue black Lab, Charlie, with her when she arrived in time on Monday to help Sebastian with the feedings and kennel cleanings.

Neither of them ended up doing much of either as Bryony and Andy showed up, too, telling Sebastian they'd work extra hours to make up for James's absence.

His crew wasn't just there to make money. They cared about the Crosswinds mission, they told him, in an impromptu little meeting in the kennel that morning. They loved the dogs.

And maybe they cared about him, too, he thought, as, fueled with energy, he left them to their tasks and took Oscar home for a PTSD session.

He'd been working with the dog since Ruby had first suggested that Oscar could be cross-trained. He'd figured trying couldn't hurt.

If it worked, he could add cross-training to the list of Crosswinds services.

The film crew and cohost interviewer weren't due until afternoon, when it would be warmest outside.

Sitting at the table, Sebastian started bumping one heel up and down on the floor. Two seconds, and Oscar was there, nudging his knee.

"Good boy!" He gave the dog a treat. And repeated the process.

He'd noticed that the heel bump was something he did when he was starting to get tense. He'd always taken the movement as a rhythmic reminder to himself to relax. But if he could teach Oscar to cue him when it started, the dog's distraction and loving attention might calm him before the tension escalated.

He knew the ropes. Had been training PTSD dogs for a few years. It was different when he was working with his dog. For himself. The thought created a curious level of anxiety.

Except that…he wasn't just doing it for himself. What if he was around his kid sometime, fell asleep and had a flipping nightmare?

If Oscar was there, if he was trained to nudge Sebastian when signs of a nightmare began, there'd be an added level of safety for the kid.

Not that he planned to have the kid around and fall asleep. He wasn't a family guy. Just the thought of not having his space to himself created a level of anxiety.

But the thought of not helping Ruby? Of not being a part of his own child's life? At first, he'd gone there automatically. Had made the logical choice. But as he'd lain in bed at night, and went about his tasks during the day, as he faced the fact that Ruby could be hurt, and that his child would, too...

Oscar nudged him.

Hard.

And he relaxed. "Good boy!" he said, giving the dog a treat. Oscar had the calming skill down. Far better than Sebastian did, apparently.

He moved on to simulate a moaning sound that he knew commonly accompanied nightmares. Ruby had told him he was moaning. Showing Oscar a treat, and moaning, and giving the dog the treat.

Oscar, who'd already mastered search-and-rescue training, caught on quickly. A couple of more moans and the dog was nudging for treats.

Figuring he'd move on to serotonin-level change, getting up to retrieve hormones that would simulate the smell, Sebastian stopped when his phone beeped a text message.

He hadn't yet heard from Ruby. She'd said she'd text when she got to work. Just so he'd know she was there.

More eager than he should have been to hear from Crosswinds's veterinarian, he grabbed his phone off the table.

YOU CARE MORE ABOUT DOGS THAN YOU DO PEOPLE

The phone number was blocked.

Tapping the newest icon on his speed dial, Sebastian got Fletcher on the first ring.

He hadn't even started his campaign and the guy was escalating.

Hitting out at him and not Ruby. Because he thought

Ruby had minded his command and stayed away the morning before?

"Bring it on," Sebastian said aloud, standing. "Come at me and we'll get this done."

Facing the danger on his own, by himself, he wasn't afraid.

He was trained.

The day flew by. Other than breaks for proper nutrition to go along with her horse-pill-size vitamins, Ruby moved efficiently from appointment to appointment, enjoying her time with each client and patient, answering questions, advising, giving lots of hugs and getting plenty of nose kisses, too. Until late afternoon, the day was the kind she liked best—all well checks. And everyone checked out well. She never scheduled surgeries on Mondays unless there was an emergency.

She was just getting ready to sit at her desk and make notes in her charting system when she got a call from the reception desk telling her that a dog injured in a car accident was on the way in. A runaway beagle had been hit on Main Street.

Three hours later, tired, but filled with satisfaction, with the sense that she was living her best life, she headed home. The beagle had lost part of an ear, and one kidney. He might walk with a slight limp, but he should fully recover and live a normal life. Barney's elderly owners had both been in tears when she'd led them back to see the boy before going home for the night.

Maria would be spending the night at the clinic and would call Ruby if anything changed with Barney before morning.

Figuring her family should be proud of her—in prior

days Ruby would have spent the night on the couch in her office and sent her technician home—Ruby was looking forward to some of Hannah's homemade vegetable soup as she pulled into the nighttime traffic. Filled with tourists all year round, Owl Creek was always a happening place during the evening hours as people came in from days of boating, fishing, skiing, or climbing and were looking for evening entertainment.

The Tides was booming, as was the brewery. She figured the nightclub just outside of town would be, too. But not for Ruby. None of it sounded good to her. Her sister had made up several individual containers of her soup for freezing and had gifted Ruby, and the rest of the family, with them the night before. Ruby was having part of her share for dinner.

And maybe she'd hear from Sebastian. More than just a text message. He'd had a marketing crew in that afternoon, she knew. But she hadn't talked to him or heard from Fletcher or Detective Steele all day.

Didn't mean nothing had happened. Only that it hadn't directly involved her.

She didn't like not knowing.

So why didn't she ask? Who said she had to wait to hear? And if she wanted to talk to Sebastian, why didn't she?

Filled with self-righteous energy, she gave the voice command to call Sebastian. And grinned in the darkness of her car's interior when he picked up on the first ring.

"Have you eaten?" she asked without preamble.

"Nope. Just coming in from the kennels for the night." He'd had a long day. She wanted to hear about it. As a volunteer in his program. Her Dr. Colton persona wanted a rundown on her patients, too.

"You like vegetable soup?" she asked before she could get ahold of herself and change her mind. She was carrying his child. He wanted to be involved. They were friends. And she wanted to see him.

"I do."

"You want to come over?"

"Of course."

"I'm not there yet. I had an emergency come in at the end of my day. Spent three hours in surgery."

What in the hell was she doing? Sharing her day with him like they were a couple or something. She always went home alone after work. Long days and not so long. Grueling and easy. Her, alone. It's how she wanted it.

"I'm leaving now," Sebastian said.

Starting to doubt herself, she almost canceled the invitation she'd just issued, but he'd hung up. Too much was changing. Too fast.

She wasn't a woman who ever had a man over after work.

Or ever.

Her home was her haven.

It was soon going to have a new human being living in it full-time.

Sebastian was an offshoot of that little person.

And a big man with an appetite to match. Her servings of vegetable soup weren't going to be enough to satisfy the mountain man who'd been working all day and hadn't had dinner. She turned into the grocery store, then ran in and grabbed a loaf of freshly baked Italian bread from the bakery and a precut vegetable tray from the deli. Paid at self-checkout and was back at her car within minutes. Her little house, right on the lake, was only another couple of minutes away and he had ten to get to town.

She'd left her nightshirt on the kitchen counter, to remind herself to do a load of laundry when she got home. And hadn't put away the rest of the supplies she'd used for Elise the day before, either, which she needed to do to set the table for dinner.

For that matter, she hadn't emptied the dishwasher.

She had not thought the evening's events through.

She wasn't a woman who could just entertain a man on a moment's notice.

"He's not a man. He's Sebastian," she said aloud as she rounded the curve to her little lakefront home. Heard the absurdity of the statement, considering the fact that his manly part had very much changed her life, and…

Lights shone to the left of her. Blinding her in her rearview mirror.

Sebastian?

Already?

The vehicle wasn't behind her.

What the…?

It was there, up to her bumper, beside her, going to hit her…

Ruby swerved. Had no shoulder to turn on. And came to an abrupt stop in the ditch.

Heart pounding, she sat for a second. "I'm fine," she said aloud, checking to make certain her assertion was correct. The airbag hadn't deployed. She hadn't hit the steering wheel. She'd felt her seat belt, but hadn't been bruised.

Glancing in her mirrors, she unbuckled herself with shaking hands. All was dark around her. The vehicle had sped on past. She could see lights shining from homes down from hers. Their little access road didn't get a lot of traffic.

Taking a deep breath, she tried to calm herself. She needed to get home. But the nose of her SUV was stuck in dirt. And with the small but sharp incline she'd headed down, there was no way she could back up.

She'd have to walk. Or wait for Sebastian. Opening her door, she pulled out her phone to call him so he didn't miss her and drive on past. She couldn't stop shaking, missing his speed dial on the first attempt and…

She screamed as arms came around her from behind. Pulling up under her armpits. She saw black gloves. "No!" She got a word into the second scream.

"I've been told that land is mine," a male voice said softly into her ear. "I will have it. God says animals are here to serve man, not for man to serve them. It's blasphemy."

Scared, trembling, unable to breathe, she flung her head back as hard as she could, hitting her assailant in the face. He released her and pushed away, and she fell to the ground.

Lights came around the corner. She had a flash of the man's face. His bloody nose. Then he turned and ran off through the trees.

Gasping for air, trembling, Ruby crawled to her tire. Pulled herself up.

Saw Sebastian.

And started to cry.

Chapter 15

Leaving Ruby's SUV nose-down in the ditch, Sebastian picked her up, cradled in his arms, grabbed her satchel and rushed them both to his truck.

"I'm fine," she said, but the way she laid her head against his chest, pushing into him, showed him the lie in her words.

He dropped her satchel to pull open the passenger door. Set her on the seat, pushed the button to ease it back, strapped her in and set her satchel on the floor of his truck as though he'd been through save-your-child's-mother basic training.

He just moved. On instinct.

Got himself in the driver's seat the same way. No thought. No feeling. Just do.

As soon as the truck was on, and headed back to Main Street, he voice-called Fletcher Colton, telling the detective in a few succinct words what he'd come upon, giving a description of the back of the fleeing man, which was all he'd seen, and let him know the direction in which the man had gone.

Fletcher had questions, spat out in the same manner.

He answered every one of them.

Including that he had Ruby and was taking her to be examined.

By the time he hung up, he was already heading toward the highway.

"I don't need to be examined." She was raising her seat as she said the words. "He didn't hurt me, Sebastian. He just scared the air out of me."

"I saw you on the ground." Emotion hit then. Hard. Full of anger. He'd find the man. And show him why he should never have touched Ruby Colton.

"I head-butted him," she said, sounding more like the woman he'd known since childhood. Controlled. Self-sufficient.

She'd been crying when he'd picked her up. It was a sight that was going to haunt him.

"I think I broke his nose." She sounded as though she might be bragging a little. "I know I made him bleed."

Sebastian's grip tightened on the wheel. "How do you know that?"

"I saw the blood coming out of his nose."

"You saw his face."

"Yeah, in your headlight as you came up the road. I think that's what made him run off." He heard the fear in her tone at the last remark. She shuddered.

And he gritted his teeth against the need powering through him to go hunt the guy down. Right then. Himself.

Because getting Ruby to the emergency room was more important.

"If you hadn't come—"

"You'd have been fine," he interrupted. He had to believe those words.

"I should talk to Fletcher," she said then, as though just coming into a full awareness of the situation. "Turn around. I'm fine, really. We need to get back so I can talk to the police. And I have to get my car out of the ditch. I have to be in early to check on Barney. And I have appointments starting at eight."

"You're pregnant, Ruby. Your SUV obviously hit the ditch with some force. And if you were close enough to head-butt the guy with enough force to land you on the ground, I have to assume he had some kind of hold on you, and then let you go in a way that caused you to fall."

She wouldn't have deliberately lain down for the guy. Sebastian would bet his life on that one.

She was fully dressed. Her clothes weren't torn. He'd just been on the phone with her ten minutes before he'd come upon her...

The man hadn't had a chance to...

He owed fate his life for sparing her...

Thoughts flew. Started and stopped.

"Fletcher and Steele will have people out casing the area. I had enough of a description for them to apprehend him if they find him soon. We need to get you checked out to make certain the baby is okay. That's more important than a police report," he told her.

They just needed the baby to be okay.

He repeated the words to himself. And then again. Until he realized just how much he had invested in the small being growing inside Ruby. Not just his biology, but the heart and soul of him.

He wasn't going to be a father. But he'd fathered a child.

And would give up his life for that tiny being, too.

She and the baby were both fine. Ruby had known they were, and yet, when the doctor came into her Connors emergency-room cubicle and told her so, she'd been flooded with relief, anyway.

There'd been no doubt, since she'd found out she was pregnant, that she was going to have the child. That moment alone with the doctor, waiting on the precipice of knowing what the ultrasound had revealed, she'd been shown just how much she wanted the baby. How deeply she already loved it.

The worried look on Sebastian's face when she approached him in the waiting room touched her heart, too.

He cared.

And that mattered.

"All good," she said, unable to stop the smile that spread on her face.

Or to stop the flip-flop her heart gave when he smiled back.

Reliving the near kidnapping, trembling, as she stepped out into the dark, she stopped her hand from sneaking around his elbow, forcing herself to keep her distance as she walked with him back to the truck.

They were friends.

Not lovers.

As she reminded herself on the forty-five-minute drive back to Owl Creek—Sebastian was all business, and there was no reason for her feelings to be hurt by that fact.

Her emotions were on overload.

She was not only hormonal due to pregnancy, but she'd also been through a near abduction. Sebastian was the guy who'd happened by to clean up the mess.

She'd be on top of the fear by morning. And would have the rest of her heart back in line by then as well. With all the upheaval she'd experienced growing up, she knew she could count on herself to be strong and step away from the drama.

As soon as they were in the truck, Sebastian started filling her in on news from Fletcher.

There'd been no sign of a man between five-ten and six feet in dark pants, a dark, long-sleeved hoodie and dark shoes anywhere in the woods or neighborhood surrounding Ruby's house. Officers canvassed houses and businesses on Main Street, too, but no one remembered seeing a man with that description.

They were requesting private security footage, both in the neighborhood and from businesses along Main Street, to go through.

"He had dark hair," Ruby said, when Sebastian paused for breath. "And he was white." She remembered his hands coming up from her sides, as his arms slid under her armpits, and shuddered again.

Glancing at her, his chin seemed to tighten, but in the darkness of the truck, she couldn't be sure.

"They found an SUV, Ruby," he said, his tone like a sergeant, reporting to the masses. She knew the tone. From Fletcher and Wade, too.

Wasn't overly fond of it.

But being one who sometimes had to be the bearer of bad news at work, she completely understood it.

"It fits the description you gave from Friday morning. It was abandoned in the woods across from your house."

"He ran me off the road," she said, as it occurred to her that Sebastian hadn't known that part. She'd been in panic mode when the father of her child had arrived. Was still trying to comprehend that she'd nearly been taken against her will.

Shivering, she wanted the memory, the horrifying sensations involved with it, to go away. Forever.

"Just like Friday morning…"

But that night she'd been in the ditch. "I wasn't able to turn out of it," she said slowly, reliving those moments, with darkness looming larger than the lights on the dash, the lights in the homes along the lake. "I sat in the ditch," she remembered. "Trying to figure out what had just happened. Deciding what to do. I was just getting out of the SUV, to flag you down, when…"

He'd grabbed her.

She was cold. Needed a warm blanket. Forced herself to think.

"My phone," she said. "I was calling you…"

He glanced her way again. Maybe it was her imagination, but he seemed pleased by those last words.

And in times of crisis, a little fantasy to get her through didn't hurt, did it?

"Fletcher's meeting us at your house." Sebastian repeated something he'd told Ruby on the way to the truck in the hospital parking lot.

She didn't respond. He wasn't sure how much she'd processed of anything he'd been telling her.

"He talked to me," she said softly, her entire body shaking, as though warding off a chill. He reached to the dash, turned up the heat in the truck. Kept his eye on his driving, and glanced at her, too. Back and forth. The road. Her. The road. Her.

She'd hadn't mentioned hearing a voice.

Was she imagining things?

It was only a couple of hours since she'd been attacked, and he knew what trauma-induced panic could do…

"It just came to me, the sound of his voice in my ear." She hugged her arms, her voice sounding almost childlike.

"What did he say?" Sebastian asked softly. With as much kindness as he had inside him.

"'I've been told that land is mine, I will have it. God says animals are here to serve man, not for man to serve them. It's blasphemy.'" The words rolled off her tongue with no intonation whatsoever. "It was him, Sebastian. Your stalker. The SUV, yeah, but those words. It was him." As she looked his way and continued talking, her tone rose, panic lacing every syllable.

And Sebastian pressed his foot on the pedal all the way to the floor.

He had to get her back to Fletcher.

And needed to hold on to her.

No way was he leaving her to drown in the panic all alone.

He knew how that felt.

And she was there because of him.

Ruby refused to go to her parents' house. Or to the police station. At ten o'clock at night, her big brother could come to her house.

She had to go home.

To be where she was the boss of the land.

She heard Sebastian relay the information to Fletcher while they were still ten minutes outside of Owl Creek.

"He doesn't think it's a good idea for you to go back to that neighborhood right now," Sebastian told her, hanging up.

"That's exactly why I *have* to go back," she retorted. "I won't let this fiend turn my home into a haunted house. Besides, if he was going to do something to me at home, he'd simply have waited until I got there," she added. "I was three houses down. If nothing else, he could have waited for me to pull into the garage and slipped inside…" Her voice trailed off as another wave of panic hit.

Sebastian shot a quick look at her. And then said, "I think you're probably right about that."

He almost sounded relieved.

"I guess it's better that tonight's…episode relates to my work at Crosswinds, rather than just that I'm unlucky enough to be the target of a second madman." Dear God, let that have meant that he wouldn't have forced himself on her.

No. She wasn't going to borrow trouble.

She had enough real boogeymen chasing her mind at the moment.

As they passed the sign announcing the turn-off for Owl Creek in two miles, Sebastian blurted out, "We have to tell Fletcher about the baby. I've been trying to figure out a way to get your cooperation on this one, and I know it's not what you want or what would be easiest for you. I get that you don't need your family breathing down on you any more than they already are, or will soon be, but I'm not backing down on this one. Not anymore."

When he finished, finally giving her a chance to get a word in, she said, "I know." And then added, "But we don't have to tell anyone that you're the father."

He'd pulled to a stop at the bottom of the highway exit ramp. They had the road to themselves, and when he glanced over at her, he didn't seem to be all that concerned about turning into town. "Are you ashamed to tell them it's me?"

"No!" She'd screamed the word once before that night. Her throat still stung from the sounds she'd made. That second time, it wasn't filled with panic. But with exclamation. "No," she said again, more calmly. "I'm thinking of you, Sebastian."

"Then you don't know me all that well." He faced forward.

"What does that mean?" She could see the set of his chin in the darkness but little else. Avoiding the strong desire to unbuckle and touch that chin—it wasn't anything she'd know how to pull off casually—she continued into the silence, "Talk to me, please," she said, in her more professional tone.

"I'm a man of honor. I don't shirk my duties. And I won't have anyone in your family thinking that I do."

She wished she hadn't asked. Her heart fell as she heard the words.

It wasn't about her.

Or their baby.

It was about Once a Marine, Always a Marine. Wade's explanation anytime she told him he was getting on her nerves with his need to fight for and defend everyone in their family anytime he was home on leave.

With a nod, she accepted his explanation and waited for him to take her home.

Chapter 16

Are you ashamed to tell them it's me? Where in the hell had that come from? If ever there was a man completely out of his element, it was Sebastian.

Fighting the enemy, he knew what to do every time. Whether that enemy was a terrorist in another land, or one in his own backyard, antagonizing his dogs. And his veterinarian.

But finding out that the night his friend had taken pity on him, he'd made her pregnant? In spite of the precautions they'd taken…

How did a confirmed bachelor go about figuring out how to deal with that? Most particularly in a small town that, along with his dogs, was the only family he had left?

She'd gone cold when he'd overreacted to her very sweet offer to keep his name out of her baby confession that evening. He'd have apologized if he hadn't thought it would make matters worse. If for no other reason than because they'd almost reached her house and had no time left to talk about it.

Her SUV was already back in the driveway, with her brother's right beside it. Fletcher climbed out as Sebastian pulled up out front. Half expecting Ruby to wish him good-night before she exited his vehicle, he was aware as she climbed down from the truck and then stood there, as though waiting for him to finish rounding the front of the vehicle.

No way he wasn't going to be present for the coming conversation. Just felt irrationally good that she'd seemed to take his presence for granted.

After giving his sister a thorough once-over glance, Fletcher took a seat at Ruby's kitchen table—still strewn with supplies from her attention to Elise the morning before—and announced that while Steele was running command on the officers out on the street, Fletcher would be recording the interview with Ruby.

Sebastian sat diagonally across from the detective and Ruby sat next to Sebastian. He didn't make anything of it.

The ten-minute conversation was straightforward. Ruby told her brother everything she'd told Sebastian in the truck. Adding more description to the man's face. With the light's glare she hadn't been able to tell an age, but she'd seen no age lines. He'd had facial hair, but no beard or mustache. Just stubble. Light-colored, not dark, like his hair. She agreed to sit with a sketch artist Fletcher was calling in from Boise in the morning.

Then Fletcher turned off the recording, putting his phone down on the table instead of back into his pocket.

Glancing between the two of him. The detective's frown, the uneasy look in his eyes, had Sebastian looking at Ruby. Gearing up to take the brunt of whatever was coming.

She seemed to be holding up fine. Hands folded on the table, tone strong. It was as though the attack had never happened.

"First, it's pretty clear to everyone that this guy tonight is the same one we've already been hunting," Fletcher started in. "The SUV they found tonight just yards from where Ruby was attacked fits the description she gave Friday morning and then again this evening." Fletcher looked at both of them. "The vehicle was stolen last Thursday from a big-box store in Connors…"

"Which means we've just lost our best chance at getting him," Sebastian guessed. "He's changing vehicles. Driving stolen ones."

"It looks that way. Which would explain why we haven't been able to find the same vehicle leaving town on all the nights there's been attacks at Crosswinds."

His enemy was a canny one.

"He's been told that the land is his," Fletcher said, glancing between him and Ruby, but settling on Sebastian. "We have to assume this means the land upon which Crosswinds is sitting. Which brings us back to the possibility that your father had a child outside of his marriage to your mother. From Ruby's description, he sounds younger as opposed to not—that would fit, too."

Sebastian nodded. He'd also gone straight to the idea of a love child after Ruby had told him what the guy had said.

"But this…" Fletcher referred to the notes he'd also

been taking on a yellow pad. "'God says that animals are there to serve men…and not for men to serve…'"

"Has to refer to the kennels," Sebastian mused. "Until James quit, there were five of us there, pretty much every day, taking care of the dogs."

"And Ruby most definitely fits the role of serving animals," Fletcher continued, glancing back at his sister.

Sebastian felt her stiffen beside him. She was no longer shaking. Whether it was because she had her fear under control, or just enough determination to remain strong in front of her brother, he couldn't be sure.

Suspected it was the latter.

The woman had certainly perfected the guise of being a rock on the outside. Growing up as she had, he couldn't blame her.

"He's after you, too, Ruby. And judging by his behavior, it would appear that he's no longer satisfied just going after the dogs and issuing warnings. Tonight's episode shows us that he's escalating. They found rope in the car. He wasn't going to just warn you and let you go."

She nodded, surprising Sebastian. And scaring him. Ruby rarely just acquiesced and that was the second time that night. First one being when he insisted on telling her brother about the baby.

But then, looking from Sebastian to her brother, she asked, "What possible reason would he have for kidnapping me? I volunteer at Crosswinds—I don't own it. I get that I've angered him. That my work has systematically undone pretty much every attempt he's made to put Crosswinds out of business, but what does he gain by taking me? There are three other veterinarians in my office alone…"

Sebastian glanced at Fletcher, who said, "How many do you think will be eager to service those dogs, knowing that they could end up like you? Or how do you think it will look in the news? 'Crosswinds veterinarian kidnapped…'"

She shook her head. "I can't believe someone would resort to such tactics…"

"He would if he was experiencing some kind of psychotic break." Sebastian issued the explanation softly, while inside, every fighting instinct he had was at the ready. "Assuming he's a result of this affair of my dad's they think they've discovered at this point…he's grown up on the outside looking in. Even if he didn't know that my dad was his father, he'd have grown up without knowing his real father. Somehow he finds out, either he's always known, or maybe his mother told him after Dad died. She could easily have known about the Owl Creek property. Maybe even told the kid he deserved to have it. For all I know some lawyer told him it was his. From what Ruby said, he seemed to have no doubt that what he'd been told was true. And yet, he gets here and finds out that I'm firmly ensconced. The only known heir, the only legal heir and running an elite training business on what he thinks is his land. Then you come along—" Sebastian looked at Ruby "—and thwart every attempt he makes to get me to tuck my tail and go."

"He hasn't done enough homework if he thinks you'd ever do that," Ruby said, her words more of a statement of fact than praise. His heart lifted a bit at the words, anyway.

"I see where you're going with this," Fletcher added then, his gaze toward Sebastian assessing. "You could be hitting it exactly right. Ruby's in his way. He's getting more and more desperate, maybe becoming more unhinged, and just sees her as someone he has to get out of the way. Which makes him even more dangerous. He's still thinking clearly enough to create all these issues without ever being seen or coming close to getting caught. He's wearing gloves, so leaving no prints. Other than the rope, there was nothing else in the car."

At her sudden intake of air, Sebastian sent her brother a look. Ruby was strong. She wasn't inhuman.

"I'm sorry," Fletcher said, then added, "But not completely. You can't stay here, Ruby. I don't care how much you argue. He clearly knows where you live."

Relieved that he wasn't the one bringing up the matter he'd been planning to discuss with her as soon as they were through with Fletcher, Sebastian said, "Your parents have state-of-the-art security. You'd be much safer there."

If her brother hadn't been sitting there, he'd have mentioned the baby. Even if she survived another attack, the baby might not get that lucky. If the man had hit her harder, if the seat belt jerked tighter across her belly, if the airbag had deployed…

He started to sweat again…as he had pretty much the entire time he'd sat in the hospital waiting room that evening. She had to see the sense in not staying home alone until the unknown man was caught. "You saw his face," he added. "He's going to know you can identify him."

"Which brings a whole new level of desperation to his thinking," Fletcher said.

"Did someone check the ground for blood splatter?" Ruby asked. "Or my hair? Maybe I got some of his DNA on me when I hit him with the back of my head."

Sebastian's tension increased. He needed her on her parents' property. Safely locked in. Not sitting here trying to solve the crime. But while Fletcher called Steele to check the dirt in the area of the attempted kidnapping for blood, Sebastian turned on his phone light and studied the back of Ruby's hair. It was tucked up in her usual messy bun.

"I hit him with the bun," she said then. He grabbed some paper towel off the rack in the kitchen and pulled out her scrunchie. He saw no sign of blood but gathered the plastic bag she told him was in the drawer, inserted the hair band and paper towel and handed it over to Fletcher when the other man completed his call.

"If your shampoo has peroxide in it, and many of them do, that will most likely falsify any result for blood testing," Fletcher said. But he added that they'd test the few hairs attached to the scrunchie, just in case.

And he asked Ruby for her clothes. Again, just in case.

While she went to change, Sebastian looked at Fletcher. "She didn't say she'd go."

The detective nodded. "If I have to, I'll stay here myself, but I'd rather meet up with Steele, compare notes, see what we can find on the few new leads we have. We know the guy was in Connors on Thursday. Maybe surveillance tapes from there can give us something."

"She can't stay here," Sebastian said. Almost bursting with the need to know that Ruby would be in a safe place.

"I can hear you," she said, joining the two and handing Fletcher a bag with her work clothes inside. She'd put on jeans and a sweatshirt. Sebastian hoped that meant she was planning to go out again that night. To her parents' house.

Ruby looked at him. A long, meaningful glance.

Gut knotting, he sat back down when she did.

"What's up?" Fletcher asked.

"I'm pregnant."

If Sebastian hadn't been so involved, so disturbed with worry and his inability to control Ruby's every move so that he could keep her safe, he might have felt a small bit of amusement from the way the detective's jaw seemed to drop down to the table.

"You don't have to look that astonished, Fletch. I have had sex now and then on occasion."

Her brother coughed. Glanced at Sebastian, as though looking to him for some kind of guy way to handle the moment. "Pregnant?" Fletcher said then.

Flipping back his chair with force the detective stood. "By who? For how long?" And then, turning a complete circle, he asked, "Tonight…is everything okay?"

"We're both fine," Ruby told him.

And that's when Sebastian jumped up. It was either that or grab the woman and hold her close and out of danger, her and his child, for the rest of his natural life.

Ruby didn't want a whole drawn-out thing. She'd had a long day. A horrible evening. And wanted her brother's piercing stare—and the knowledge that he was going home to their parents' house—gone.

She needed some peace. Time to recover. To relax, if she could. To think.

Standing, with her arms crossed, she said, "The father's a friend. A good one. The baby is the result of one night that was filled with tension, just like this one. We used protection. It didn't work. I was shocked when I first found out. I'm already in love with the child. Intend to raise it on my own, my choice, and Hannah and Lizzie know, but no one else does, and I really need you to keep this quiet." She finished the spiel she'd been working on, mostly subconsciously, for the past week, then added, "I've got enough on my plate at the moment."

"You have to tell Mom and Dad," Fletcher replied. "You're going to be staying with them."

The baby was one of the reasons she'd been fighting with herself to stay home. There was no way she could live with her mother, a nurse, and not have Jenny figure out something. The first time Ruby smelled coffee and threw up would do it.

"And how good a friend is this guy if he's letting you take this on all alone?" Fletcher's tone was sharp, but faded at the end. He glanced at Sebastian. "A night filled with tension just like this one." Fletcher repeated her words. And then added, "He's not leaving you to take this on all alone, is he?" The question was meant for Ruby, but her brother hadn't moved since he'd locked eyes with Sebastian.

"No, he is not," Sebastian answered for her. He wasn't moving, either.

The two men were like… She didn't know what— opposing forces that didn't ever back down or lose. And the last thing she needed at the moment.

When Fletcher said, "Okay," and took a step back, Ruby was the one standing with her mouth open. "And now that I know the full detail—" he very clearly meant just one "—I understand why we need to keep this quiet. We absolutely do not want this guy getting any idea that there's another heir in the making."

Ruby cringed and looked away, fearing Sebastian's reaction to the casually dropped phrase, until she felt his hand on her shoulder. "I do agree that your parents should know, though," he said, increasing the tension he'd just deescalated with his touch. "She can't stay there without them being aware..."

"Hello, I'm right here," she said, frowning at both of them. But deep inside, where she didn't want to look at the moment, she knew they were right.

But... "I'll make a deal with you," she said. "I stay here tonight. One of you stay with me. And tomorrow we go to Mom and Dad's. And we tell them about the baby. I just don't have it tonight to deal with them. Not on top of everything else. Please."

"I'll stay," both men said at once.

Ruby glanced at Sebastian, making her choice clear. And Fletcher let himself out.

Chapter 17

Sebastian heard the door close as Ruby's brother departed. He didn't watch the man go. He couldn't take his gaze from Ruby. The past few minutes, the entire evening, had been so fraught with tension, and being alone with the slimly built, green-eyed woman, with her long golden blond hair, was doing things to him that weren't right.

Not given the circumstances.

Those being that he was her friend.

And nothing more.

In dress pants and doctor's coat, makeup fresh and hair shiny clean, or in jeans and a sweatshirt after a near kidnapping, she was a vixen, luring him into space he knew he could not occupy.

"How about some of that vegetable soup?" Ruby broke the spell, turning away, toward the kitchen. She mentioned a grocery bag that, last she knew, had been on the front passenger seat of her SUV, and he gladly went to retrieve it for her. To breathe the nippy fresh night air, which cooled his body, but not his mind. Outside, he was a soldier, checking every inch of Ruby's small property, knowing that he was on duty for the rest of the night.

So thinking, he called the night security team manning Crosswinds, had them coax Oscar through his doggy door and lock him in the big kennel room with that officer for the night. He didn't want the boy letting himself out in the middle of the night in the event of an intruder. Sebastian had been closing off Oscar's personal entryway into the house every night before bedtime.

By the time he returned inside, Ruby had the soup heated. He cut bread while she unwrapped the veggie tray and set the table.

Growing up, he'd been the one to set the table. Until he'd deemed the chore not manly enough and then been assigned to do the dishes every night after dinner.

Then he'd learned to cook and was the one who'd prepared dinner. More often than not, he'd eaten it alone. With his plate on his mother's expensive side table, he'd sit on the couch with Jerry right next to him, watch what he wanted on television, or play video games, taking bites as it suited him.

Good memories of easier times.

Much easier than being part of an intimate twosome preparing a meal in the smallest kitchen he'd ever done any food service in.

Ruby talked while she worked. Telling him about Barney, the dog who'd been hit by a car that evening, causing her to stay late at work. Which gave him pause.

Their attacker couldn't have hit the dog on purpose, could he? To keep Ruby late? So that he could attack, as always, at night?

The theory was far-fetched, he silently acknowledged. But he texted Fletcher, anyway, suggesting that they contact the dog's owners and get a rundown of the incident. If it *was* their guy, maybe there was surveillance-camera footage...

Figuring it would be too rude to eat standing at the kitchen counter, which was what he'd have felt more comfortable doing, Sebastian sat across from Ruby, as she indicated which place was his. He put his napkin in his lap as his parents had taught him. And wiped after every spoonful of soup inevitably left drops on his beard.

He'd been on more dates than he could count. Had spent full weekends in the company of whatever woman he'd been seeing. He had never, not even once, been self-conscious sharing a meal with any of them.

Or with Ruby, either, in the past.

He'd never been having a child with any of them.

"This is good," he said, motioning toward the soup.

Ruby nodded. Looked at him, and said, "It's weird, though, isn't it?"

"The soup?" He knew that wasn't what she'd meant. Was not eager for the conversation that was coming. Her brother knew she was pregnant and Sebastian was the father of her child.

Her parents were going to know in less than twenty-four hours.

"We've never even been on a date," she said then. "I've never had a man in my home for a meal, either," she added. Took another bite, almost as though glad for the distraction.

He knew he was. Helped himself to a celery stick and another piece of bread, too. And did what he'd been trained to do—march into battle, not run from it.

"Tell me how you want to play this," he said. "If you want everyone to think we've been secretly dating, or that we were dating and broke up—whatever you need to tell them, give it to me and I'll back you up. One hundred percent. You have family to answer to—I don't. So whatever you need our story to be, that's what it will be."

Ruby took a bite. Then glanced at him, her gaze soft. "I've been sitting here trying to figure out how to tell them that we aren't a couple, aren't in love, have never dated, and are having a baby," she said, her tone as gentle as her look. "And you're right—we don't owe anyone our intimate truths. We just give them what works for us, while staying within boundaries of the truth." Her sudden smile, like she'd solved the problems of the world, pulled an answering smile from Sebastian.

The woman had a way with him that no one else had ever had.

He prayed that it didn't turn out to be what killed him.

"We've been together a lot these past months, with my volunteering at Crosswinds. One thing led to another, and now we're having a baby." With Sebastian sitting across from her in her small dining room, late at night, smiling that way, the words just rolled off Ruby's tongue.

Funny how what had seemed impossible was easy, when shared with a friend. A caring, yet different perspective, that didn't try to force one particular way down her throat.

"Whether we're dating or not isn't anyone's business. We're friends. We know that, in whatever fashion you choose, you're going to be involved in the child's life. So we present ourselves as friendly with each other, sharing a child. Done. End of what they need to know."

She liked it. A lot. Felt a bit easier inside. Took a bite of bread. Enjoyed the homemade, feel-good taste.

"And when your father asks me when the wedding's going to be?"

Chewed bread stuck in her throat. She washed it down with the decaffeinated iced tea she'd served them both.

"We haven't set a date?" she asked, but was only half-serious. He was right. Their situation was bigger than she was making it out to be.

"We're adults, Sebastian," she told him then. "We simply tell him that at this time we aren't planning on getting married. I'll tell him when I tell them that I'm pregnant."

"He's still going to come to me," he said. "I'm not complaining here. Or trying to get you to do anything. I know your father well enough and have heard way more stories from Wade over the years to know that he's traditional. He cares about how he and his family look to others. Appearances matter to him more than, say, being close to your mother. And while he loves you all very much, he's not beyond a little ruthlessness if that's what it takes to make the world what he thinks it should be."

Setting her spoon in her not quite empty bowl, Ruby stared at him. Not sure whether she was angry with him for…what? His honesty? Because he'd been spot on.

But no one was perfect, and Robert Colton was her father. She should defend him.

So why wasn't she?

"He's going to try to force me, somehow, to convince you to marry me."

Force—no, her father wouldn't go that far. But he did wield a lot of power. And had the gift of persuasion down pat.

Robert was also traditional enough, old-fashioned enough, to think that a man could still sweeten a pot enough to get a woman to marry him.

As though being alone was not the better choice.

Enough. Enough. Enough. Enough was enough.

"How about if you come with me in the morning? We tell them together, and I make it very clear to my father that it is my choice not to marry and that there is nothing you can do, say or offer that would make me change my mind?"

She respected Robert. She didn't agree with him a lot of the time. And had no problem standing up to him. Most particularly when it came to the way he took her mother for granted.

He, in return, gave her space and supported her endeavors, even while he had her brothers keeping an eagle eye over her.

And did so himself as well.

Ready to pick up the pieces in case she failed.

At least, that was her take on their relationship. She couldn't speak for any of her siblings.

Sebastian held his bowl up to his mouth to scoop out the last bite. Set the bowl down. Wiped his mouth. And, hands on the table, very quietly said, "I don't need you to handle your father on my behalf, Ruby. Not now. Not ever. I will talk to him man-to-man. I'm asking how you want our story to be so that I have your back."

She blinked. Wasn't sure what to say. Except... "I didn't mean to offend you."

"I'm not offended." He gave an easy shrug. "But I'm also not having you bear the brunt of awkwardness due to our situation. I was fifty percent of the creation, and I will carry fifty percent of the burden." He stopped. Held her gaze, and then said, "There are obvious things that you have to do, like actually giving birth to the child, giving them a home, but I can handle all of the child's financial details, rather than a fifty-fifty split like the law generally requires. And anything else, as yet unknown, you're going to need from me along the way. Right now, I'll be standing right beside you as your parents find out about the baby, and later, when the town does."

Tears pooled in her eyes. She didn't mean them to. Hadn't known they were coming. Didn't know why they were there.

But she knew why Sebastian suddenly leaned over and ran a thumb softly along her cheekbone. It wasn't a gesture of love. Or even of affection.

He'd simply been wiping away the moisture on her face.

Apparently, he intended to reveal his future plans to himself in spurts without thinking ahead.

Sebastian hadn't considered the town, his employees, or anyone but Ruby's family finding out about the baby. Just hadn't gotten that far.

But there he was. Standing by her through all of it.

And feeling completely right about doing so.

"How do we do this?" Ruby asked, turning to him in the kitchen as she stood at the sink rinsing soup bowls.

As soon as he'd seen her tears, and attempted to wipe them, she'd jumped up and grabbed their dishes and spoons.

He'd gathered up the rest of the meal and had been silently seeing to storing it.

When she leaned back against the sink, he took a rest against the opposite counter, facing her. "I don't know," he said. "I guess we just do it."

How did they give answers to questions they didn't yet know?

Or explain what they hadn't yet figured out for themselves.

"One step at a time," he added, because that was what he knew. You assessed the enemy, or the problem, you figured out your end goal. And you took the first step toward reaching that goal. Sometimes the step was face-to-face meetings to reach a satisfactory conclusion for all involved. Sometimes mediation was necessary. And if all else failed, you fought.

Ruby's nod lessened some of the tightening in his gut. "For now, it's just my parents. And we tell them…" When her voice faded off, she was still looking at him, and Sebastian got all tight inside again.

"What?" he asked.

"How do you feel about the baby?"

Not the step he was expecting. "I'm not sure what you mean," he said, anyway. "I'd die for it, if that's what you're asking."

Her lips trembled on their way to a small smile. "That pretty much covers it," she said. And then added, "Are you angry?"

"No." Straight up.

"Sad?"

"No."

She nodded. He was relieved he'd passed her test.

"Happy?"

Of course not. The words were there. Didn't come out. "I'm not happy that it's creating such havoc for you," he told her honestly.

"And for you."

He shook his head. "The only havoc in my life where the child is concerned is this damned Crosswinds stalker and keeping the two of you safe until he's caught. And what telling your parents is going to do to you." Truth.

"Are you happy there's going to be another Cross, your flesh and blood, coming into the world?"

"Yes."

Oh. Well then. He was happy about the baby. He'd arrived in a new place. Because she'd known him well enough to know how to get him there.

She grinned at him.

And he grinned back.

That grin.

Not sure what to do with herself now that they'd eaten and the kitchen was clean, Ruby continued to lean against the counter, facing Sebastian. Wanting to get lost in his smile.

Just for a little bit.

She had a two-bedroom home, but only one of them held a bed.

Fletcher had said the couch was really comfortable.

But the night she'd spent at Sebastian's, he'd shared his bed with her. She wouldn't mind having him in hers. It wasn't like they hadn't done it before.

Or would have repercussions...

Feeling heat rise up inside her, she halted the thoughts. Prayed Sebastian hadn't gotten any hint of what she'd been thinking.

"I'm thinking we tell my parents the truth," she blurted. "That we're happy about the baby. That we are both independent people who never want to get married. And that we're going to be raising the child together."

As soon as she heard the word *raising* come out of her mouth, she froze. Stared at him.

He was nodding. His expression...calm. Easy. "I'm good with that."

He *was*?

He didn't just want to be a help to her, he wanted to be involved in raising his child?

"Why do you look so surprised?" he asked. "I told you I'd go with whatever story you needed to tell."

Story. Her heart sank.

Chapter 18

Ruby, still standing against the sink, heard Sebastian say he was going out to do one more perimeter check.

Nodding, she went to get a sheet, pillow and blanket for the couch.

Having a furious conversation with herself as she did so. What in the hell was she doing? Building some kind of fantasy where Sebastian was a fully engaged, participating father to her baby? Was that what she was really hoping? That they were going to engage in shared parenting? That he'd be by her side, figuratively if not physically, for the tough moments?

Telling herself she was perfectly fine doing it alone... Had she been lying?

By the time she was in the living room, dropping the pillow on top of the bedding she'd just tucked in, she'd calmed some.

She hadn't been lying. She really could see herself mothering the child alone. Knew that she'd be fine. Happy. That she'd be a good mother.

"I was wondering," Sebastian said, coming back in through the kitchen. "Maybe we could…"

He stopped. Stared at the couch.

As if to put the bow on her handiwork, she dropped a sealed toothbrush and paste packet on the pillow. "I collect them from hotels," she said inanely. "When they're complimentary, I bring them home…"

Her words dropped off. And she asked, "Maybe we could…what?"

He looked at the couch. "You're ready to get some rest," he said. "I'm sorry, I should have realized…with all you've been through tonight, and being pregnant…" He shook his head. "I guess I'm going to need some practice at the support role."

"Maybe we could…what?" She repeated her question. And then, as though it made some kind of statement, she sat down in the middle of the bed she'd just made for him.

With a shrug, he sat down beside her. Leaving a few feet between them. "I was thinking we could talk about what the future might look at in terms of my role. But I wasn't thinking about your long day with the late emergency, the ordeal, you needing to get up in the morning and being pregnant."

"I'm fine," she said, feeling much better now that he was sitting there, talking to her. "Tired, but not ready to sleep just yet."

"I was thinking about talking to your parents. Maybe it would be easier if we started to talk about it all. You know. Just between us."

His voice, the look in his eyes, the shaggy dark blond hair… Those muscles…everywhere… Ruby liked every bit of it. A lot.

She particularly liked the *just between us.* Her life was overflowing with people, with family. But to be a part of something that belonged to no one but her and one other person—her and Sebastian…

The flood of warmth that the moment invoked in her was brand-new.

And like the seed he'd let loose inside her to make her pregnant, Ruby had a feeling that Sebastian had once again altered the course of her future.

She just had no idea where his road led.

And that scared her more than the attempted kidnapping had.

The expressions crossing Ruby's face were like a jigsaw puzzle. Sebastian watched them all, but wasn't sure how to put them together.

Or how to answer the question she posed in the midst of them.

"What kind of involvement do you want?" The medical-professional tone she'd adopted each time they'd reached this conversation in the past was absent.

He'd have done better with its presence. With veneers stripped away, all he had was "I have no idea."

"Would you want to know if the baby got sick?"

"Of course."

"To the point of a call in the middle of the night?"

"Absolutely." What did any of that have to do with their future, though? He wasn't getting it. "I already told you, I'm always here to support you, every step of the way."

"Say the child likes soccer. Would you want to be at games?"

He hadn't thought that far ahead. In terms of his own wants. But… "If we could work that out, sure." Who wouldn't enjoy that?

She shook her head. "What's there to work out? You're there or you aren't."

And it hit him. The problem.

"Who do we tell the kid I am?" As soon as he asked the question, he wanted to take it back. He didn't allow insecurities.

And most definitely did not take on anything that he couldn't handle full out.

Ruby's frown sent his turmoil into tornado mode. "I don't get it," she said.

"If this baby knows that I'm the father, then why am I not being a father?" He had the questions, but no answers.

Only…more sweat. More discomfort.

Mouth open, Ruby stared at him for long seconds. Too long. Way, way too long. "You intend to tell my family, and the town, that you're the father of my child, but you didn't think the child would know?"

"It's a baby," he said weakly. Hating his lack of attention to detail. His failure to have all the answers.

Or any at all.

The child was going to grow.

Would look up to those in their life for example.

He'd had a thoracic surgeon to model himself after. A man who'd spent a good deal of his adult life in operating rooms saving lives—and in his spare time, had taught others how to do so.

And Sebastian's kid?

He looked straight at her. "You really want your child to have me as a role model? The ex-Marine who had a panic attack when his dog was shot and in the midst of it, had sex with the angel who'd appeared to save him and got her pregnant?"

He didn't.

Ruby's day melted off from her as she sat there in the aftermath of Sebastian's painfully honest question. Heart open, she felt the compassion, the caring, emerge from her and pour outward, toward him. In an effort to flood him with it.

Used to allowing herself to give her whole heart to the animals she cared for, to all the dogs in her life, she wasn't quite sure what to do with herself.

How to act.

Who to be.

"Maybe you need to hire a different writer for your story," she said softly. Talking because the words were there and she had no other ideas present. "Maybe the example is one of a friendship between two loners, there for each other without question in time of need, and fate steps in and gives them both a human being to love as their own."

Intensity shone from his sharp blue eyes. Pulling more words out of her. "In that story it wasn't just the ex-Marine who got the woman pregnant. She needed something from him that night, too, which he so tenderly and unselfishly gave, and she was equally responsible for what happened."

For a man who wasn't moving at all, Sebastian managed to bathe the room in emotion. So much that she had to start swimming or drown.

"Now might not be the best time to say this, or maybe it's the exact right time, I don't know, but I need to rest, Sebastian…"

Of course. He stood, blinked, and it was as though he turned off the faucet and sucked all the fluid out of the room. "I'll just…"

"What?" she asked him, feeling a strange kind of power as she sat there looking up at the strong mountain of a man. "I'm sitting on your bed. There's not much you can do." Her words were almost a challenge as, empowered by the knowledge that her friend and co-parent had a whole lot of him hidden inside.

And had shown her a huge chunk.

Crossing his arms on that massive chest, he stared her down.

When she didn't do anything but stare back, he said, "Finish what you were going to say."

"What I got that night… I could use another dose. I'm finding that I don't want to go to bed without it."

He started, his head jerking back sharply, maybe in horror. But at her eye level, he had a different response. "Are you actually sitting there telling me you want to have sex with me tonight?" he asked.

She was saying far more than that.

She'd already given him too much. More than she'd ever given anyone.

Which scared her.

So for starters… "I'm not much in a position to have it with anyone else now, am I?" She had to be strong.

To keep her wits about her.

"No, I guess not, so, if that's what you want, then, of course…"

No way. Uh-uh.

"Is that what you want?"

"This isn't about me."

There. That bothered her.

"So it's not a good thing when you're in need, and I help, but it's okay if I'm in need and you help."

He sat back down. "We aren't talking about sex here, are we?"

She looked him in the eye. "Yes." And said, "On a practical level, I was mishandled by a man tonight. I'd like to have a pleasant male-female physical experience to replace the repulsion my skin is feeling. On another similarly practical level, I think you and I did sex remarkably well, and it makes sense for two friends who understand and respect each other, friends who don't ever want to marry, to be able to share physical pleasure with each other. And there's the third aspect, which I've already mentioned… The awkwardness of me having sex with another man when I'm pregnant with your child…"

She was losing control of the situation. She could feel it.

And see it in his expression, too. The shift in power.

Teetering on just letting go, Ruby pulled herself back. Something much larger than winning and losing, than staying strong and maintaining independence, hovered around them.

We aren't talking about sex here, are we…?

"And no," she said, giving him the deeper answer to his question. "The friendship you gave so tenderly, so unselfishly that night… I need it again, Sebastian. Tonight, at least. As you said, it's been a rough day…"

She hadn't finished speaking when Sebastian reached for her, sliding his arms under her knees and back, just as he had earlier that evening.

But this time when he carried her, it wasn't to drop her alone in a car seat.

Or to deposit her anywhere.

He strode to her room, sat and then lay down with her on her bed.

Never letting her go.

For the night only, she knew.

As his lips came down on hers, and she closed her eyes, opening her mouth to welcome him, her last conscious thought was a reminder to herself.

It was only for the night.

Sebastian was at his best Monday night. Holding Ruby in his arms, pleasing her, letting go and consciously allowing himself to take what she had to give him, energized him in a whole new way. She strengthened him, even as they wore each other out.

He entered her differently, too. Slowly. Reverently. Aware that in another space inside her, his child was growing into life.

He was a part of the two of them.

They were a part of him.

What it would all end up looking like, what it meant in a real-world sense, he had no idea. He didn't ask. For those hours in her bed, he just lived.

After she fell asleep, he allowed himself the light doze that came with living in a battle zone. He slept, but always aware that he was protecting precious cargo.

And yet, he rested better than he had in a long while.

Which was a good thing, he realized, when, just after six, Fletcher called to say that both Robert and Jenny wanted a meeting with Ruby at seven that morning, in the kitchen of the family home.

"You see how he played that?" Ruby asked, in her

work clothes, as she sat beside him in his truck. He'd showered, brushed his teeth, turned his underwear inside out. He had nothing but the jeans, button-down shirt and dirty socks from the day before.

"Telling your parents that you had to talk to them?" Sebastian asked, admiring the detective's grit where his sister was concerned. Ruby was not easy to love when it came to worrying about her.

Not that he loved her.

He was in the unique position of being a friend who'd made a baby with her who also happened to own a business being targeted, with her getting caught in the crossfire. He could see how it would be hard to also love her when she was so independent and mostly refused to let people tell her what to do.

As a friend, and co-loner—as she'd sort of called them in her little story from the night before—he admired her independence and spunk. Understood it, even.

Better to go down on your own terms than to live a life that wasn't right for you.

As long as you didn't get closed-minded and forget that you weren't always right. As long as you always sought the evidence and looked at it with an eye to finding truth.

He'd known Ruby Colton, peripherally, since she was a kid. "Did you know that you used to irritate the hell out of Wade, always asking questions about everything, wanting to know how he knew something, verifying facts?" he asked as they drew closer to Hollister Hills, the affluent neighborhood of mansions where her parents lived in the five-bedroom, three-bath lake home Jenny had designed.

He knew Jenny was behind the home choices because Ruby had mentioned the dark green that colored every building at Crosswinds the night they'd tended to Oscar. She preferred his color to the gray wood and dark gray trim of her parents' lovely home…and figured she was the only person on earth who didn't find the exquisite beauty in the grayness.

He pulled to a stop at a light. Looked over when she didn't answer his Wade question. Figured he'd stepped in his own crap again. But wasn't sure how to get out of it.

"Does it irritate you?" she finally asked. Not at all what he'd expected.

"It comforts me." The truth fell out with his relief. "You get the facts, rather than let yourself be swayed, and because you're open to the truth, you make good decisions."

Relief dissipated as he heard his own words. And saw the surprised look on her face.

Thankfully, the light turned green, and he didn't have to keep staring into that expression.

"I think that's the nicest thing anyone has ever said to me." Her words settled over him. Gave him added confidence as he prepared to square up with her father.

"And for the record," she continued, "of course, I knew. You think Wade would be irritated and not let it be known? Ad nauseam?" Sebastian heard the words and heard the note of deep compassion in her tone, too.

And was envious.

Not because he wanted her affection toward Wade for himself. Or in any way begrudged all her siblings her love. But because, in the end, no matter what happened between the two of them, she'd always have her family.

And he'd always be without one.

Chapter 19

Ruby had made a deliberate choice in accepting Sebastian's offer of a ride to her folks' place. Her SUV was drivable. He'd be taking her back to it in time for her to get to work.

She'd ridden with him because it meant she could leave with him. If things went bad—and she gave a fifty-fifty on that—she didn't want to send Sebastian off alone without a chance to talk about things.

And thinking of which…

"Do we need to talk about last night?"

He'd already been in the shower when she'd woken up alone in her bed that morning.

"We didn't talk about it last time."

"Right." But had it been the right way to handle it?

"Do you need to talk about it?" His question surprised her. She'd thought they were done.

"No, unless you're regretting it." He'd been so distant. But then, he'd had the call from Fletcher before they'd even seen each other that morning.

He turned into her parents' neighborhood. "No regrets here."

"Good."

"It was good, wasn't it?" He didn't take his eyes off the road, but he seemed to be playing with a grin.

"Very." She didn't even try to rein in her smile.

Until he pulled into her parents' place. Then she shoved his teasing words into her private thoughts.

"You ready for this?" she asked, as she walked beside Sebastian up to the door.

His shrug, his easy stride, was so... Sebastian. He was who he was, no apologies. But no airs, either. She'd always liked that about him.

Figured his parents had done something right in that they'd raised a man filled with quiet self-confidence.

Real confidence. Not bravado.

Ruby had gained her own confidence through sheer determination and hard work. She'd had to prove to herself who she was. What she was made of.

And refused to revert back to being the girl who always had to please her parents as she walked into their home with a quick knock and headed straight to the kitchen. Sebastian had been in the home before, with Wade. For some reason, the idea was a comfort.

Taking his hand would have been a greater one.

She purposefully did not do so. She had to stand on her own two feet.

Her parents both rose as they stepped into the room, Jenny rushing forward, grabbing for Ruby's hands, looking her over with concern, checking her over, as she said how worried she'd been. While Robert, who joined them as well, kept up appearances in his welcome to Sebastian. Not expressing the surprise that he had to be experiencing.

Over her mother's shoulder, Ruby saw the coffee cups on the table—along with her father's Irish cream liqueur—and stopped short.

"This isn't exactly how I wanted to go about this, but can you please remove the coffee cups from the table?" she asked, not wanting to chance another step closer.

Frowning, Jenny studied her harder, like a nurse studied a patient, and then did as asked, taking her cup to the kitchen island before motioning Ruby and Sebastian to seats. Robert, retrieving his cup, stood with it at the island, then began sipping. "What's going on?" he asked in the commanding tone that had been giving Ruby security, and intimidating her, since childhood.

"I'm pregnant," she told them both. Just dropped it out there. "The smell of coffee makes me throw up." She could have worded it better.

Jenny stared at her, her mouth hanging open. "You're pregnant?" Shock was evident in her tone. Concern. And possibly a slight bit of pleasure, too. It was no secret that Jenny Colton, who'd basically raised ten children and only had one grandchild, wanted more.

Robert, cup frozen halfway to his mouth, bellowed, "You're what?"

"She's pregnant, sir." Sebastian's calm words made it sound like a piece of good news. "And I'm the father."

In that moment, going up against her parents with her, he was her child's father, but he was much more than that. He was her hero.

* * *

There were some tense moments, but overall, "That went well," Sebastian said as he and Ruby headed down the walk toward his truck.

As predicted, Robert had asked about marriage, a wedding. Ruby had preempted Sebastian's ready reply with a version of what she'd said the night before about them being happy about the baby, independent people who never wanted to marry, and raising the child together.

"It went amazing," she said, grinning at him over her shoulder. She'd been leading the way all morning. He'd been fine to have her do so. Knew better than to help her climb up into the truck, but he did stand by the door and closed it behind her.

"That's the first time in my life I had someone sharing my situation as I faced off with my parents," she said, still grinning at him as he climbed into the driver's side.

"You had five siblings," he reminded her. "Surely there were times when you all banded together to further a cause." He'd always envisioned Wade and his brothers and sisters that way.

"Not really, no," she told him. "What just happened there, Mom and Dad meeting us together, that's not the norm. I'd have a session with Dad, or a session with Mom. They weren't close, you know. Didn't present a united front for us kids. The only time I can remember having the attention of both of them was when I announced that I was buying my house."

How being a member of a family with six kids and two parents could sound lonely, he didn't know. But right then, it did.

"My folks were gone a lot of the time, pursuing their separate professional interests, but when they were home at the same time, when there was some big decision or announcement to make in my life, they always presented it together. We'd talk things out, the three of us. All three opinions on the table, being heard." Something he'd taken for granted until just that moment.

"Not here," Ruby said, nodding toward the gorgeous lakefront home with walls of windows providing beautiful views of the water. "Maybe because there were so many of us...so much going on. But Mom and Dad... Sometimes I wonder how they ever made six babies. They're more like strangers in the same house, or business partners, than lovers."

Sebastian glanced over at her as he put the truck in Reverse. Had he just seen a glimpse of why Ruby preferred to live alone?

Not that the *why* mattered. She preferred it. He preferred it. And that made them a good team.

A team. He and Ruby Colton. A baby-having team.

Surprised at how much he liked the idea, he glanced at the other member of his unusual partnership. "I agree with them that I'd worry less if you weren't going in to work, but with the security you have there, and being right in the middle of town, and this guy only hitting at night so far, you're probably fine to go."

"There's a lot of security at Mom and Dad's and I see the sense in staying there at night, especially with Fletcher there, but it's right on the lake, Sebastian, and this guy...the way he got to the dogs—it really does sound like he approached from the lake. I figure I'm safer at work than alone out at their place all day."

He liked that they could talk to each other. Be honest. Maybe the future really was going to work as well as they'd just led her parents to believe it would.

He wanted it to.

And believed that she did, too.

"You sure don't let your father intimidate you any," he told her. "Telling him that he had no room to talk about you still working full-time while you're pregnant—did he really have a minor stroke four years ago?"

"Yes, he did. Doctors had been after him for years about the sallowness of his skin, the pouch. Years of working all hours, being on the road for a week at a time, hard living, eating red meat every day, the whiskey he consumes, those daily cigars… They took their toll."

"And he hasn't given any of it up?" Sebastian clarified what Ruby had hollered at her father when he'd tried to put his foot down with her. He'd seen the Irish cream whiskey on the counter.

"Nope."

"I'm surprised, with your mother being a nurse, she doesn't have something to say about that."

"I think she gave up trying years ago. As you noticed, he doesn't listen to her much."

"I like her," Sebastian said, feeling generous with his emotions. He'd been welcomed back to the Colton home, been invited for dinner every night that Ruby was going to be staying there, and had been told to come and go, treat the house as his own, for the duration as well. Robert had stopped short of saying he was welcome to spend the night, but in the end, the real-estate magnate had been gracious.

And, Sebastian thought, sincere.

The man might be hardheaded, but he knew when to capitulate. Both qualities necessary to build a small hardware store into an empire that owned half of Owl Creek and still be well thought of in the town he'd taken over.

"Mom's the best," Ruby said. "She's wealthy enough to travel the world and she's still here, looking after all of us, and Uncle Buck, and doing some private nursing, too. She just sometimes wants different things for me than I do."

"I'm guessing our kid will want differently from us as well." The statement just came off his tongue. He'd been in the role, being the dad, for her parents, sharing everything with her and...

He had to go. Get back to Crosswinds. To Oscar and the rest of his dogs. To his employees. He couldn't expect, or allow, Della and the others to carry his weight.

He couldn't leave Ruby alone at her house. He'd agreed, in front of her parents, to wait while she packed. He'd do it even if he hadn't agreed. He also thought he should follow her to the clinic to make sure she made it okay.

And then he had to go.

They were getting in too deep. Sleeping together. Spending the night together. Visiting her parents together. He'd even been invited to her uncle's birthday party.

He'd accepted the invitation. Had actually wanted to go. With her.

Like a real date.

He was letting the vague description of their future that they'd delivered to her parents lure him into a place he didn't belong.

Ruby didn't want to marry any more than he did. Watching her parents together, he kind of understood that—though, of course, all unions weren't like that. Still, she'd spent the first eighteen years of her life surrounded by a plethora of needs all vying for attention. Still had to brace herself against all the lovingly offered, but still intrusive, interference in her life.

She needed her independence. He'd just watched her go up against Robert Colton to defend it.

And Sebastian needed his, too. For different reasons, but the result was the same. She'd pegged it the night before. He was a loner.

Which made them perfect for each other.

As long as he kept his distance.

He'd been doing it for thirty-two years with complete success.

No reason to think he couldn't get it done for the rest of his life.

With his thoughts firmly back in line, Sebastian waited comfortably in his truck, parked outside Ruby's house while she packed.

He helped her carry her things to the back of her SUV.

Followed her to work.

And went home.

Where he belonged.

Alone.

Over the next couple of days, Ruby watched her back constantly. She didn't go anywhere alone, other than to drive to work, and wasn't at the clinic by herself, either. Until the kidnapper was caught, she was his prisoner.

She missed Sebastian like crazy. Which made no sense to her. He was in touch. Making sure she was okay. Asking if she needed anything.

It wasn't the same as the two of them alone together taking care of his dogs. Or eating soup. She wasn't safe at Crosswinds. And he wasn't coming into town.

He had a handler coming in from out west and, apparently, a load of work to go through, video to view and approve for the marketing campaign he was launching to try to lure out his stalker.

She heard more about his plans from her brother than she'd ever heard from Sebastian. With Ruby's attempted kidnapping, the Owl Creek police were planning to do all they could to help with Sebastian's plan, including having extra patrols in the area, both on land and on the lake.

The city had agreed on Tuesday to allow posters to be hung and distributed, too, advertising the celebration for Sebastian and his parents in Boise later in the month, with tickets available to attend the black-tie event. She'd heard from Fletcher that the honor was a real one. Sebastian had turned it down in the past.

Her brother talked as though she knew all about it. He'd just been reiterating details in terms of the investigation. Fletcher seemed to think she was going to the event.

Sebastian had never even mentioned it to her, let alone invited her to accompany him.

Because they weren't a couple. They were just friends who'd made a baby and were dealing with the situation as best they could.

Which was exactly how she wanted it.

Except that…she didn't.

She didn't blame him for withdrawing from her after spending time with her parents. She had a tendency to do the same after even a normal day at home.

And Sebastian's time with the Coltons had been anything but that. Their daughter was in danger because of someone stalking his business. And she was pregnant by him.

He'd handled the whole thing like a pro.

He didn't need her lying in bed panicking about him needing some space.

So on Tuesday night, she turned over and went to sleep. On Wednesday night, too. But she dreamed of him.

Of them together.

And woke up with growing discomfort regarding the future.

The time she and Sebastian had spent alone together over the past couple of weeks, the personal conversations, even when they got intense, eating together, touching…she craved more.

And yet…she loved her little house. Needed a place where she didn't have to fight to have her way. Her psyche relied on the peace she found there.

The baby was going to change a lot of that. Starting with no full night's sleep for a while. But she'd still have the final say in the house. Still be paying the bills. Making the choices. She'd still be in control.

Lying in her bed at her parents in the wee hours of Thursday morning, she remembered being out of control a couple of nights before, in her bed, with Sebastian.

Her thoughts flowed freely in the dark, and for a while there, she entertained the idea of a lifetime of out-of-control moments.

With desire pooling at dangerously high levels, she finally slid from beneath the sheets to wake herself up and find her reality, and was suddenly beset with the strangest feeling. Like someone was watching her.

Her gaze went immediately to the corners of her room. There were no cameras there. She knew that. But after days of living with the need for surveillance to keep herself safe, she sensed the presence of cameras everywhere.

Watching them.

Watching her.

Was that a twinkling out on the lake? The nighttime view from the lovely wall of windows across from her bed was generally dark. She blinked.

Had a spotlight just flashed across her wall?

She waited for it to come again. Some kind of talisman for a lost boat, she told herself. Or surveillance out on the lake.

Closing her eyes, she stood against the wall on the side of the window, hiding behind the curtains, and tried to picture what she'd seen in her blink. Had there really been a flash of light?

Not liking the darkness behind her eyes, she peered out at the lake again. Where was the small light she'd seen moments before? Had it been a boat?

Someone night fishing?

Or a lonely person locked in a private hell of their own smoking a cigarette on a dock?

She was tired. Exhausted. From lack of restful sleep, but more from all the uncertainty in a life that had been carefully planned to avoid all chance of surprise.

A streak of white spread across the water. The moon came out from behind clouds. She recognized it. Welcomed it, even, in its normalcy.

For all she knew, she'd seen the moon's glow in her mind's eye as she'd blinked, and not a flash on her wall at all.

So, thinking, she went back to bed, pulled the covers up to her chin and forced herself to breathe deeply, to replay an old TV show rerun in her mind over and over until it bored her to sleep.

The boogeyman was not going to win.

Chapter 20

Sebastian woke up before dawn on Friday morning to the sound of his text message notification. *Ruby.* Phone in hand before he'd fully opened his eyes, his heart pounded as he pushed to open the app. This early, it couldn't be good.

It was a text, not a call, so not an immediate trauma. He was just reassuring himself as the message popped up on screen.

THE LAND IS MINE GOD SAYS PRIDE COMETH BEFORE THE FALL AND YOU ARE ABOUT TO FALL BIG FOR YOUR PRIDEFUL WAYS

He read, and read again. Calming even as adrenaline pumped through his veins. The two previous texts, one to Ruby and one to him, had come from burner phones.

Pinging from the Owl Creek tower. Whether the man was in town only in the dark hours, or full-time, no one knew, but it was likely he was close by.

After texting Fletcher, Sebastian was out of bed and into jeans, a flannel shirt and cowboy boots by the time he had a response. Ruby's brother was on his way out. Commercials had run on the local television station the previous day and were scheduled throughout the weekend, talking about Crosswinds, featuring photos of people who'd been saved by Sebastian's search-and-rescue dogs. One had a testimonial from a veteran who was able to take up life again thanks to a PTSD dog. Posters about the dinner honoring Sebastian and his parents were up all over town.

They'd pushed the guy's button another notch. His current text, all caps like the previous two, was less to the point. It was longer, more preachy, like someone who'd reached a stage of rambling thoughts.

If they were lucky, they'd have him in cuffs in the next hour.

And Ruby had to stay home.

He didn't even try to get an agreement through text. He dialed her cell phone.

And felt a twinge of fear when he heard her voice. If anything happened to her...

"He's on the move," Sebastian said, not even attempting to tone down his tension. "Fletcher's on his way out. The plan is working. And I'm going to beg if I have to, but please stay out of sight today, Ruby. Please."

The long pause on the line didn't bode well. Antsy to get outside, Sebastian stood in his kitchen, ready to remain in that spot for as long as it took.

"I've egged him on," he said. "I've purposely pushed

him over the edge. Please let us get this done without giving him a chance to get to you."

"Okay."

Knees suddenly weakened, Sebastian said, "Did you just say *okay*?"

"Yes. What you say makes sense. I'll ask Wade to come spend the day with me, at least until we get the all clear," she told him.

And Sebastian actually smiled. He was going to get his guy. And until he did, Ruby would be protected by the best of the best.

The woman knew him well. Knew how to deliver exactly what he needed. Just as he hoped he was able to do for her.

"Thank you."

"Anytime," she said, but the word wasn't issued lightly. There was a message there.

He just wasn't ready to hear it yet.

Ruby tried to go back to sleep. But the more she forced herself to lie still, the less sleepy she felt. Her stomach was in knots, and as they grew tighter, they started to swirl, too. Not wanting to wake her parents, she made a quick stop at the bathroom, and headed down to the kitchen for saltine crackers.

Her brother had left a light on during his hurried departure. She worried for him. And for Sebastian. Told herself over and over again that Steele and his men would be there, too. They were all well-trained.

Many against one.

But the one knew who and where they were, while they were against a phantom.

"Ruby? You okay, sweetie?"

Jenny, a few gray streaks in her dark blond hair, came into the room, her pajama pants and long-sleeved T-shirt top showing the body of the slim, fit woman.

"I'm fine, Mom. You don't need to be up at this hour."

"I heard Fletcher leave."

Because, of course, Jenny was on call in her home, for her children, 24/7.

Would Ruby ever be able to be half the mother her own mom was?

The thought almost tipped her stomach over the edge. She took a bite of the cracker she'd just pulled out of the wrap.

"You want to talk about it?"

"About what? Morning sickness?"

"If that's what's on your mind."

The shrewd look her mother gave her reminded Ruby that she was alone because she chose to be. Jenny was always available.

Having a seat on the kitchen stool, she asked, "How did you do it? All those kids. Social functions with Dad. Taking over for Jessie when she ran off, mothering her kids, too, and still having your own career?"

Jenny poured two glasses of milk, put one on the island in front of Ruby and kept the other in her hand as she perched on the stool next to her. With a shrug, looking at her milk, she said, "Love."

What? Ruby frowned. "Love," she repeated.

"I loved your father, wanted to spend my life with him, so I married him. Our love gave us six kids. When each one of you were born, I fell in love in a way I'd never imagined. You start to feel it when you get pregnant, but once that baby is out of you and you're holding this tiny little human…it's like a wand waves over you, sprinkling you with gold that doesn't ever get lost. No matter what happens, you just know that as long as your child is alive, you have the jackpot. Not in money. But in love. It's the love jackpot."

Her mother had never been a wordy woman. Transfixed, Ruby homed in on the glow in Jenny's eyes. "Way more than money has ever done, the love I was blessed with for each of you kids has carried me through every tired day, every sleepless night, every chore and every tear. And with poor Buck... I loved my sister. I was happy when they married. And I loved their kids. Love is what does it, Ruby. In the end, it's all that really matters."

And was it love that kept Jenny with Robert? Despite the chill in their mutual treatment of each other? Deep down, did her mother get strength from spending her life with the man she'd fallen in love with all those years ago?

Jenny didn't say. Ruby was afraid to ask. Not sure she wanted to hear the answer, either way.

"Do you love Sebastian?" Jenny's gaze wasn't judgmental. But it was direct. And filled with compassion.

Ruby shook her head. But couldn't get the word *no* to rise up through her throat. "I don't know," she told her mother. What was love?

She loved her entire family. Deeply. But didn't want to spend her life with any of them, in the same house, forever.

"He makes you feel things you've never felt before."

Was Jenny guessing? Or telling? Did her mother, in all her wisdom, see something Ruby was missing?

"Doesn't mean it's love."

"No." Jenny's head tilted to the side a bit, and then

straightened. "But if it is, fighting it is a losing cause, sweetie. Love comes through the heart, not the mind, and there's nothing your mind can do to stop it from coming."

Ruby wasn't sure she'd gained any clarity in thought, or even in understanding, but as she took a sip of the milk her mom had poured for her, her stomach settled some. And her heart felt stronger.

She might not get all of life's choices right.

But she'd make them.

And be able to live with them.

Sebastian saw the brief trail of sparks in the air and Fletcher had yet to make it to his place. After calling the security company on site until daybreak, he'd grabbed his gun, jumped in his four-wheeler and sped out to the kennel. Dialed 911 to report a fire, and then Fletcher, as he drove, then circled the big building housing his dogs and turned his vehicle toward the lake.

He could see the blaze already, an acre away. After jumping out of the off-roader, he grabbed a shovel out of the back and started to dig. Some of his land was going to burn. He'd likely lose some trees. But he was not losing any buildings.

Sweating in the early morning chill, he dug eighteen inches wide, and then down to mineral soil, his only illumination coming from the vehicle's headlights. One man, by himself, he might make enough of a difference to at least divert the flames. Della, Bryony and Adam should be on their way to get the dogs up to his house. And to be prepared to vacate the premises altogether if necessary. Fletcher had said he'd make that call.

And police were heading toward him by lake, as

well. They'd be looking at both sides of the shore for the detonator. He'd told Fletcher the flare had not come from his land.

He'd only dug about a yard before he started to see the flames coming toward him, far faster than a grass fire in the spring should have done.

Like it was following some kind of accelerant...

Heart pounding, shovel in hand, he ran toward the flame, stopping half an acre away to check the ground in line with it. And with the light from his phone, saw the primer cord lying in the unmowed mange.

He shoved his phone in his pocket with one hand, raising his shovel high with the other, and with both hands and arms fully engaged, slammed the tip of the blade into the line, again and again, so angry he felt as though he could have ripped the thing in half with his bare hands. He wouldn't be able to stop the fire. But if he could prevent the speedy projectile to his buildings...

He would prevent it.

The fire was coming toward him. More rapidly than he'd assessed. Bearing down. He slammed the shovel again and again, watched the flames continue to speed at him.

He slammed the shovel. Jumped on it. And felt a snap.

Digging with his bare hands, he took hold of one end of the line in both hands, the end leading toward the building, and, pulling so hard his muscles stung, he ran toward the lake. He didn't have time to get to the buildings, to the end of the line, but if he could get his section far enough away from the fire...

He heard sirens. Didn't turn to look. He just kept running.

For his dogs. For Crosswinds. For all of the people who'd yet to become lost and needed to be found. For the veterans who'd sacrificed all for country and come back broken. For Ruby.

For his little baby.

The human yet to be born that was as much a part of him as he'd been a part of his father.

Ruby heard from Fletcher while she and Jenny were still sitting in the kitchen. Her brother needed her to phone Della to get to Crosswinds and move the dogs. He'd said that Sebastian wanted his trainer to call in Bryony and Adam, too.

Ruby made those last two phone calls instead, letting Della concentrate on getting dressed and out to Sebastian's place.

And then she stood.

"Where are you going?"

"To Crosswinds," she said. "I have to help. The dogs will be panicked. They know me. And I can tranquilize anyone who might try to run. I can treat any if the fire…" Her words broke off as she reached the stairs.

"You can't go out there, Ruby. You're a target. Think of the baby."

The baby.

She stopped, one foot on the stairs.

Why hadn't she thought of the baby?

She'd been thinking about the dogs.

Thinking.

Not feeling.

And as she sat on the bottom step, calling one of the veterinarians on her staff and asking her to head out to Crosswinds, she had an inclination that she'd just been given a lesson in what her mother had been talking about.

Love came from the heart, not the mind.

She was smart. Learned. And she trusted her mind.

Her life was cerebral by choice.

But if she was going to make it as a mother, she had to let her heart take the reins.

No matter how scary that might be.

Someone was watching him. Sebastian slowed to a walk, still heading toward the river with the highly flammable line in his hand, but took in the area around him as though he was back in Afghanistan, in the desert during the night, expecting an attack at any moment, from any direction.

A leaf fluttered down out of a tree, and he stopped.

If the enemy was in the tree, he'd be dead in seconds. His gun would do him no good when he didn't know where to aim. He could shoot into the tree and hope.

The enemy could shoot right at him and win.

He was in the open. The other was not.

And it hit him. The line.

Resuming his trek to the lake, he veered on a diagonal. Threw the rope up over a branch and shot it all in one move.

The tree lit up in an instant blaze.

Giving Sebastian a view of wide eyes filled with horror, just before a skinny male body hurled down at him. The fiend had the advantage of gravity. Sebastian had the superior height, weight, muscular build and a trained warrior's mind filled with intent.

Taking the brunt of the man's weight with a severe blow to his chest, he dropped his gun, grabbed hold with both arms and rolled, while the fire blazed right above them.

He had to get to his gun before his assailant did. The enemy may have been skinny, but he was a wild man, kicking and throwing punches, hurling his body around, reaching toward Sebastian's gun.

The smaller hand got there first, grabbed hold, and just as he was raising his arm, Sebastian's hand slammed down on the man's wrist, lifting it again, and slamming it down, until the gun was free. With complete focus and clear thought, he grabbed his gun and pushed into the attempted kidnapper's chest, pulling back the hammer all in one move.

He heard voices in the distance. Had flashing lights in his peripheral vision. All just distant background.

"Who are you?"

"Your brother, come to save you from your sins…" The voice came out strong and solid. Deep, as though the man was channeling a sacred tone.

With a hand at the chest of the man's hooded sweatshirt, right next to the barrel of his handgun, Sebastian pulled up and slammed the man back down.

"Your name," he growled, feeling nothing but a need to take the man down. But he couldn't let go until he knew the truth.

"Leon."

"Who's your father?"

"God is my father and you are a sinner, worshipping animals instead of God. This land is…"

"Sebastian!" Fletcher's voice sounded from outside Sebastian's sphere, cutting off his prisoner's tirade. "Hold on, man," Fletcher said, running up to them. Aware of other feet starting to circle them, Sebastian felt a hand at his back. "I've got this, brother," Fletcher said, more softly.

Brother.

One on the ground beneath his gun.

And one who would never be his, not even in law.

With a knee on the man's chest, holding him down, he kept the gun firmly pointed, but handed it to Fletcher Colton. Nodding at Glen Steele and other officers as he stood, Sebastian turned his back on the man on the ground, the half brother he'd never known, and walked away.

He didn't look back.

His job was done.

Ruby was safe. The child she carried was safe.

His only living relative in the world was being taken into custody.

He had to get back to his dogs. To make sure everyone was okay.

They needed him.

And he needed them, too.

Chapter 21

Sebastian wasn't picking up. Ruby had tried several times that day. He texted each time, to make certain she was okay, but didn't engage any further, even by text.

Fletcher had called shortly after dawn to let her know that since she didn't need Wade's protection, their brother was going to be at Crosswinds, helping to clear out fire debris with other townspeople.

An impromptu volunteer service for a member of their community family. Her brother had thought she'd already heard from Sebastian.

For some reason she didn't want to think about, she'd let her detective brother go on thinking she knew what was going on. And had called Sebastian.

And received a text asking if she was okay. Her *fine*, followed by a question to him, went unanswered.

Jenny had ended up being the one to tell her that her

kidnapper was behind bars. She'd heard from Chase, who'd heard from Robert after Glen Steele had called him at work to let him know that his daughter was safe.

She'd heard all about Sebastian's heroic actions, trapping the kidnapper in a tree, and then fighting him physically to subdue him until police arrived.

And she knew that the man who'd tried to ruin him was his half brother.

Sebastian Cross had family after all.

He had to be taking it hard. To find out he had a living relative, only to have the man be a criminal who'd attempted to kidnap the mother of his baby, and could have killed the baby, too.

A brother who'd tried to kill several of his dogs. More than once.

A man with evil inside him. One who wanted to take, not give. To steal, not earn.

Saddest part was, if the man had simply approached Sebastian, she'd bet her life savings that Sebastian would have gladly shared the land with his younger sibling.

Instead, on their first meeting, he'd held a cocked gun to the man's chest until law enforcement arrived.

Ruby moved back home. After only a short time away, the place seemed like a long-lost friend to her. She walked through it. Absorbing the peace she'd created through color choice and beautiful objects. She showered. And, instead of having to call off, she went to work.

At lunch, she drove herself to the police station next to the fire station at the west end of Main Street and was shown to a room to identify the man who'd attacked her.

He'd seemed smaller to her at the station, but Fletcher

said that wasn't unusual, given that he'd grabbed her from behind. He'd have seemed like a big specter at her back that night. The man, according to her brother, was incredibly strong. If she hadn't head-butted him, much worse things could have happened.

She'd reminded him that she'd been well trained through a myriad of self-defense classes. Her brother had helped her find the best ones.

She'd had a glimpse of the man's face on Monday night. In the dark, with headlights shining. The only thing she'd recognized, the only thing she'd really seen, other than the dark blue hoodie that he'd apparently been arrested in, had been the wild, glazed look in his eyes.

It was still there. Even sitting alone in a police interrogation room.

Fletcher offered to take her to lunch after the ID procedure was over. She'd been afraid she'd throw it up, so she went back to work and had an apple. And later some crackers and an orange. Thanking the fates that her sisters weren't there to see what she was consuming. Or rather, how much she wasn't.

By late afternoon, when she'd seen her last scheduled client and her most recent call to Sebastian went to voice mail, she signed herself out. Exchanging her white doctor's coat for a dark purple fleece coat, over light purple scrubs, she grabbed her satchel, climbed in her SUV and headed straight out to Crosswinds.

Being busy was one thing. Ghosting her was not okay. He got a point for keeping in touch to ensure she was well.

And dozens of them for the trauma, the emotional tension, the life-changing news of the past weeks. Things she mentally relived during the ten-minute drive out to his place.

The points in his favor were catapulted by him finding out that the love-child theory he and others had tossed around had become deadly reality.

Her frustration with him had pretty much dissipated by the time she pulled onto Cross Road. Along with any self-righteous anger that might have been mixed in there.

When she saw the land, by the lake, the charred remains of some trees and the blackened ground, she felt tears prick the backs of her eyes. She had no idea which tree might have been the one that Sebastian had lit afire himself. From what she'd been told, the police had run their prisoner away from the burning embers and a fire crew had taken their place, but that didn't mean they'd managed to put out the fire before the tree had burned to the ground.

Needing something to be normal, she pulled into her usual parking space, relieved that it could be hers again. That their attacker was safely, and quite firmly, from what she understood, in custody. The man was in chains and was assigned a twenty-four-hour watch. Not for his own good, but the peace of mind of all those who'd sought him. And for those who'd suffered at his hands.

There'd be no worry of escape.

Because she was there, she peeked into the medical building, but had already heard from her colleague, who'd returned to the clinic, that no dogs were injured in the morning's attack. The building was empty. From there she walked up to Sebastian's house. He'd been up since well before dawn. Had, from what she'd heard, trained that day. And had helped with fire cleanup, too.

Oscar greeted her at the door. As did Turbine, a dog leaving them that week to be adopted by a female veteran pilot whose plane had been shot down. She'd managed to land the plane safely, to get her and her crew out, but had been taken hostage overnight before her rescue.

"Where is he, boys?" she asked softly, stooping to pet them both as she looked around.

"I'm right here."

Rounding the corner into the kitchen, she almost wept as she saw Sebastian, in jeans and a checked, long-sleeved shirt and tennis shoes, standing at the stove, stirring a big wok, with his three other burners filled with huge saucepans.

He was okay. He'd come through the day and was either making himself a freezer's worth of meals, or was cooking for a very large gathering.

"Can I help?" she asked, walking over to look in his pots.

"I'm almost done," he told her. A nonanswer that she took as a *no*. He'd barely glanced her way. It could have been because he was clearly quite occupied, but she didn't think so.

"Is this it, then? We're done?"

"Now's not the time, Ruby." She got that, but her emotions wouldn't settle with the logic. The man had to be suffering. And even if he wasn't, he'd been distant since long before the day's activities. Ever since they'd been to her parents' house, to be exact.

"When is the time?" she asked, taking a seat at the kitchen table, quite sure that if she waited for an invitation she'd be standing until she grew tired and left.

"I can't make you be a part of my life, Sebastian. I wouldn't even want to. But I'm not going away until you tell me that our friendship is over, and you want no part of the baby's life."

She'd been through a hell of a lot, too. It would be a long time before she drove down her own road and didn't avoid looking at the ditch where her SUV ended up. Didn't shudder with the memory of those arms coming up behind her.

Sebastian just stirred. Browning what had to be several pounds of what smelled like—judging by the meat packages she could see in the trash—minced chicken.

"You having a party of some kind?" she asked then, getting frustrated with him again. And maybe a little panicked.

She could do the baby thing alone. She didn't doubt that for a second.

But the thought of not having Sebastian in her world, understanding the loner parts of her no one else got, was more than a little unsettling.

"I'm making dog food," he told her. "They've been through a hellish two months, continued to work hard, and so for the next few days, they're going to eat like the kings and queens, princesses and princes, that they are."

She teared up. Quickly blinked away the moisture. Asked about the recipe he was using.

And found out it was one of hers, posted on her website.

She should have known from glancing in his pans. The chicken. The rice. Mixed vegetables, also minced.

Perhaps she wasn't doing as well as she'd thought she was. Maybe not any better than he was. Just different. She was reaching out…to him. Only to him.

Needing him to be wrapped in compassion.

As she'd been that morning.

Her mind froze as she reached a new place. The major difference between her and Sebastian. He'd known it already. She put pieces together as thoughts and memories of conversations tumbled on top of each other. She'd never known a single day of her life without her family in her background.

Being surrounded by people who cared even when she didn't think she wanted them there. Having a mother who'd get up in the middle of the night, pour her a glass of milk and sit on a stool with her.

She was a loner by choice, always knowing she had her family.

Sebastian was a loner because…he was alone. Maybe even more so, having just held a gun to his newfound little brother's chest. Having just had confirmation that the man who'd fathered him, the man who'd taught him what family was, had had a separate son somewhere else.

Seeing the big can of dog nutrients on the counter— the brand she recommended, something she should have noticed walking in the door, something she *would* have noticed if she'd been as together as she'd thought she was—she picked it up, grabbed the scoop she needed and started dropping scoops into the rice Sebastian had just drained.

"You brought Turbine in with you," she said as he dumped the ingredients of his pots into two huge bowls, handed her a big metal spoon and took another for himself.

His silence was hard to take. But she did it. Stirred right alongside him.

If he didn't want to talk about why he'd opted to take home his best-trained PTSD dog for the night, that was his choice. Still didn't change the fact that he'd done so.

Or that she knew why.

Sometimes, that's what friends did. They knew and just stirred food in a bowl.

Being a friend, a daughter, a sister, a cousin, a parent—none of it was going to be easy all the time. Jenny was a living testimony to that.

And yet, if Ruby ever wanted to emulate another woman, ever wanted to hope she'd one day be as shining an example as any one woman she'd ever met, heard of, or read about, it would be her mother.

Jenny got up every single day to tend to those she loved. No matter what.

Those she loved…

Ruby looked at the tall, broad, bearded man standing next to her and could no longer deny what Jenny Colton had already seen in her daughter.

She loved him.

They'd used the four-wheeler to cart the containers of dog food down to the kennels, filling bowls and putting the rest in the refrigerator. And then, feeling as though he owed her a good turn, Sebastian offered Ruby a homemade chicken-salad sandwich.

He'd saved the cooked chicken and she cut up grapes while he diced onion and celery. He made the dressing from scratch. She spooned it over their mixture. Sitting at his kitchen table with glasses of milk, they consumed the entire bowl. She'd had hers on crackers. He'd had three sandwiches.

He hadn't eaten all day.

Hadn't been hungry.

He figured she was sitting there needing more from

him than chicken salad. And he was just waiting for her to leave.

She was safe.

He'd captured her kidnapper.

And cooked.

He'd done what he was trained to do.

What he could do.

They cleaned up the kitchen together. And she still didn't pick up her satchel to go. As he hung the dish towel on the oven-door handle, Sebastian was trying to figure out the best way to tell her he needed to call it a night.

And said, "He didn't look anything like me."

"I didn't think so, either."

Ruby leaned back against the sink, reminding him of the night at her house. The night of the attempted kidnapping.

The night they'd talked about the future.

The night they'd had sex.

The night that everything had flown out of control.

And... *I didn't think so, either?*

"You saw him?"

"Fletcher had me go to the station at lunchtime to identify him."

"Why didn't I know that?" He, of all people, should have been told. The woman carrying his child, facing her kidnapper? His half brother. "I should have been there."

"You didn't answer my call."

Since it was part of the case, Fletcher should have let him know. "You could have texted the information."

"You could have answered your phone."

Swallowing, he met her gaze, full on, for the first time

since he'd driven her away from her parents' house on Tuesday morning.

It felt like coming home. Shock waves went through his system.

The start of an episode? The panic after the attack was done? Turbine wasn't indicating, yet.

"Were you able to give the ID?" He belonged next to her, supporting her as she stared through the glass at the man who'd attacked her.

"He matches the description I gave that night. Today, all I could remember for certain was that glassy, wild look in his eyes. Your headlights were bright, and every time I think of those seconds, it's those eyes that get me."

And, selfish ass that Sebastian had been, he hadn't answered her repeated calls that day. Thinking that she was checking up on him.

And that he couldn't encourage her to expect more from him than he'd be able to deliver. After they'd left her parents, he'd been talking as if the two of them would be parents, together, to the child they'd created. He'd had to take a break from the situation to get himself in check. The idea of disappointing her, which those comments had set him up to do, was worse than any PTSD nightmare.

"I'm sorry I didn't answer my phone. I will always do my best in the future to answer any call that comes in from you."

She smiled then.

And he hoped he'd redeemed himself a little.

Chapter 22

"Fletcher says he's not talking." Ruby stayed by the sink, just leaning there, a friend in conversation before heading out. Wanting Sebastian to know that he wasn't alone in his suffering. That even if they didn't talk about it all, she was aware.

And cared.

Something she'd learned from her mother just that morning. And through the rest of her life, too, she supposed. She'd just been too set in her own thinking to realize what else had been there.

"He told me he's my brother."

She'd heard that, too. Could only imagine the shock that must have reverberated through Sebastian in that second. But according to her brother, who'd been watching from afar as he ran to the scene, Sebastian hadn't so much as twitched the entire time he had the younger man on the ground.

"I'm sorry it turned out this way."

"Sorry that your child is related to an unhinged criminal?"

"Stop it, Sebastian."

"Stop what? Speaking the truth? You're the Coltons. Your reputations matter."

"Stop putting thoughts in my head. That man is not a reflection on you. He never even met you. There's no way you could have had any influence on him, or, for that matter, him on you. He was deserted by your father, not raised by him. And he had a different mother."

"Who's dead," Sebastian said. "Fletcher said they'd tracked down the woman my father was meeting with in that hotel. She died a couple of years after their last visit."

"And she had a son."

"Yes."

"Is your father listed on the birth record?"

"No. And the rest was sealed. He was adopted out after his mother died."

"I wonder if your father even knew about him?"

He shrugged. "Leon knew about me…"

Leon. Her kidnapper had a name. She swallowed. "He must have found your connection through one of the DNA companies…or maybe his mother left him something that his adoptive parents gave him when he turned eighteen. Maybe they knew all along…" She was there for him. Not to get herself worked up again.

Her part was done. The ordeal was over.

Sebastian's chin jutted, but otherwise he gave no reaction to her words. Because he didn't care how Leon had found him? Or because he was just that good at hiding the turmoil inside him?

He rubbed at the beard on his chin as he said, "Fletcher said the only question he's answered, period, is when they asked him who his father was. He just keeps saying God is his father now. And that God will save him because he's righteous." With a shake of his head, Sebastian ended with, "When he told me he was my brother, he said he'd come to save me from my sins. Which, apparently, have to do with worshipping animals..."

"He needs help," Ruby said then, glad that the threat was done. Fearing that Sebastian would be a long time in healing from the ordeal.

Turbine, who'd been lying on the floor, stood and moved to Sebastian's side, nudging his hand. Sebastian pet the dog as he said, "He needs a good lawyer. And I'm thinking about paying for it." His gaze challenged her.

Ruby just kept looking at Sebastian's hand on the dog's head. Petting, just lying there, petting again. And Turbine, leaning up against him.

The dog was working.

Sebastian's stress level had just raised.

She looked at him. "You think I'm going to have a problem with that," she guessed, glancing at the dog again, and then met Sebastian's gaze.

"Seems like a traitorous thing to do, from your point of view," he said then. "Paying for the defense of the man who's terrorized your life."

Yet he was going to do it, anyway. "So why are you?" Her tone was neutral. She wasn't sure how she felt.

"My reasons are twofold." As soon as he started talking, she knew he'd given the matter enough thought. He'd already made his decision. And was worried about her.

Just as she'd worried about her family's reactions when she'd known she was going to do something they wouldn't like.

Their opinion mattered because she cared about them.

Sebastian cared about her.

Ruby's heart softened, and filled.

"First," Sebastian continued, "I want to make sure that he has the best defense first time out so that when they put him away, he stays there." His words were clearly stated. His expression unflinching. "And second, I grew up with my father's love and all the financial benefits I'd ever need. He's been denied the love, but I can still see that money that morally should have been shared with him, benefits him."

Which just confirmed what she'd already figured. If Leon had just gone to Sebastian, his older half brother would have given him part of the land.

Just as Sebastian would always be there for her child. Sharing what he had. In any way he could.

She felt her expression lighten as her heart did.

He frowned. "Why are you smiling? I thought you'd be upset."

"I'm happy that you're the father of this child," she said, holding her still-flat belly.

And looked him straight in the eye so he'd know she meant every word.

She was happy he was the father of her child?

Sebastian didn't doubt Ruby. He just didn't get it.

Why couldn't she see that he wasn't great father material? He lived a far-from-traditional life.

When he was alone in that life, Sebastian was good.

He liked himself and the life he'd built. Around Ruby, all he could seem to think about were the areas where he was lacking.

Which made no sense to him. He'd never been a poor-me guy. Not when he'd watched his friend die. Not when his parents had been killed.

He'd suffered. But others had suffered far more.

"We aren't getting married. Aren't moving in together. The child is going to grow up in a single-parent home..."

"But this baby is going to be loved and protected and given opportunities to succeed," Ruby said. "I'm seeing it more clearly now," she continued. "In a way, Leon did us a favor, showing us what matters most. It's not the license or where our bedrooms are, or how many adults are in the house when a child goes to sleep at night. It's having someone there, having people to turn to, to be able to count on, to believe in you, support you, help you grow and you do all of that, Sebastian. All the time."

If he wasn't careful, she was going to have him believing he could celebrate his child's birth without guilt. Without feeling like a failure.

Without doubting his every move.

"We're human beings, not cookie cutters," she said then. "We're not all meant to be the same, feel the same, want the same. But we are all deserving and needing of love."

Throat tight, he had to restrain himself from reaching out to her, pulling her into his arms and spending the night showing her how very much he valued her.

"And you know what I need right now?" she asked.

"What?" He wasn't afraid to ask. She knew his limitations. Respected them. And, best of all, had her own set of rules by which she insisted on living her life.

She was as stubborn as he was.

"I need to put these past weeks behind me. To feel no fear. To have some hours in the darkness where only pleasure and happiness exist."

She wanted to go to bed with him.

If ever there had been a woman made for him, Ruby was it.

And... "I can't risk it, Ruby, not tonight. After what happened out there today, I'm like a time bomb here, ticking off until I have a panic attack, or go to sleep and transport myself to hell."

"You have Turbine and Oscar here. They'll be in the room with us. And if I have to jump out of bed, then I do."

"I can't risk hurting you." And it wasn't only the results of PTSD that scared him. He was a loner. He didn't answer his phone every time it rang. Or enjoy being surrounded by people all the time.

"There are some hurts that are worse than physical ones," she told him. "That cut deeper."

He was between a rock and a hard place. Needing to please her. Wanting her to please him. And trying to prevent a future of failure.

He didn't walk into losing battles.

"I need to know that you won't suffer because of me."

"Then invite me to spend the night with you."

She wasn't backing down. He couldn't, either.

"I've spent the past several nights in stark fear, Sebastian. Lying awake, reliving it all. And the only thing that takes away the ugliness is thoughts of you. Please, even if you don't touch me, just let me stay and get a good night's rest."

It was like she was reading his mind. Facing the night ahead alone—with visions of his half brother's wild eyes glaring up at him, with the internal fight to accept that he *had* a half brother, that his whole life with his father had somehow been a lie—he needed more than Oscar.

He needed human conversation to sort out the chaos inside him.

Ultimately, he needed to support her and their child. He'd made the promise.

And he was not going to fail.

"Just for tonight," he told her, and, opening his arms, grabbed her close as she fell against him.

His touch was urgent. Needy. Giving. Tender. And for a few hours, Ruby let herself believe that as she gave him her love, he gave his back.

She didn't weave fantasies about living together. Or marriage.

Her entire being was geared toward avoiding both.

But as she was lying beside Sebastian, fully satiated, wanting to know that she'd be in his bed again sometimes, she needed more than they'd agreed to share.

As exhausted as he had to have been, he wasn't sleeping, either.

"Fear's an insidious thing," she dropped softly between them. With the dogs at the end of the extra large king-size bed, she drew from their silent support. "It's the root of PTSD and panic attacks. And stops us from reaching higher, trying for more."

"You're talking about us."

Turning, the sheet up under her armpits, she looked at his head on the pillow next to her. His ear was facing her. She studied the half of his face she could see.

"I'm talking about all of it," she said. "There has to

be a balance. The dangers we run from, and the ones we take on because if we don't, we lose too much."

He didn't agree. But he didn't argue, either.

"And sometimes," she continued, "you manage them."

"I need to know what, in particular, you're hoping to manage."

She did, too. Wasn't quite there yet. But since he was listening, seemed to be open to consideration, she reached inside herself and found, "Like tomorrow night, for instance. Uncle Buck's birthday. It's going to be a pretty big affair. Lots of people we both know. And there's no longer any reason to keep my pregnancy a secret, or to not announce you as the father..."

She started out bigger than she'd meant to go, or even wanted.

He hadn't left the bed.

"I'm not suggesting any kind of formal announcement," she quickly added, for her own sake as much as his. "But maybe we attend together. Not holding hands, or arm in arm, just...together. And when I start to show and news of the baby gets around—which, with my family, it will—we just continue appearing together on occasion. We show the world who we are. Friends who enjoy each other's company and are going to be raising a baby to whom they are both parents."

The announcement—too much. The plan she's just laid out...not enough.

"We've both spent our adult lives carving out the existences we've wanted. We've established ourselves as the people we want to be. We're strong-minded enough to carry this off. There's no reason why we have to define ourselves or explain to anyone. We just continue to be who we are."

Except that she was deeply afraid that she was changing.

Fear again.

"You make it sound easy."

Yeah. But they both knew it wouldn't be.

Still… "What's the alternative? We live in a small town. We work together. Even if you decided not to have anything to do with me, you're never going to abandon your child, Sebastian."

The reality was right there. Both of them knew it. "We're in control of how this goes, is all I'm saying," she finished, as much for herself as for him.

"I'm never going to decide not to have anything to do with you." He turned his head then, looking at her. "You've become a part of me."

Her heart flooded and she blinked back tears. Reached out and touched his face, running a finger along the lines under his eyes. "You've become a part of me, too."

He kissed her. Long and full.

She kissed him back, pouring herself into the silent communication.

And for that night, it was enough.

Chapter 23

Before Ruby left early Saturday morning, she'd asked Sebastian if he'd be at her uncle Buck's birthday party that night. Looking in her eyes, he gave her the only answer that he could get out, telling her he'd be there. And felt good about doing so when he saw the brief flash of relief, and then the pleasure in her eyes.

The Coltons were her family, so technically, they were her problem, not his. But this child was going to be a Colton. And he'd impregnated a Colton. He couldn't leave her standing by herself, period, let alone in a very public crowd.

His father had always told him that he gave his all to everything, which meant that he'd succeed at whatever he tried. Certainly, his time in the Marines had played out that way right up until his friend had died instead of him. And Crosswinds put truth to his dad's words.

And, he supposed, Ruby did, too. Leave it up to him to impregnate a woman whose father owned half the town. Could sic the entire town on him for what he'd done.

He fed the dogs. Got some training in. Cleaned up a bit more residue from the fire. Thanked his employees again for all their support over the past couple of months. Giving every one of them generous bonus checks for having done so.

And he tried not to think about the evening's event at Colton Ranch. His gut knew he didn't want to go. His mind knew it, too.

A new tension related to Ruby pushed at his back all day, calling him to the ranch. To be there to stand beside the mother of his child.

More, to support his very, very good friend.

Friend.

There would be baby talk now that everyone who knew also knew there was no longer any reason to keep the baby a secret. Sebastian realized he couldn't show up at Buck's place without telling his lifelong very good friend of a different nature.

Wade.

By two that afternoon, he'd been unable to fight off the emotions over which he kept such tight control. After calling Ruby to let her know what he was doing, to give her a chance to voice disapproval, he then drove over to Colton Ranch and told Wade that he was having a child with Wade's younger sister.

As talks between them went, it could have gone better. Compared to sparring they'd done in the past, it hadn't been so bad.

Once Wade knew his father and mother had been

told, and that all hell hadn't broken loose, he could hardly try to condemn Sebastian himself. And when he called Ruby, to hear from her that she was happy with the way things were turning out, Wade held out his hand to Sebastian and congratulated him on becoming a father.

That was when Sebastian should have felt a lightening inside him. Relief, certainly. And satisfaction with the reassurance that he and Ruby really were going to pull off the parenting thing without having to change their lifestyles all that much.

It was what they both wanted. And it was working.

The stalker had been caught.

Life was good again.

So why didn't his step feel any lighter?

The question hit him again early that evening as Hannah Colton came up to congratulate him. "I was scared to death for her when she wouldn't say who the father was, but when I found out it was you… I'm happy for both of you."

He smiled. Glanced at Ruby, who was in conversation with a couple from town he knew only peripherally, and then forgot the moment for a bit as he was pulled into conversation with Malcolm.

The evening wore on, and he and Ruby gravitated to each other more and more, as they stood together and received congratulations for news that had spread as quickly as he'd figured it would. But he was left more and more unsettled.

People were accepting. Excited. Seemingly truly happy for them. Showing no misgivings over their unusual arrangement—friends living apart and having a child. Even when he wasn't with Ruby, people came up to Sebastian and offered words of encouragement and advice. He couldn't have scripted it any better. But felt more deflated than not.

Those who knew about the crimes at Crosswinds, and Ruby's near kidnapping, were congratulating them both on a successful conclusion to a very bad situation.

It was obvious to Sebastian that people cared.

That he was one of them. A couple even mentioned his parents, saying they used to come into their shop every summer, saying how proud they'd been of Sebastian. And how much they'd have loved having a grandchild.

The words left him feeling gratified. And strangely empty, too.

Because the investigation was still ongoing until the perpetrator was formally charged, the police weren't yet releasing any information on the suspect. No one knew, yet, that Sebastian had a half brother.

Until nightfall, people mingled outside with an open bar and live music. Tables were set up in a barn with food in warming trays, buffet style. Balloons and banners gave the party a festive air. A mammoth cake sat in the middle of a table surrounded by small plates, napkins and forks.

Sebastian was glad he'd come. Most particularly when he was with Ruby. The woman had a way of lighting up the space around her. And not just because she was a Colton or owned the town's veterinary clinic. She was unique and strong and…

Jenny Colton brushed by him carrying a large birthday present toward the front of the room, where a microphone had been set up. Robert, across the room, was holding court with a group of five or six people circled around him.

"Here, Mrs. Colton, let me help you with that," Sebastian jumped in, then carried the package, and caught Ruby watching him. She smiled.

He smiled back.

And wanted more.

Jenny, Buck and Robert were the first to go through the food line. And had gone in that order. When Jenny sat at Buck's table to eat, and Robert headed over to a table on the other side of the barn with a group of people in line with him, Sebastian found himself thinking about his own parents. How, even during major social events, they'd always eaten together. And had a dance together, too.

Had his mother known about the affair?

Been hurt by it?

He and Ruby went through the food line together. He hadn't asked her to wait for him. Wasn't sure she had. But he liked them there. Doing that.

Even the fact that he'd noticed such a thing didn't make sense to him.

He was just leaning down to point out the vegetable soup to Ruby—more of what they'd shared at her house, he knew, because her sister Hannah had catered the event—when there was a commotion at the far side of the room.

Chairs pushing back. A collective gasp.

"Call 911!" Shouts came one after the other.

And beside him, Ruby dropped her plate.

"It's my father!" she cried, and ran off toward the crowd gathering around.

For the rest of her life Ruby would be grateful to Sebastian for his quiet presence during the couple of hours that followed her father's collapse. The big mountain man insisted on driving her to the hospital in Connors, where the ambulance was taking her father.

Once she'd seen that her brothers and sisters were traveling together in one vehicle, she'd gratefully climbed up with Sebastian. All that collective fear together in one vehicle would be too much for her.

Buck and Jenny, who'd both been at Robert's side almost as soon as he'd passed out, had ridden together in the ambulance.

Her cousins, with hugs, concern and pleas to be kept informed, had stayed back at the ranch to see off the guests and clean up, as best they could.

He's alive. Sebastian's words as they'd pulled out behind the ambulance came back to Ruby again and again while they waited to hear any news at all.

Buck and Jenny were inside the emergency room cubicle, where they'd first taken Robert. The rest of them sat in various chairs in the waiting room. Hannah called her sitter to let her know she might need her overnight. And she then sat holding hands with Lizzie, their heads bent together as they talked softly.

Wade was by himself, reading a magazine. Chase kept checking at the desk for news. And Fletcher was scrolling on his phone.

Ruby sat with Sebastian, not touching, but so glad he was there. After an hour passed with no real news, other than that Robert had not yet regained consciousness, but was breathing on his own, and tests were being run, Ruby reluctantly told Sebastian, "You don't have to stay. I can catch a ride home with either Mom and Buck, or the crew." She motioned toward her various siblings scattered about.

And yet, all together, too.

When Sebastian said he was fine right where he was, she didn't question him. Or offer again. She found herself more calm—frightened, but not panicked—with him sitting next to her.

Sebastian felt as relieved as if he'd been sitting vigil over his own family member when Jenny finally came out to tell her children that their father had suffered another stroke, but that he'd regained consciousness a couple of times and was holding steady.

The slim blond woman was clearly concerned—for her children as well as their father.

"Buck and I are both going to stay the night with him," she said then. "The doctor said each of you can come in for a minute, but that's it. They'll be moving him to a room and you can all come up tomorrow," she said, even glancing at Sebastian as she did so.

As though, because he'd fathered a Colton child, he was one of them.

He nodded at Ruby's mother, touched her shoulder as she passed and made a silent promise to her to watch over Ruby. Wanting to tell her that Robert would pull through just as he had four years before.

Like Sebastian, or Robert, had the ability to control fate.

He waited outside the emergency-room door as the siblings went in three at a time, to give their dad love, and was moved when Ruby, who came out first, looked to him as soon as she exited the door.

"I need to stop by Mom and Dad's," she said as they wished her siblings good-night and headed out into the night. "Mom wants me to pack a few things, including her pills, to bring up in the morning."

All business. Keeping a stiff upper lip. That was his Ruby.

He knew now, though, that underneath, she was as scared as the rest of them. He'd seen the chinks in her armor that no one else ever saw. With the exception, he suspected, of Jenny.

"I left my SUV there, anyway," she continued without a pause as they approached his truck. "I went over to help Mom load up decorations this afternoon, and rode to the party with her. Dad came straight from the office."

Sebastian wanted to just nod, keep his mouth shut. But said, "I can drive out to let Oscar out and put him in the kennel and meet you back at your place if you'd like." He didn't want her to be alone. Didn't think she wanted to be alone.

And since she didn't have a husband or boyfriend to call on, a friend was the next best thing.

He tried to wrap it all up nice and clean, but knew that he needed to be with her. To share the anguish with her, just as she'd sat with him through his own on a couple of occasions.

If ever a panic attack or nightmare could be better than another. Those two times with Ruby would qualify.

She hadn't given him a response and as he pulled out of the parking lot, he saw her wiping at her eyes. He stopped.

She glanced at him. Nodded.

And gave him the saddest smile he'd ever seen.

Ruby wanted more.

Seeing her father in that hospital bed, knowing he

could have easily died that night, could still die, had brought it all home to her.

Life didn't come with a single guarantee, other than that it would, at some point, end. Robert wasn't the perfect husband. He'd been an absentee father much of the time. But he loved them all. Had gone to battle for every one of them when they'd needed it growing up. Had always provided well, both in advice and monetary advantages.

"I just realized something tonight," she said aloud. "My dad, he's lived his whole life big. If not for his over-the-top dreams, maybe over-the-top energy, his need to always reach for more…we probably wouldn't even still all be together. He'd be running the hardware store with Uncle Buck. There'd be no ranch. No Colton Properties. Owl Creek would be the small town with no industry that it had always been. Maybe even be dwindling into nothing, if not for my father's vision of it as a tourist town. Us kids, if we'd been lucky enough to afford a college education, would have had to move elsewhere to get good-paying professional jobs. I sure would have had to. At least as far as Connors. If I'd even been lucky enough to get to go to veterinary school. Without the example I had, to dream big, to reach for what I wanted, I might not even have considered the possibility that I could be a vet…"

She was rambling. She knew it. Had to do it, anyway.

And wasn't the least bit worried about it, either. Sometime in the past weeks, or maybe slowly, over a period of years, Sebastian had become her safe place.

She wasn't looking at him. Stared at the road ahead of them, the headlights on pavement in a sea of darkness.

"I think that once I reached that dream, becoming

a vet, I quit reaching," she said then. "I do good work, that I love, that completes me, and I go home where I feel peaceful. But, you know, there'll be plenty of time for peace when I pass on to the next life, right?"

Sebastian glanced at her. "If you want to do more with your life, you absolutely should," he agreed.

"If you spend your life avoiding turmoil, if you don't take risks, then you miss out on the possibility that you could have it all, instead of settling for peace."

It was all becoming clear, there in the darkness.

"What more do you want?"

She wanted him. As a husband. A lover. A boyfriend. The father to her child. A housemate. Or, if all he could give her was friendship, she'd grab at that for all she was worth.

"I want love," she told him, remembering what Jenny had said the other day in the kitchen. "I want love," she repeated, almost to herself, with total conviction. "And if that means my siblings drive me up the wall, then, oh, well. What goes up, has to come down, right? I want this baby. I want to be the best mother I can possibly be. It's going to be messy and unpredictable, but I want it, Sebastian. More than that, I think I need it."

His hands were gripping the steering wheel so tightly she could see the whites of his knuckles in the dash lights.

"I want you, too," she told him then. Taking the biggest risk of all. "However we work it out, so it's good for both of us, I want you."

Chapter 24

Sebastian had no words. His friend was in pain. Pouring her heart out. And he had no words. He'd known the time would come.

Her father had just collapsed and was in the hospital. Could yet die. She was pregnant with Sebastian's child. She'd been nearly abducted that week. Had IDd her kidnapper the day before.

And she wanted him.

Say something, dammit.

"I'll be here for you, for as long as you want me to be." More than he'd ever said to anyone.

And, he was sure, not nearly enough.

"I know."

She didn't sound like she was settling.

But like she knew better than to ask for anything more.

"It's not enough, is it?"

When she didn't answer right away, his gut sank. They shouldn't be having the conversation right then. They'd been through so much. Were both tired. She had to be worried sick about Robert.

Should probably be with the siblings who shared her agony as acutely.

But…he knew what it felt like to lose a parent. "No matter what happens, you'll get through it, Ruby," he told her then. "If you risk and fail, or risk and get an entirely different result than you planned… If you need your father's advice someday and he's not there to give it…you'll get through. You'll learn. And you'll grow. And you'll have a future in front of you, too." He'd found words. Maybe not the right ones, but they were better than a deafening, potentially hurtful, silence.

"If one thing doesn't work, you'll take another risk. You're as determined as I am to chart your own course, and I can promise you that what I'm saying is true. When my folks died, I was lost. I sat in our home in Boise, knowing that I was the only family left within those walls, and felt like I was through. I was having nightmares, and panic attacks, and couldn't see a future. I came to Owl Creek just to get away from those walls. The cabin was mine, no one would come looking for me there, or visit, like they were in Boise. And look at me now," he said, not in a bragging way, but in an attempt to give her hope where he'd just snatched it away. "I've got Crosswinds, a career that I love, a town that is peripheral family to me, a baby on the way…and I've got you."

He bit off the last bit quickly. They'd reached Owl Creek.

Would soon be at her parents' home.

"You've got me, too," he said then, restless, frustrated as hell. Filling with tension that he knew he couldn't assuage.

Pulling into the Colton community of Hollister Hills, he slowed the truck. "It's not enough, is it?" he asked again, when he knew the timing wasn't right.

Because he knew, too, that she'd needed to have the conversation. Which was why she'd brought it up.

Once again, she didn't answer.

So Sebastian did what he said he'd do. He pulled into her parents' drive. Dropping her off as she'd asked him to do. "Do you still want me to come over tonight?"

She nodded, jumped down, put her satchel on her shoulder and turned back to him. "You'll always be enough, Sebastian. You are who you are, and I want you in my life. I need your friendship. There just might be someone else, too. Sometime down the road."

With that, she shut the passenger door and walked, head high, with steady steps up to the Colton mansion front door.

He waited until she was inside, wishing he'd said differently. More.

But didn't know what he'd add.

Backing out of the driveway, he headed out to tend to Oscar.

She wanted him with her that night.

And so he would be.

She wasn't going to let herself cry. Her father was probably going to be just fine. He'd survived his last stroke without any adverse effects. The same could happen again.

He'd just been to the doctor, she reminded herself,

comforted herself. His tests had come back no worse than previously.

Yes, according to Jenny, Robert's doctor had continued with grave warnings in the event that Robert didn't change his habits, but the man was only fifty-nine.

And other than the effects of his hard living he was in good health.

And the rest of it?

She was out of danger, thank God!

As she climbed the stairs up to her mother's room, to collect the things on the list Jenny had texted to her, she made herself focus on the good in her life.

Thoughts of Sebastian's words, the deep honesty in them, as he'd told her about coming home from Afghanistan, having to leave the Marines early, to deal with his parents' tragic and unexpected deaths.

The Sebastian she'd always known never spoke of such things.

And the picture he'd painted—a man all alone, suffering from what was probably, at that time, acute PTSD, to have pulled himself up and out and built Crosswinds from the ground up, who spent his life giving to other veterans, and training dogs to save lives of those who've gone missing... She'd fallen in love with a good man.

She wasn't sorry about that. Nor was she sorry she was having his baby. To the contrary, she felt honored to be the mother of Sebastian Cross's child.

And she wanted more. She wanted love.

Maybe Sebastian loved her and just couldn't tell her. But she wanted marriage, too.

She was, after all, Robert Colton's daughter. She

wasn't going to settle for peace and quiet. She was going to risk failure to try to have it all.

To live big, as her dad did.

She'd reached Jenny's room. Found the overnight zipper bag right where her mother had told her it would be. Didn't recognize the black leather satchel, but saw it as something her mother would use. There was a change of underwear inside already, so she crossed that off her mother's list.

She wondered where Jenny had been overnight. As far as she knew, her mom hadn't left town in over a year.

Sitting on her mother's bed for a moment, she remembered a night when she'd awoken with a nightmare and crawled in bed with her mother. Jenny had wrapped her arms around little Ruby and she'd fallen back to sleep safe and secure.

She'd grown up in a home filled with chaos, but she'd been well loved. Had never doubted that.

It was that assurance, more than anything else, that she wanted to give her child. Whatever she had to do to accomplish the mammoth feat.

She took her time packing.

The pants and blouse were right where Jenny had said they'd be. The hospital was providing a toothbrush and paste for the night, but Jenny wanted her own in the morning, just in case she had to stay another night.

Her mom's hormone pills were in the cabinet.

And she added the few makeup items and the hairbrush Jenny had requested.

If Sebastian hadn't been coming over, she'd have driven the bag back that night. To sit with Jenny as her mother had been there for her so many times in her life. But Uncle Buck was with Jenny, and maybe it was best for the two of them to have some time alone with Robert. They'd all grown up together right there in Owl Creek.

Had gone to high school together.

Where, of course, Robert had been quarterback on the high-school football team.

Her dad was a competitor. A fighter. He was going to be fine.

With the bag on her shoulder, she wandered into Robert's room next door.

Separate rooms.

When had that happened?

After Lizzie was born?

Or had it been that way from the beginning?

Looking around, noticing the burned butt of a cigar in the ashtray on the nightstand by her father's bed, Ruby frowned, trying to remember how old she'd been when they'd lived in a house big enough for her parents to have separate rooms.

And then frowned again as she smelled something.

It was familiar.

And she didn't like it.

Heart pounding, she opened her father's nightstand drawer. Was she really searching her father's things for drugs? Of the illegal variety?

She'd been around marijuana in college. Had strongly disliked the sickly sweet smell.

It was illegal for any use in Idaho.

Or maybe it was just cut grass she was smelling. Leaving the drawers, she went to her father's open closet door, thinking maybe he'd been golfing earlier that day.

A Saturday in late April, made perfect sense to her…

"And now, my pretty, I've got you!" The familiar

male voice reverberated through her brain, through the clothes in her father's closet, as a gloved hand reached out from between them and grabbed her wrist.

Sebastian took his time getting back to Crosswinds. It was late. Traffic was nonexistent. The night was peaceful. And he wanted to give Ruby time to get home and have a minute in her own space.

It was an act of selflessness.

What he wanted to do was turn around and follow her home.

Just to be by her side.

Life had spiraled in so many directions. For both of them.

The two of them together was the constant. Through all of it.

The attacks were on Crosswinds, and her.

The baby was equal parts of both of them.

He had a half brother. Her father had a stroke.

For years, they'd been living peaceful, productive lives. Side by side, through her brother, and then through work, but separate. And suddenly, they implode together. It was like fate was out to force them together.

The last thought triggered a self-deprecating grunt. He was so tired he was getting punchy.

Oscar greeted him with happy whines and a wagging body when he walked in the door. He fed the boy, and found a sense of rightness within himself, too.

Dogs were another thing he and Ruby had in common. A deep understanding of the relationship between canines and humans. Of the bond that existed between them.

"You want to go for a ride?" he asked Oscar then.

He'd take the dog to Ruby's with him. Oscar would bridge the gap of need between them.

She'd told him once that she'd love to have a dog of her own, but just couldn't subject a precious canine to a life spent mostly alone. He'd suggested she take the dog to work with her every day. She'd seemed open to the idea. And then Oscar had been shot and he and Ruby had slept together and they'd quit talking like friends.

Grabbing food for the dog for the morning, and a clean pair of underwear and his toothbrush, Sebastian was just bagging his items to head out the door when his phone rang.

He'd only left Ruby a brief fifteen minutes before…

His entire being stopped flowing as he saw Steele's name come up. Close to midnight?

"What?" he answered.

"Working late here, and heard you were in Connors with the Coltons, so figured it wasn't too late to call," the detective began.

Get on with it. Sebastian kept his impatience to himself. Holding the phone to his ear with his shoulder, he shoved his things between paper handles, motioned for Oscar, and was heading out the door as Steele said, "A report just came through from Boise. Your father wasn't having an affair. The woman he was seeing was a patient. She didn't have health insurance and couldn't afford a hospital stay. He paid for her hotel and treated her there, on and off for a couple of years. When she got pregnant, he told her it would likely kill her to have the baby. She opted to have it, anyway. And when she died, the child was adopted out."

"Leon."

"That's what we thought because we thought he was

your brother, but we haven't been able to confirm that. It's what we were after when we had Boise checking on the woman. We still haven't been able to positively ID this guy. He's got no driver's license, his prints aren't in the system. We've sent out DNA samples but haven't heard back."

Sebastian's mind was ticking. His father hadn't had an affair. He had to tell Ruby. And… "If he's not my brother, why does he think the land is his?"

"We're still working on that. He's not talking. Just keeps saying God is his father. And spitting out renditions of bible verse that aren't accurate. Our theory right now is that he did some amateur checking and somehow thinks you're his brother."

The young man sounded delusional.

"Has his attorney been in to see him?"

"Today. Of course, I have no idea what was said."

Right. And knowing the kid was in good hands— hands Sebastian would continue to pay for now that he'd started—he could walk away.

And he did.

Ruby screamed, "No-o-o-o!" burst out of her as the man in the closet held a vise grip on her wrist. She kicked her elbow out like a chicken wing, striking him under his chin, and twisted her arm with a purposeful jerk as she did so.

In the split second that his grasp loosened, she was free. Slamming the closet door, she ran for the room's exit, pushing the lock in the knob as she shut that, too.

The lock wouldn't hold. The door was solid wood, and the jambs were standard, attached to trim wood. Her attacker was strong. She had two minutes, max.

Too late, she identified the stench.

The smell of the man who'd grabbed her from behind in the dark.

He'd been smoking dope before he attacked her.

Her kidnapper wasn't in jail.

He was right there in her parents' house. Like he'd been lying in wait. Watching all of them. Had he followed her to the hospital, and back?

He'd smelled like pot the night of the attempted abduction. How could she have forgotten that?

How he had gotten out of jail, and how long it would be before anyone knew, she had no idea. Just knew she had a baby to protect.

She had to stay alive.

She'd left her purse downstairs. Had to get to her phone. Her parents, like so many, no longer had a landline. Thoughts flew as she moved down the hall.

Seconds later, she passed the bedroom she'd recently used and was turning toward the stairs when she heard the loud crack of wood behind her.

Her attacker was already free, just around the corner.

She'd never make it down the stairs in time.

Instead, she slipped behind the door in the bathroom, prayed that he'd run past her toward the stairs.

Her heart thumped. Pressed against the wall behind the door, she could hear the beat in her head, feel the ends of every nerve. She could hardly breathe, but had to keep thinking.

To keep focused.

She was alone. Had to save herself.

She knew the house. The fiend after her did not.

How long would it be until Fletcher got home?

Her brother had a gun in his room. Fletcher was

wearing his personal gun in town, and had showed her the nine-millimeter, for her use if she needed it to stay alive, the first night she'd stayed with him and her parents.

She was going to need it to stay alive.

Doors banged against walls down the hall, followed by seconds of silence. The kidnapper searching rooms? He was coming closer. If he banged her door, she'd be dead.

Turning her cheek to the wall, she prayed for all she was worth. And saw the sink. The cupboard under it was empty. She'd stored her toiletries there.

Hearing another door slam, figuring she had seconds while the intruder was in the guest room, she used those seconds to crawl inside the small cupboard, scrunching up, with her head tilted to avoid the drain.

The door just outside her space slammed.

If he opened the cupboard, found her, she had one shot. A kick straight to the groin, or she was done.

She had to wait for him to open the door. To be that close, facing the cupboard, or she wouldn't have a shot at incapacitating him.

She could hear the man's heavy breathing.

Could feel his incensed desire to lay his hands on her.

And held her breath.

Chapter 25

Sebastian wasn't even up Cross Road before he voice-dialed Ruby to tell her about Steele's call. Her kidnapper wasn't his brother.

Though, logically, he'd known the relationship wasn't his fault—wasn't a reflection on him, as Ruby had pointed out—the relief was palpable. Coursing through him with a newness of life. His child was not going to have an uncle in prison for heinous crimes against the child's mother.

Expecting her to pick up on the first ring, as she generally did lately, he waited impatiently through the second.

And then the third.

After the night she'd had, he was antsy to give her some good news.

By the fourth ring, Sebastian was fully focused.

The young man in jail sounded delusional. Was quoting bible verses wrong. He must have done his amateur sleuthing incorrectly to have come to the conclusion that Sebastian was his brother.

Even with desperation driving escalated behavior, the man in jail did not resemble a stalker shrewd enough to elude investigators, leaving no clues at all, for more than two months.

A kid spouting religious rhetoric. Like the kidnapper had spewed to Ruby the night of her attempted abduction, and to him via text, and with a clever plan to torch his place that fit the man's method of operation. Calling him brother. Maybe he was overreacting.

It would be way too much of a coincidence, some kid just happening to torch his place after he'd initiated a campaign to squeeze out the stalking kidnapper.

And it hit him.

With cold certainty.

A man who'd been pushed past his limit, who'd been forced out of his carefully calculated plans, might hire someone to be in one place, while he would lie in wait for what he'd obviously determined was the root of all of his problems. Ruby.

Why the guy wanted his land, why he thought Crosswinds belonged to him, he had no idea. And at the moment, didn't care.

Calling Steele back, Sebastian told the man to get to Ruby's house, while he broke all speed limits to get there himself.

She thought she heard her phone ringing.

Would it draw her attacker down the stairs?

What about the security system?

Where was Fletcher?

Her kidnapper had shoved the bathroom door against the wall. And then…nothing.

Had he left?

Was he standing there? Staring at the cupboard?

Had she left a trail?

Did he know she was in there?

Chest tight, she couldn't breathe. Hurt everywhere.

And…she heard the screech of rings against metal just feet away as he pushed aside the shower curtain.

He was going to find her.

Sebastian had just reached the outskirts of Owl Creek when his phone rang again. Steele.

"She's not at her house."

The words sparked a fear in him that he couldn't contain. Gunning his engine, he spit out the words: "Her parents." And, turning his wheel sharply to the left, screeching his tires, he told Oscar to hang on as he entered the private neighborhood of mansions.

Feeling sick, ready to kill or die, he saw Ruby's SUV still in the drive of her parents' home. And saw the light on upstairs.

"Please, God, let her be in Jenny's room, taking her time collecting things. Needing to be close to her mother."

Comforted himself with the thought of the security system.

He dialed her again as he pulled up the drive, stopping right behind her vehicle. Told Oscar to stay and was already heading up the walk as he heard the ring of the connected call. He could see her satchel through the window. On an ottoman not far from the front door.

And knew with dead certainty that something was wrong.

Very wrong.

With her father in the emergency room, Ruby would not let her phone go unanswered unless she had no other choice.

Not knowing if she'd fallen, was hurt, or if his worst suspicions were true and the man in jail was not their stalker, and the kidnapper had Ruby, he picked up a rock and broke the front window, using his shirted arm to swipe away enough glass to get inside.

Gun out, he surveyed the space, looking for... *Oh, God, not blood.*

"Ruby!" The call was a cry from the heart.

Then he saw curtains blowing through an open window in the back of the house.

And went into full battle mode.

She might already be gone.

He had to check the house first.

Maybe he wasn't too late.

Maybe there would be a clue to who had her, where he'd taken her.

He'd quickly canvassed the downstairs, was heading upstairs when he heard what sounded like wood slamming against a wall.

Gun pointed, ready to take out the fiend with one bullet to the head, he took the stairs three at a time, heard a grunt. Fear made adrenaline race through him as he rounded the corner.

"You..." A man's voice.

He swung around. Saw a jean-clad backside and shot.

The wall at the end of the hall.

It was enough to make the man stand upright for

the split second it took Sebastian to shove the barrel of his gun to the back of the intruder's head. "Move and you're dead."

Ruby saw blood drip to the hallway floor. And didn't move.

Move and you're dead.

She'd heard Sebastian's voice but could only see the intruder.

And blood.

After looking in the bath, her kidnapper had left the bathroom. Ruby had breathed a full breath. She'd heard the door slam against the wall. And then nothing.

Until she'd heard Sebastian call her name.

Tears had flooded her eyes. She'd bit her lip to keep from making a sound.

And had heard her kidnapper as he whispered, "I know where you are. You're going to come out of there nice and slow..."

He was going to use her as a human shield. She just knew.

Would hold her up and make Sebastian let them walk away.

The cupboard had opened.

She'd kicked, but the evil man had been ready for her, keeping himself back far enough to ward off any self-defensive blow. Her foot landed on his shin.

Painful, but not debilitating.

That's when she'd seen the gun. Held low, in one hand, it was pointed straight at her. Still.

Did Sebastian know? He was behind the man. Could he see the gun?

Did she warn him?

Hoping that Sebastian was a quicker shot than the man who'd been eluding police for more than two months?

The kidnapper had escaped chains and jail.

Her parents' security system...

She was going to die, right there in front of Sebastian...

"Turn around slowly." Sebastian's controlled, commanding tone brought more tears. If his voice was the last one she heard, she'd take it with her forever.

Staring unblinkingly at the intruder's feet, she waited for them to move.

They didn't.

She was still staring at a gun barrel.

She was going to die.

Sebastian would never know his baby.

Never give himself another chance to have a family of his own.

If he didn't know about the gun, he'd never forgive himself when Ruby got shot.

Her only chance was to take a chance.

The gun was two feet away.

She'd get one move. And it had to be quicker than a trigger pull.

She'd positioned herself to kick out and up. If she could knock the gun...

A quick movement, and the feet in front of her suddenly twisted away. "Drop the gun, you..." Sebastian's curse words sounded. She waited for the sound of another shot.

Heard... Was that Fletcher?

And Detective Steele?

"We've got this..."

"Ruby..."

Sebastian's voice. Warm. Worried.

She wanted to tell him she was fine.

But she lay there, curled up, her back to the wall, a drain in front of her face, her arms cradling her baby, and couldn't move.

She was shaking. But breathing. Reaching a steady hand in, Sebastian felt for a pulse. It was rapid, but strong.

Her gaze didn't seem to be focusing.

Fear struck through him again. "Ruby?"

When that beautiful, deep green-eyed gaze moved to him, he felt tears prick his eyes. He hadn't cried since Jerry had died.

While everything inside of him wanted to rip the vanity apart and lift her up against him, never to let her go, he remained on his haunches, holding her gaze. "Are you hurt?"

If the man had…

She was fully dressed in the same red jeans and black pullover sweater she'd had on all night.

"No."

She still didn't move.

And he understood. The chaos right outside the bathroom door. The sounds of police voices, sirens in the distance. He shut the door.

Flipped on the bathroom light.

And met her gaze again, immediately.

"You want to come out now?"

She shook her head. "Not until he's gone."

"Ruby!" Fletcher's voice sounded panicked, followed by a strong knock on the door.

Standing, Sebastian opened the door.

"Her vitals are fine. She's scared to death. Stay with

her," he said, taking the stairs down two at a time, and racing for his truck.

"Come on, boy," he said, slapping his thigh and racing back toward the house. The blue-hooded man was in cuffs, being led out of the house. Sebastian didn't look at him. Just slapped his thigh again and took the stairs back up, with Oscar keeping pace beside him.

"It's okay, sis, it's over." Sebastian heard Fletcher's voice.

And when there was no reply, he tapped the detective on the shoulder and motioned for him to make room. Seeing Oscar, Fletcher stood.

It took strength for Sebastian to stand back and let Oscar rescue the mother of his child. He watched as the dog put a paw on Ruby's leg, and then moved closer, laying his front paws in as much of her lap as he could get to.

But when he saw her hand move to Oscar's head, and then slowly start to pet the dog, he knew she was going to be okay.

And dropped to his knees with relief.

Chapter 26

Ruby had no need for medical attention. An EMT on scene checked her out, but she'd have refused to head back to the ER in Connors even if it had been recommended.

Standing in her parents' front yard, looking at the crime-scene tape, the flashing lights, she could only think of one place she wanted to be.

"Take me home with you," she said to Sebastian, her hand on Oscar's head. "Please."

Her brother was going to be at the police station for a while. If she didn't detest the fiend who'd been terrorizing them for months, she'd have felt sorry for him. Fletcher was not going to leave the man alone until he had every answer he wanted out of him.

He'd do it legally. But her brother would not give up.

He'd also said he was going to head up to the hospital in the morning to speak with their parents. Or at least Jenny, if Robert wasn't well enough to hear what had happened.

Steele agreed to put off that particular notification for the night.

By morning, they should have answers to give Jenny—like how the kidnapper got past the security system—along with the bad news that her beautiful home was a crime scene. Or even, who the kidnapper was. In the meantime, officers were going to secure the house for the night. Tape cardboard to windows and assign a watch so the place didn't get vandalized.

It wasn't until she and Sebastian were in the truck, on their way out to Crosswinds—Oscar sitting in the back seat with his head popping over the back of the seat—that Ruby remembered the blood.

"Did you crack him with the butt of the gun?" she asked. She'd heard his report to Steele and Fletcher, right after she'd given her own without Sebastian present.

They'd both been told to stay close in case they'd need to come in for further questioning in the morning.

"Nope. No way I was risking any chance that man has any cause to come after me again. I played it fully by the book."

She glanced at him. "I saw blood drip on the floor."

When Sebastian pulled up his red-checked flannel sleeve, showing her the gash on his forearm, she gasped. "Why didn't you have the EMT look at that?" she asked him. "It needs attention, Sebastian."

"And I have someone perfectly capable of taking care of it, if that's the case," he said, adding, "Right here in the truck with me." He glanced over at her. "I needed to get you out of there."

Yeah. Even just five minutes down the road, she was feeling better. Breathing easier. Her chest felt lighter.

"I think it's just surface," he said then, sounding calm. But she saw those white knuckles on the steering wheel.

In his own way, Sebastian was as agitated as she was. And she thought of something she'd just heard.

"Leon isn't your brother." He had to be feeling good about that.

He nodded. Gave her nothing more on the subject.

And then they were pulling into Crosswinds. She insisted on a stop at the medical building so she could check out his arm—cut from breaking the front window glass in her parents' home. She found herself picking out a couple of shards—remembering when she'd been similarly engaged treating Elise not so long before—and could hardly comprehend that it was really over.

She'd thought it was. Trusted it was.

But it hadn't been.

Sebastian didn't need stitches. She'd have insisted on a trip into Connors if he had. She patched him up with butterfly strips and looked up at him, to see if he was satisfied, only to catch him staring at her with the most intent look in his eyes.

An expression she didn't recognize.

And couldn't look away.

He didn't say anything. Just looked at her.

And then lowered his lips to hers. Showing her what he was feeling.

Because that was who he was and what he had to give.

And when she'd needed him, he was there.

He'd saved her life. Not once, but twice.

Maybe she wasn't meant to get married. Maybe a good friend, hopefully occasional lover and co-parent was all she was ever going to have.

Because she wasn't going to walk away from Sebastian.

Ever.

There was no one else on earth whose presence made her world okay. No one else who seemed to take the same comfort from her own nearness.

So what he had to give was going to have to be enough.

Lying in his bed with Ruby that night, Sebastian watched the expressions chase themselves across her face. Frowns. Looks of pain.

No smiles.

He'd dozed some. Had definitely rested, with her body lightly touching his. He'd refused to allow himself deep sleep. After all the trauma of the past few days— culminating that night when he'd seen the gun in the kidnapper's hands and had thought, for a split second, that he could very well lose Ruby and the baby—there'd been too much chance of a nightmare.

He'd been surprised at just how relaxed he'd been, from the moment they stripped down to their underwear and crawled in bed together.

There'd been no sex. She'd given him no hint at all that she wanted it. And he'd had no inclination for it, either.

They'd been through too much to put themselves through any more emotional upheaval. Even ecstasy.

But as dawn neared, he wished he'd made love to her. To have that be her last moments before sleeping, to chase away the demons that seemed to be haunting her in her sleep.

To have a pleasant memory be the first thing on her mind when she woke up.

And right then, in that moment, lying there watching her, focusing solely on her, he knew. And bent down to kiss her.

Her lips moved beneath his before her eyes opened.

And then she was lying there staring up at him, completely open. No filters.

It was a second that would be locked in his memory for life. The thing he would be striving to achieve for the rest of his days.

"Marry me," he said then. So easily.

She blinked. And when her eyes opened again, the smart, assessing, closed-off woman he knew was staring back at him.

"Don't, Sebastian."

Absolutely the furthest reaction he'd expected to get.

"Don't what?"

"All of it—just don't." She slid from the bed.

And he followed right behind her. "I thought you'd changed your mind, that you wanted to get married someday," he said as she pulled a flannel shirt out of his closet and slid her arms into it on the way to the kitchen.

He wasn't going to panic. He was going to be there. Period.

Turning, she stopped him in his tracks. "I want you," she said. "The real you. Not someone who gives me what I want when it doesn't fit. That's a recipe for failure."

Something she'd been afraid of her whole life, he realized. Thinking of all her questions, always. Needing to know. To be sure. To limit...

And he took a deep breath.

"Last night, when I saw his gun…"

She hissed in a breath, but he didn't stop. "I knew I could lose you. And that if I did, the light in my life would go out. You are my constant, Ruby. And… I saved your life. I was able to protect you, in spite of myself. You said not too long ago that there are dangers we run from and those we choose to manage. I'm asking you to take on the potential danger of living with a man with PTSD. I've started training Oscar. Our awareness of the situation, the potential triggers and a dog trained to stop me before I escalate out of control could be how we manage that. And when our child is young, I'm never left alone all night, or at least, I never go to sleep, without another adult present, just in case. I know your stubbornness, your strength, and know that if I'm ever out of control when you're there, the first thing you'll do is see to our child."

She was shaking her head. Not smiling.

He didn't get it.

"I love you, Sebastian," she told him, as if she'd said the words many times before. "And right now, I need you to take me home. To get a shower and head to Connors to see my mom and dad. And you need to feed dogs and train…"

"Della's going to cover Crosswinds for me," he told her. "I texted her last night when you were in seeing your father." And then, with his newly opened heart shattering a bit, he said, "I'm fine to take you home. I'd like it better if you'd let me get a quick shower, first. And then I can come to the hospital with you. Just in case."

He left that "in case" hanging there. Just in case there

were questions about Ruby's near kidnapping the night before. Or, just in case Robert wasn't doing as well as expected. She could take her pick. Both were there.

And when she nodded, saying, "I'll feed Oscar while you're showering," his heart started to piece itself back together again.

The man already owned her heart. There was no reason for him to give up his own path to walk hers. As badly as Ruby had wanted to throw caution to the wind, reach for what she most wanted and suggest that she and Sebastian go to the courthouse that day to complete marriage paperwork, she couldn't.

Maybe she'd never be a person like her father. One who could just take what he wanted, create what he needed by hard work, dedication and sheer force of will, and deal with the consequences later.

She was a woman who'd been too shut in, too cautious to dare to dream. But she was also one who needed to look for possible consequences and be prepared to deal with them in the event her reaching, her risk, brought them about.

And the consequences of marrying Sebastian, when he was so definitely not a marrying man, were too brutal to consider. She could lose him entirely.

She'd rather be his friend for life than his enemy.

Or, worse, his nothing at all.

An early morning proposal, out of the blue, after the night they'd had, preceded by the weeks they'd had... She'd have been nothing but selfish to accept.

But she kissed him when he came out of the shower. Deep. Long. Like a lifetime lover would do. Squeezed his arm before she got out of his truck at her folks' house and got into her own SUV. She waited for him to pull into her garage after her and walked with him into her house.

And smiled, an expression she felt to her soul, when he was waiting for her with breakfast made when she came out of her room. He pulled her into his arms then, kissing her as deeply as she'd kissed him earlier, and she started to rest a little easier inside.

They were going to find their way.

It might not be traditional. Or be exactly what she thought she wanted.

But in the end, what she wanted was him.

And if he wanted her as badly, they'd find a way to make it work.

Fletcher called just as they were getting ready to leave for the hospital. He was heading up after a shower, and asked that she wait to tell their parents what had happened until he got there.

A condition with which she was quite happy to comply.

She put him on speakerphone then, as he relayed what had transpired during the night. Sebastian drove, as they heard, together, that her kidnapper's name was Bob Thompson.

"I know that name," Sebastian said.

"His lawyer approached you six months ago with an offer to buy your five acres on the lake," Fletcher said. And Sebastian and Ruby frowned together.

"All of this is because Sebastian wouldn't sell his land?" she asked, incredulous. No matter how much research, how many questions asked, or how many foreseen risks she might have turned up on a land offer, she'd never, in a million years, have come up with such a potentially deadly consequence.

"Yes and no. Yes, if Sebastian had sold the land, the man wouldn't have gone after the two of you. But he'd have been living right here in Owl Creek and that would not have been good," Fletcher continued. And Ruby grew more and more incredulous, and horrified, too, as she listened. "He's an Ever After Church member, and claims that God told him that the property belonged to the church. That God wanted the land for a new church."

"I've never even heard of the Ever After Church," she said, glancing at Sebastian, who shook his head.

"Neither had we. Supposedly it was founded by some guy named Markus Acker. But this is where it really gets weird. This guy, Thompson, has a record. He ran an illegal gambling ring for years without getting caught. And when he was apprehended, he made a deal to turn in some of his clients who were mobsters to stay out of jail. Apparently, the second chance turned his life around, he found religion and has dedicated his life to the service of Ever After Church, claiming it saved him. To the point that he was willing to risk going back to jail to follow what he claims are God's edicts. He's been living in plain sight, staying at a cabin on the lake. Dressed in expensive clothes. Golfing. The blue hoodie was for his nighttime persona. Using a rowboat along the shore in the dark to access Crosswinds. He's a smart guy. Too smart for his own good. He was able to hack into the Wi-Fi on Mom and Dad's security system so if it went off, it dialed his number instead of the security company or police. He'd done that the day after the kidnapping, when you started staying there. He'd been following you ever since."

Ruby had no words.

Sebastian's were off-color. And pretty much expressed her own feelings. Shivering, she put her hand on the console between them, and he laced his big, warm fingers through hers.

"He's still claiming that we're all sinners and that God will make us pay," Fletcher said.

Consequences again. The thought hit Ruby. They were everywhere, those things that happened due to choices made. She was never going to be able to control them all.

And she sure as hell didn't want to try and end up losing sight of reality, as Bob Thompson surely had.

"What about Leon?" Sebastian's question brought her back to the moment at hand. And the man at her side. One who'd asked her to marry him when marriage hadn't even been a dot on his radar. And who'd been rejected by her.

"When he saw Thompson in handcuffs, being led by his open door…"

"Your suggestion, I'm sure," Ruby butt in.

"Yeah, well, when Leon saw Thompson, and knew that he'd been arrested, he was only too happy to tell us that Thompson had been a visiting minister at his church on and off, and had approached Leon, saying he'd had a vision, that God had chosen Leon to do a hard part of His work…"

"He duped the kid into setting my place on fire," Sebastian said. "But what about saying I was his brother?"

"This kid believes that all people on earth are brothers and sisters, per his bible readings. His last name's

Connolly. Turns out his dad's in prison. His mom abandoned him. He's been in and out of foster homes his whole life. Some of them abusive. And, in high school, landed in the home of a couple of zealots, who took him to a small, very strict church. He'd been looking for something to believe in, someone to believe, his whole life, and he thought he'd found his family. His home."

There it was again. Family.

Home. She placed her other hand over her stomach. Cradled her tiny but growing baby.

"And hey, sis, you'll be the first in the family to know—I've been offered lead detective here in Owl Creek. And I've accepted. I'm moving home!"

Ruby burst out with enthusiasm without even thinking about how it would be with one more sibling watching her. Giving her their opinion of her life choices. Butting in. Instead, she let herself be happy to have someone she loved back home.

And after they hung up, she asked Sebastian to pull into a mountain park not far from Connors.

He stopped in a small, deserted lot by a hiking trail. "What's up?" he asked, turning to run a finger through a few strands of hair that had fallen out of her always loose bun.

"Why did you ask me to marry you? Full-out honesty here, Sebastian…" she said, her tone filled with warning. Though she couldn't have told him to save her life what the consequences would be if he didn't comply.

Because the heart knew what it knew.

And was strong enough to deal with the consequences.

"Because I realized something last night on my way back to Owl Creek," he told her, looking her straight in the eye, his fingers remaining in her hair. "You and I—we're a constant. When life flew out of control for both of us, others were involved, in the picture, helping, but you and I were my constant. Us. Together. I'm good alone. I'm better with you. And I think you're better with me, too."

Her eyes flooded with tears. Her lips were trembling so much, her throat so tight, she couldn't speak.

"I love you, Ruby Colton. As much as I'm going to love that kid you're carrying. I don't want to go to bed at night without you, wondering about you. Or wake up in the morning thinking of you, when I could be lying there with you. This morning, it was all…just there. The battle I'd been fighting, to be independent and live alone… Maybe I was just afraid of losing love again. Maybe I was just plain uninformed. But I lost the battle, Ruby. I don't need to fight it anymore."

She swallowed. Tried to speak. And when she couldn't, she threw her body over the console, her top half landing against Sebastian, and her butt on the hard cover between their seats. It wasn't a well-thought-out plan. Or elegant.

It didn't work well.

And she didn't care.

Because it got her where she most needed to be. Her body in the arms of the man she loved. And her arms around the human who needed her just as badly.

He lowered his lips as she raised hers. And in that kiss, she found her future.

It wouldn't be perfect.

There'd be hardship and pain along the way.

Their child would grow up to disagree with them, go out into the world and take their own risks. And if they had more than one…then they'd all eventually go and there would be even more risks.

She had to take them.

When they both finally came up for air—only because they couldn't go any further to assuage their physical needs on the driver's seat of his truck—she whispered, "Ask me again."

"Marry me," he said, and this time she smiled.

He hadn't asked the first time.

He'd commanded.

If she'd heard that, she'd have understood.

Because she knew Sebastian Cross. He hadn't been commanding her. He'd just been that sure of his own personal course going forward. And that's all she'd needed to know.

"Marry me," she said back, in just as forceful a tone.

And this time, when they kissed, they did so around the smiles on their lips.

* * * * *

Get 3 FREE REWARDS!

We'll send you 2 FREE Books <u>plus</u> a FREE Mystery Gift.

FREE Value Over **$20**

Both the **Harlequin Intrigue®** and **Harlequin® Romantic Suspense** series feature compelling novels filled with heart-racing action-packed romance that will keep you on the edge of your seat.